SAY YOU WON'T GO

SAY YOU WON'T GO

EMERALD COVE BOOK 2

HEIDI MCCAHAN

Heidi McCahan

Snug Corner Cove Press

Raleigh, North Carolina

Contents

1

Copper Mountain, Colorado

Alyssa Huard was on top of the world.

From her vantage point in the starting gate, she adjusted her goggles and let her gaze travel across the slopestyle snowboarding course, taking it all in. Living in the moment—always her mantra. A front of gray-white clouds blanketed the snow-capped mountains rimming the resort, hinting at another storm. Ribbons of fog threaded across the lower half of the course, blotting out the rowdy crowd but not completely stifling their cheers and her father's ever-present cowbell.

Hayley McFadden had cut the lead by an uncomfortable margin after the qualifying rounds, but Alyssa had saved her best moves for this run. A win at this prestigious event—on the heels of her Olympic gold medal finish last February—would solidify her position as the number one American female slopestyle snowboarder.

Three, two, one ... now.

She tapped her helmet two times for good luck, then leaned forward, propelling her snowboard over the slick, hard-packed snow. The icy wind nipped at her cheeks as she focused on nailing this final ride of the competition. *This is it.* Only a few jumps and rails stood between her and first place. Where she belonged.

Crouched low and tight, she rocketed toward the far side of the hill, then rode up the snow-encrusted ramp. Sailing off the lip, she kicked her board into the air, the world flying by in a blur as she went airborne, pulling off a sky-high three hundred sixty-degree turn. Adrenaline ricocheted through her veins. Cheers erupted from the spectators as she hit the snow. *Sweet. Stomped it.*

Buoyed by the crowd's excitement, confidence filled her chest with warmth. Alyssa cut hard on her toe edge, gaining speed for her next trick: a five-forty off the obstacle looming in her path, a huge platform of snow situated in the middle of the course. This slick ride had

1

challenged previous riders, even resulted in a serious injury earlier. No worries. If all went like she'd planned, it would set her up for a gnarly midair board grab designed to dazzle the judges and gain a boatload of points.

But the men's competition before this had trounced the course. Gone was the smooth powder that had fallen overnight, chewed up by the dozen or so runs before hers. She flew toward the box more quickly than even she preferred. *Easy. Don't panic.* Relaxed and confident, that's what had gotten her this far. The judges would evaluate both technique and creative presentation. The world's best riders knew how to morph and adjust to combat whatever came their way. Alyssa had been doing that her whole life, shifting and changing to fit in, like a chameleon blending to match her environment. Second to snowboarding, it was her specialty.

She spun around, her backside facing downhill as she zinged sideways across the top of the platform. Not what she had in mind. Entering the five-forty backward added a whole new level of difficulty. *C'mon. You've got this.* She couldn't afford to bail, or she'd risk a face-plant or worse—slamming her torso into the obstacle and cracking a rib. At the last second, she rotated her hips and propelled her body into the air. As she spun one and a half times, the edge of her snowboard miraculously came within reach of her hands, and she locked her gloved fingers around it. Another cheer, a delicious wave of praise that washed over her, rose from the crowd. Releasing her grip on the snowboard's edge, she landed, front-facing. *Perfect.* Take that, Hayley McFadden.

Alyssa's final trick was one she could pull off in her sleep. On a whim, she changed it up, throwing in a little flair to impress her friends and fellow riders. Their opinion shouldn't matter. But it did. *Always.* Sometimes more than it should.

When she reached the end of the course, she cruised to a stop at the plastic barrier separating the bleachers from the competition. Chest heaving, she looked past the corporate sponsor banners to where the judges sat perched in their box.

Hurry. Adrenaline still hummed through her veins, and her leg muscles burned as she impatiently anticipated her scores. Up in the stands, she could just make out the familiar shape of her parents huddled together, Dad's obnoxious cowbell clanging as he rang it for all to hear. Even at the age of twenty-five, she still craved her adoptive parents' support and attention.

Nearby, several of the guys from the men's team stood in a semicircle, staring at someone's phone. Nick Porter held court in the center, ringleader that he was, a broad grin stretched across his face. He looked up at Alyssa and when their eyes met, his smile became a smirk, and he quickly tucked his phone inside his parka. Weird. They were tight, weren't they? Especially lately. She popped her boots out of her bindings, picked up her board, and headed toward the guys. Nick said something she couldn't quite hear, and laughter rippled through their little clan. Alyssa's stomach churned, more from the expressions on their faces than from the anticipation of the judges' posting their scores. This didn't feel right.

"What's up, gorgeous?" Ethan Young called out as she drew closer.

Nick shushed him with a subtle elbow to the ribs. With an appreciative gaze sweeping over Alyssa, Ethan held his ground.

She stopped and planted the end of her board in the snow. "What's going on, Nick?"

"Nothing, babe." Nick cleared his throat and looked away. His friends snorted and stamped the snow down with their boots.

"Nice pictures, Alyssa. Where have you been hiding curves like that?" Ethan's eyes twinkled.

"Shut up, Ethan." Nick's voice hardened, and he gave his teammate a shove. Ethan stumbled sideways, laughing.

Alyssa couldn't breathe. Her vision narrowed, and the sounds of the crowd faded as the blood pounded in her ears. Fragmented images from last night's party replayed in her mind. She'd wanted to chill, maybe sit in the hot tub under the stars and relax. Instead, she'd let Nick talk her into going to a party with the rest of the snowboarders. Then he kept bringing her drinks—insisting there was "hardly any rum" mixed with the soda—and convinced her to stay. They'd danced in the crowded living room until the party spilled out onto the back deck. Was she the first one to pull off her dress and jump in the hot tub? Other girls had followed, hadn't they? She couldn't remember. But a fuzzy image of her bikini top lying on the cement filtered through her mind, and echoes of Nick laughing as he lifted his phone and snapped a picture of her smiling at him over her bare shoulder sent a shameful heat climbing onto her cheeks.

"Nick?" Her voice cracked. "Did you post those pictures? From the hot tub?"

"Oh, yeah, he did." Ethan leered, tugging his phone from his jacket pocket. "Good thing I grabbed a screenshot."

No.

Nick only stared back, mouth pressed into a thin slash. His silence confirmed her worst fears.

A sob broke from her lips. She pressed her gloved hand to her mouth, snatched her board, and shoved past them.

"Alyssa, wait. It's not a big deal. You…" The roar of the crowd drowned out Nick's voice. Results were probably up, but she didn't even glance at the scoreboard. She had to get out of there. *Now.* Tears blurred her vision as she broke into a jog and hurried toward the resort. She'd text her parents from the airport, let them know she'd gone someplace safe, someplace where Nick couldn't hurt her.

***

Jeremy Tully wiped the grease from his fingers on an old T-shirt and stared up at the ski hill. The lights from the quad chairlift cast bright orbs across the fresh snow. Fat, wet flakes had started falling after lunch and didn't show any sign of stopping.

At least eighteen inches had fallen on Emerald Cove, Alaska, in the last twenty-four hours. Jeremy's pulse quickened. He needed to get back to town. He'd promised Blake, his brother, and sister-in-law Lauren that he'd stop by for dinner tonight and discuss the future of their whitewater rafting and kayaking business.

But he couldn't leave yet, not with fresh powder calling his name.

The tiny hairs on the back of his neck prickled. The unsettling feeling that bad news was looming had dogged him all day. What if Blake and Lauren wanted to dissolve their partnership? He tossed the soiled T-shirt inside the shed. Blake had hinted he and Lauren were hoping to have a baby soon. No arguments from Jeremy—he loved kids. But after six successful summers leading tours and guiding people down the rapids, why give up a good thing?

He glanced at the mountain again. He'd promised himself he'd get back on his skis this season. But if he didn't show up at Blake and Lauren's, Jeremy'd never hear the end of it. And he didn't need his older brother accusing him of blowing off a meeting. Things between them were dicey enough already.

One run down the mountain couldn't hurt, right?

Besides, he'd earned it. He'd spent most of the day tinkering with the snowcat, changing the oil and then checking the sprockets and inspecting the tracks for damage—everything he'd learned in his certification class last winter. Chuck Malone, Jeremy's boss and the manager of Chugach Backcountry Adventures, insisted the refurbished all-terrain vehicle was their top priority. Apparently "high-end" clients had booked the first expedition of the season. Jeremy couldn't get any more information out of him. The rumor circulating around town indicated it was some hotshot snowboarders and a crew who wanted to film a movie here. His stomach clenched at the memory of the last time production crews came to Emerald Cove. It hadn't gone well. But he'd been caught in the vortex of rumors enough to know you couldn't believe everything you heard.

He stowed his toolbox then grabbed his gear from the corner by the workbench and tried to ignore the irritating hum of anxiety building within.

It's only one run. C'mon, man. You've got this.

Jeremy squeezed his eyes shut, desperate to claim victory over the regrets that plagued him. Showing up on time for dinner was the right thing to do. The current conditions on the mountain were too good to pass up, though.

Opening his eyes, he swallowed hard and tightened his grip on his skis. Baby steps, right? The psychiatrist he saw in Anchorage counseled him not to restrict activities. To do all the things he loved. It about killed him to admit at his last visit that he'd still not slept through the night. That his life revolved around a simple routine and making sure he took his meds. Sure, he had a job and hung out with his family, but he hadn't taken a decent photograph since the accident, and the nightmares taunted him.

Today was a day for a breakthrough. He could feel it. The fresh snow and the mountain air calling his name—it was all too perfect to ignore.

In a matter of minutes, his skis dangled beneath him as he let the chairlift carry him up the side of Miller's Ridge, one of Emerald Cove Resort's more challenging runs. An icy wind buffeted his face, and he breathed deeply, letting the cold air fill his lungs. Once he crested the hill, the lights from the ongoing remodeling of the lodge gleamed in the distance. Guilt knifed at his chest. Maybe he should've resisted the urge to put on his skis. After all, if it weren't for him, the original lodge would still be standing, and the owners wouldn't have to deal with an expensive renovation.

But just for a few minutes, he needed to forget his demons—to savor the adrenaline rush of conquering the ski slope.

To not feel like such a loser.

Jeremy gritted his teeth against the tired, old message that played on an endless loop in his head, threatening to suck him into the dark abyss of hopelessness.

Please, let me be okay.

The prayer was simple—more of a plea, really. One he'd offered up again and again, but relief never came. God didn't seem to be listening. Or maybe He didn't care. The next wave of anxiety crashed in eventually, as powerful as the last, and it was all he could do to keep moving forward.

His heart leaped into his throat as the chairlift crested the top of the run, the doubts swirling inside like snowflakes in a blizzard. This was his chance to bail—to tell Gunnar, the lift operator, that something came up, and he needed a ride down to the bottom of the hill.

No.

Jeremy planted his poles in the snow and skied away, mad at himself for almost giving in. Observing life from the sidelines wasn't a role he wanted to keep playing. Time to carve some fresh lines. There wasn't a single thing he could do to change the past. So why not have a little fun?

He tucked his poles under his arms, adjusted his goggles, and surveyed the scene. Only a handful of skiers dotted the run. Most people were at work on a Wednesday afternoon, and kids were probably just getting out of school. Might be nice to have the place to himself, in case he wiped out.

Jeremy drew a ragged breath, then pushed off, pointing his skis downhill. Snow fell even harder now, marking his goggles with soggy flakes and obscuring his view of the lower half of the run. Zigzagging from one side of the hill to the other, he concentrated on keeping his knees bent and his balance centered. With every turn, the tension in his chest loosened. See? *This is exactly what I needed.* His pulse sped as he angled toward the first mogul in his path.

Suddenly, a petite snowboarder in a bright pink jacket rocketed into his line of sight. With her back to him, she had no idea she'd just cut him off.

"Look out!" was all he could manage before he slammed into her, knocking her off-balance.

"Oof," she grunted, and he threw his arms around her in a desperate attempt to cushion the impact. His stomach plummeted as she tumbled face-first into the snow, and he landed on top of her. This was bad. Really, really bad.

The world flew by in a blur of gray as they log-rolled downhill in a tangle of limbs, poles, skis, and a snowboard. When they stopped, blood pounding in his head and his chest heaving, she was pancaked across him, her cheek pressed against his jacket, silent and unmoving.

Oh no. No, no, no. Knocking a stranger unconscious wasn't part of the plan. Jeremy cocooned her in his arms, desperate to somehow protect her. As if the damage wasn't already done. He quickly scanned her body, checking for any obvious broken bones. Thankfully, her legs—and his—looked okay. He'd lost his skis, but she still had her board, its edge anchored firmly in the snow at their feet. His gaze traveled. Two long brown braids trailed from either side of her black helmet. Slowly, she lifted her head, only inches from his, then yanked off her goggles. Irritation etched her delicate features.

Wait a minute. He shook his head, trying in vain to clear his vision. Was she…? No. It couldn't be.

"Let *go*," she said a muscle in her jaw twitching.

Jeremy searched her face again. It had to be her. How many female professional snowboarders were there with different colored eyes?

"Hello?" One blue eye and one green eye bore into him. "Anybody home? I said, 'let go'."

He let go of her parka. "Yeah, I heard you. I'm sorry. You're not hurt, are you?"

The young woman dropped a string of colorful words as she scrambled to get up. He reached to loosen her boots from her snowboard. "Why don't you take your—"

She scooted away. "Don't touch me. I think you've done enough already."

"I said I was sorry."

"You wrecked my run. What the heck? You're lucky I didn't break both my arms."

"Wrecked your run?" Jeremy scoffed. "You came out of nowhere."

"Are you kidding me? You took me down, dude. Not cool."

Even as daylight faded toward dusk, he couldn't ignore her full lips and upturned nose. Dang, she was adorable. Even if she was irate.

"If you're injured, I can call for help. My name's Jeremy, by the way. What's yours?" As if he didn't already know. He'd seen her posters plastered on his sister Megan's wall, not to mention the cover of *Sports Illustrated* after the Olympics, the gold medal dangling from her neck.

Ignoring his introduction, she stared at her wrists as she twisted them both in slow circles. "If I can't ride tomorrow, it's your fault."

He pushed to his feet, then reached down to help her up. "Let me walk you to the bottom of the hill."

"I don't want your help."

"And I don't want to leave you sitting up here with two sprained wrists."

"Who said my wrists are sprained?"

Oy. He dropped his hands to his sides. "You accused me of almost breaking your arms. If you're concerned about an injury, I'll ski down and grab the bag of splints from the shed. It will take me less than ten minutes to get back—"

"I told you I don't want your help."

Jeremy jammed his boots back into his bindings and bit back the harsh words flitting through his head. Man, he'd love to tell her exactly what he thought of her snotty attitude. Maybe in Lake Tahoe or Beaver Creek or wherever she hung out, skiers plowed into you, then took off. But that wasn't his style. He couldn't leave her here.

"I'm going for help." He retrieved his poles and skied down to the shed, eager to call Gunnar on the radio for assistance. She was an elite athlete. Probably had endured hundreds of spills over the years. Was she really okay, or just pretending and brushing him off because she was scared?

Given her snarky response to his offer, he'd love to let her sit in the snow and pout, but he couldn't shake the nagging concern that she might have a significant injury. He'd be late for dinner now for sure. And Blake would have yet another reason to be disappointed with him. Helping an injured stranger was more important, though. He had to make sure she got off the hill safely.

***

Alyssa sat in the middle of the ski hill, dime-size snowflakes falling around her, coating her pants and jacket in a thick layer. Normally, this kind of powder was cause for celebration. But her collision with the hot skier left her flustered. Those ruddy cheeks. And that angular jaw. Concern evident in his eyes. Why was she so rude? He'd only tried to help. She couldn't hold him responsible for some other guy's thoughtless actions. But the venom had spewed out of her. So she'd succeeded in running him off, making him believe she didn't need him.

Now what?

She looked down and rotated her wrists in circles again, wincing as her forearms throbbed. Her left knee hurt worse than her arms. She probably twisted it when that stupid skier slammed into her.

Her parents were right. She shouldn't have come here alone. Not that she'd admit that to them. *Ever.* They'd warned her about so many things, including getting involved with Nick. She'd assured them she could handle him. That Nick's bad-boy reputation was a bunch of hype.

Too bad she was wrong.

Tears pricked her eyelids, more from the heartache than her soreness from falling. Nick had obliterated her—sharing those pictures with his friends, then posting them on social media for the whole freaking world to see. She'd considered leaving the country and hiding out in New Zealand for a while—at least until the season officially started. But that meant blowing off this endorsement deal with Verge Snowboards, and her bank account couldn't take that kind of a hit. Besides, who wanted to ring in the new year with a bunch of strangers? Not her. That sounded like all kinds of lonely.

She squinted down the hill, able to make out the faint outline of a small building in the distance. Light spilled out of the open door. She hated depending on anyone, but that tiny shack might be her best option if she wanted a ride back to town. If only she'd brought her phone.

Unfortunately, she'd left her connection to the civilized world at the bed and breakfast on purpose. She'd craved a brief respite from the nasty tweets, texts, and Instagram posts that ruled her life these days. It was like driving by a wreck on the interstate—you knew you weren't supposed to stare, yet you couldn't stop yourself. Every time her phone chimed, she had to look. Then the tears and humiliation started all over again. Her sisters all texted her and told her to delete her accounts. Part of her wanted to believe that would help. If she couldn't see the disgusting things those scumbags said about her, then this would all blow over, right?

The cold was beginning to seep through her pants. Alyssa clipped her boot back into her binding and slowly pushed to a stand. Her knee immediately protested. *Crap.* Tempted to sink to the snow again, panic squeezed her chest. There was no way she was going to admit to that skier that she needed him. If he came back, she didn't want to be sitting there, waiting for him to rescue her. She'd scoot all the way to the parking lot on her butt before she'd give him the satisfaction. Gritting her teeth, she leaned on the edge of her snowboard and forced herself to glide slowly down the hill. It wasn't that far. The pain made her breath catch, but she forced herself to keep going all the way to the end of the run.

At the bottom of the hill, she freed her boots from her bindings, grabbed her board, and hobbled toward the parking lot. A steady line of cars, trucks, and SUVs streamed up the hill, headlights bouncing across the snowbanks and roof racks loaded with skis and boards. Dang. This was the place to be. Finding a ride now might be tough. She glanced over her shoulder at the lodge nestled on a ridge. A wall of windows glowed brightly, beckoning weary skiers indoors. Her mouth watered at the thought of curling up beside the fire with a grande mocha in hand. Maybe she'd hang out there for a while.

"Hey, where are you going?" A male voice called out from behind her, snow squeaking under his boots as he moved closer.

She turned around. Shoot. The skier who'd taken her out then offered to rescue her. He held a red emergency kit in one hand. Man, he wasn't giving up on that splint thing. Hadn't she made it clear she didn't want him to help?

"I radioed for Gunnar to ski down and check on you." His gaze flitted to her arm. "Is everything okay?"

Alyssa lifted one shoulder. "I've had enough of this bunny hill for one day. Please tell me there's coffee inside. You do have espresso around here, right, Jason?"

"It's Jeremy, actually, and I'd hardly call it a bunny hill. This is going to be a world-class skiing destination very soon."

"Yeah, well, I'd say you've got a long way to go."

"Thanks for the vote of confidence. Sorry, no coffee out here. The lodge hasn't reopened yet since the fire. New Year's Eve is our big night."

"What fire?" She narrowed her gaze. Was he messing with her?

"A fire destroyed the original lodge."

"For real?"

"True story. Trust me, I wouldn't joke about something like that." His expression hardened, and he pulled his keys from his pocket. "I'm headed back to town if you'd like a ride."

She pondered his offer. And if she declined? How long would it take to find a phone and call a taxi? Or wait for someone else to call it a night and go home?

"Where are you staying?" Jeremy reached for her snowboard.

She let him take it. "I rented a room in town. I forget the name. It's up on a hill, with lots of logs and a moose's head over the fireplace."

It was exactly the kind of place she expected to find—cozy, rustic, and situated right smack in the middle of nowhere.

"The Carters? Inn at the Cove?"

"That's the one." Alyssa fisted his shoulder. "You do know what you're talking about."

Jeremy's eyes shifted from her hand to her face, a smirk twitching one corner of his mouth.

Oh. That was dumb. She looked away. Why did she touch him?

"The Carters are good friends of mine."

"So does everyone in this town know each other?"

"Pretty much. The locals, anyway." With her board tucked under his arm, he led the way to the first row of parked cars.

They stopped next to a truck, the kind she imagined every Alaskan male drove, large and gray and practically invincible.

"It's unlocked. Do you want to sit inside and warm up while I put your board on the rack?"

Before she could answer, pain knifed through her knee and she stumbled, her hand clawing at the air for something to hold on to. Oh, perfect. Her body would choose this exact moment to betray her, wouldn't it? Despite her best intentions *not* to need him, she found herself leaning against his solid frame, her legs like cooked spaghetti as she struggled to maintain her balance.

"Take a minute if you need to." His voice was calm in her ear, putting all her senses on high alert. The warmth of his arm at her waist made her feel safe. Cared for. Once again, she was only inches from those ruddy cheeks, her breath melding with his in a puff of white vapor.

"I'm fine," she said, teeth clenched, and let go of him. If she could just get inside the truck, and sit down—

"Are you sure you don't have a concussion?"

"No. I'm probably dehydrated, that's all." He really was too uptight about this whole thing.

"When was the last time you had anything to eat or drink?"

His gentle voice contrasted with his confident strength as he helped her into the front passenger seat. Her mouth dry, she gritted her teeth and cursed the warmth that flooded through her. Did her heart remember nothing of the pain and humiliation she'd endured at the thoughtless actions of a man?

Obviously not, based on the way she reacted to Jeremy's touch.

"Alyssa?" Jeremy squeezed her shoulder. "Would you like some water? There's an unopened bottle in the center console."

She only managed a quick nod, not trusting herself to speak.

"I'll take you back to the inn." He closed the door and jogged around the front, then opened the driver's door and leaned in. "I'll start it so you can keep warm. It's going to take me a few minutes to secure our gear and return this splint bag to the shed."

"Okay. Thanks." Why was he being so kind? And how did he know her name? Before she could ask, he started the truck's engine, then slammed the door.

She pulled off her gloves and dropped them at her feet. Plucking the bottle of water from the console, she twisted the cap off and took a long sip. The cool liquid soothed her dry throat.

Jeremy was behind the wheel in record time. He smelled good. Like fresh air and hard work. *Seriously, Alyssa.* She shook her head at her own stupidity and downed another sip of water.

A thick blanket of snow coated the windshield already. He turned on the wipers and cranked the defroster.

"What do you do for fun besides ski?" Alyssa asked.

Jeremy shifted into drive. "Anything outdoors. There's hiking, fishing, and whitewater rafting in the summer. But most people prefer their precipitation frozen this time of year. Cross-country or downhill skiing, snowmobile rides, snowshoeing…"

"What if people around here don't like to be outside?"

"Then I guess it's a long winter."

"What about parties? Clubs? Where do you go out in this podunk town, anyway?" She squinted through the window as Jeremy eased the truck onto the highway. Miles of nothingness stretched out in the semi-darkness. Although she'd noticed the harbor and the waterfront on her flight into town, and had only been to the airport, the inn to check in to her room, and the ski hill, her first impressions of Emerald Cove had been unremarkable. It felt dull. Almost lifeless.

"Watch yourself, South Lake Tahoe. We're small and off the beaten path, but we know how to have a good time."

She flinched. Silence filled the space between them. "How do you know where I'm from?"

"Believe it or not, we do have television here. I've watched the Dew Tour on ESPN."

Her pulse pounded. "What else did you see?"

He stared straight ahead, leaning toward the windshield. A snowplow filled the lane in front of them, kicking up a spray of snow onto the shoulder of the road. Its taillights glowed red, like two beacons in the midst of the snowstorm. "I haven't watched much lately. I thought your last ride in the Olympics was gnarly. Definitely medal worthy."

She let out the breath she'd held. Maybe he wasn't into social media. "Thank you."

"Are you in pain?"

"A little. Nothing a muscle relaxant can't fix." She envisioned the small bottle tucked away inside her carry-on. Her ticket to sweet relief and a good night's sleep.

"You're kidding, right?"

She shrugged. "It's what I always do. That or an Ambien. Out like a light."

He drummed his thumbs on the steering wheel. "Why don't you let me take you to see Dr. Wheeler? He's amazing. You aren't the first world-class athlete to break a bone on—"

"Nothing's broken." Geez. Not this again. Did he *want* her to have a fracture?

"Wouldn't you want to confirm that sooner rather than later?"

"Later. No country doc is putting his hands on me."

"He's not a quack, if that's what you're worried about. Ask anyone in town. He's the best."

"And you know this how?"

"Because he saved my brother's life."

Oh. Interesting. "What happened?"

"My brother is into whitewater rafting. A few years ago, he got caught in a complex situation. Things got out of control. Everyone survived but he had a severe head injury, and it was touch and go there for a while. If it weren't for Dr. Wheeler, I'm not sure that story would have a happy ending."

"Wow. That must've been awful. I'm glad it all worked out."

"Me, too." Jeremy glanced her way again. "Did I persuade you to go see the good doctor?"

"Thanks, but no thanks. If I need to see someone, I'll go when I get back … home." That was only partly true. She didn't have any plans to go home. Not now. Her parents would only lecture her, and her sisters would give her those disapproving looks she'd grown to detest. The thought of spending Christmas anywhere but her parents' house filled her with a hollow ache.

But it was time to put on her big girl panties, right? Maybe the owner at the inn would give her a couple of bags of ice. She'd figure this out on her own. She needed to stay far away from the people she loved the most. They'd only remind her how foolish she'd been to trust Nick.

2

Jeremy eased his truck into his brother's freshly cleared driveway. The clock on his dashboard reminded him he was an hour late. Crud. Somehow, he'd managed to lose his phone, too. He should've asked Mrs. Carter to borrow hers when he dropped Alyssa off at the inn.

Blake was going to flip out.

He sighed. *Too little, too late. As usual.* Part of him wanted to turn around and go home before someone reminded him—again—that he'd missed the mark. Instead, he turned off the ignition and then climbed out, the roar of a snowblower greeting him.

Because the only thing that would make Blake angrier would be listening to Jeremy's excuses.

A trail of snow zinged out of the snowblower's chute next door as Blake and Lauren's neighbor cleared the driveway. Jeremy waved and trudged toward his brother's front door.

Lauren answered his knock. Light spilling from the lamp in the foyer revealed her weary expression. "Hey. What's up?"

"I know, I know. I'm late. I'm sorry." He held up both palms. "I can explain."

Lauren smirked but said nothing as she stepped back and welcomed him in.

Jeremy toed off his wet boots and unzipped his jacket. "I have a good reason to be late this time. I was helping an injured snowboarder off the mountain. Hopefully she'll—"

"She?" Lauren's smirk transformed into a knowing smile. "Tell me more."

He batted away mental images of Alyssa's braids and mysterious eyes. "I had to drop her off at the inn, and I can't find my phone, and I—anyway… I'm sorry I didn't get here sooner."

"Don't worry about it. When you didn't answer my text, I figured

17

you were running late, so I sent Blake to the store to get cheese and sour cream for the chili."

Great. Blake hated it when he "blew off" a text message, too. He silenced a groan and slung his jacket over the back of a kitchen chair. The aroma of chili mixed with the sweet scent of fresh cornbread filled the air. "Can I help with anything?"

"Nope, we're all set." Lauren flashed him a tired smile. "I'll handle Blake. Why don't you grab something to drink?"

Jeremy padded into the kitchen and opened the fridge. Through the window over the sink, he caught a glimpse of his brother's SUV pulling into the driveway. His gut cinched tighter. He wasn't looking for a fight, but Blake could be ridiculous when someone had failed to meet his incredibly high expectations.

A timer rang, and Lauren pulled the cornbread muffins out of the oven, while he grabbed a Sprite and popped the top open. Maybe tonight didn't have to be so tense. What if he gave Blake what he wanted and avoided the conflict? Admit that Blake was the cautious one, while Jeremy was the reckless and impulsive middle child who never took responsibility for his actions.

That *was* what Blake wanted, right?

Jeremy leaned against the counter and took a sip of his pop, but it didn't do much for his dry throat.

The front door opened and then closed. Blake walked into the kitchen, a plastic grocery bag crinkling in his hand.

Jeremy felt the weight of his brother's steely gaze.

"I thought we had a deal."

Blake's icy tone grated on Jeremy's nerves. They were grown men, not adolescents. He could do without the accusations and marked disapproval.

"Blake." Lauren's voice was soft but firm. "It's fine. Please. Relax."

Blake set the cheese and the sour cream on the counter. "Why didn't you call or answer Lauren's texts?"

"Sorry, *Mom*, I left my phone back at my place."

A muscle in Blake's jaw knotted and he shook his head. "Of course you did."

"Jeremy, here's your chili. I'll let you add your own toppings."

Lauren stepped between them, fired a worried glance at her husband, and set a steaming bowl on the granite countertop.

"Thanks." Jeremy glared at Blake, waiting him for to qualify his snarky comment.

"So where were you?" Blake dunked a spoon in the sour cream. "Outrunning an avalanche? Singlehandedly rebuilding the snowcat's engine? Or …wait, let me guess—rescuing a damsel in distress?"

Oh, here we go. Blake was pushing all his buttons tonight. Jeremy refused to engage. He took another long sip of his Sprite, just to aggravate him, then set the can on the counter. "Are you done?"

Blake shrugged. "Just wondering which tired excuse you're going to toss at us this time."

"Blake," Lauren warned. "That's enough."

"Dude, what's your problem?" Jeremy gripped the edge of the counter with his hands. "Why do you care what I do with my time? It doesn't have anything to do with our business. I'm a certified snowcat operator. Chuck has backcountry skiing clients booked from now until March. We're working hard to make the deadline for the resort's grand reopening."

Did he have to remind his brother of everything positive he'd done? Somehow Blake always managed to emphasize the negative.

"A reopening that probably would've happened already if you'd taken responsibility for your actions."

"Blake!" Lauren pressed her hand to her husband's arm.

"Nice," Jeremy scoffed, tipping his head back and staring at the ceiling. He teetered on the edge of saying something he'd regret later. Besides, he'd apologized a bazillion times for his bad days. It wasn't like he'd set out to destroy anyone's livelihood. Sometimes he just found himself in the worst possible circumstances—like he was a magnet for trouble. When would his efforts to help rebuild the lodge be enough? He glared at his brother again. "What's this really about?"

Blake fished three more spoons from the drawer. A heavy silence filled the kitchen.

Realization dawned, like a punch to the gut. *He doesn't trust me.* "I told you I'm going to my appointments, exercising, showing up for work on time…" Jeremy stopped short of confessing he'd almost had another panic attack on the chairlift. "I'm doing everything I can to get it together, and if you don't want me around—"

"I never said we didn't want you around." Blake met his gaze, but his expression betrayed his real feelings. "Look, this thing Chuck is doing, this backcountry adventure gig, it's still a big risk. Storms or lawsuits or … I'd hate to see you out of a job because of more foolish decisions."

Foolish? Spots peppered Jeremy's vision, and he stole a quick glance at Lauren, who stood next to the oven with a plate of muffins and watched their whole interaction like a spectator at a tennis match. Where was this coming from? Did they think he wasn't qualified to do his job? That he was a liability on the river or in a kayak? "If this is your way of telling me you want to dissolve our partnership, then go ahead and say it."

Blake shook his head. "It's not about that. You haven't been the same since … the accident. We've given you space, time to process whatever went wrong there—"

"You don't remember, do you?" Jeremy cleared his throat. Why did his voice have to come out that way? Rough and jagged like his emotions were about to get the better of him.

Blake squinted at him. "Remember what?"

"How it felt to wait. Then wait some more—never knowing for sure if circumstances are going to change. But you just keep waiting. Hoping." He swallowed hard. Of all people, Blake should empathize. He'd lived apart from Lauren for almost eleven years before she came back.

Blake's expression softened. "What are you waiting for?"

"Never mind. It doesn't matter." Jeremy pushed off from the counter and brushed past his brother. His heartache would only look like an excuse at this point. Blake was the last person he wanted to talk to about his feelings, anyway.

"Hold on a sec."

Blake's simple command stopped him.

"If you're serious about meeting with us, will you—"

"All right, boys. I've heard enough." Lauren stepped in front of him, blocking his path to the door. "Stay for dinner. Please. I know you're hungry, and you probably don't have anything good to eat at your place, anyway."

His stomach rumbled in response. Could he and Blake tolerate sharing a meal together? "I don't…"

She turned away and dumped cheese and sour cream on his bowl of chili, obviously not taking no for answer.

Visions of another evening spent eating reheated leftovers with only the television and his dog, Hazel, to keep him company made him hesitate. He didn't want to fight. Really, he didn't. And as much as he hated being locked in to a commitment, he owed it to Blake and Lauren to map out a business plan for next summer.

Jeremy turned slowly, avoiding Blake's gaze, and reached for the plate of muffins.

Lauren offered him an appreciative look. "If you'll carry those to the table, I'll bring the rest."

"Got it." He led the way toward the round table, the weight of his uncertainty gnawing at him. Despite his brother's uncanny ability to pour acidic words into Jeremy's chronic emotional wounds, he kept going back for more. Even though they could barely communicate without arguing, Jeremy ached for connection with his older brother. Because his family was all he had left.

***

"Hashtag hot tub hottie?" Alyssa whispered, staring at her phone. "Nick. *Why?*"

She sank onto the bed in her rented room, clutching her phone in her hand. A sour taste coated her throat. Why was he doing this? She scrolled through Instagram, her stomach churning at all the pictures he'd posted with that gross hashtag. She'd hoped he would give up and eventually delete all the pictures, but by the time her plane landed in Emerald Cove, he'd posted more and tagged her again. Then he'd moved on to Twitter, humiliating her just for sport. How many pictures had he taken, anyway? She didn't even want to think about the number of screenshots sickos had taken and probably reposted. Fresh tears pressed against her eyelids and this time she gave in, falling back against the red-and-white quilt and letting the moisture trickle from the corners of her eyes and seep into her hair.

I hate him.

But the ache in her heart confirmed that wasn't true. She'd fallen hard for the guy who'd wooed her at the last winter Olympics—making her laugh when the pressure of being in medal contention was too much to take. He'd folded her into his tight-knit group, and they'd toured the world, partying hard. Living the dream. Even in the midst of her hurt and confusion, she couldn't turn off her feelings for him. He was the first man she'd ever loved.

She quickly reported the pictures Nick posted as inappropriate, closed the app, and checked the list of missed calls instead: three from her parents and two from her manager, Lance. Even though she owed him an explanation, it wouldn't hurt to put the call off until tomorrow. Or maybe longer. She couldn't ignore him forever, but she wasn't in the mood for his questions. If the production company wasn't coming until next week to film the commercial, she could afford to lay low. Figure out how to salvage what was left of her reputation.

An incoming call drew her eyes to the numbers illuminating the screen. *Nick.* With trembling fingers, she declined the call. Choice words tumbled through her weary brain as she flung her phone in the general direction of her duffle bag slouched on the floor.

Her phone chimed. Then again. Three, four, five more times. She smiled through her tears. Only one person sent that many text messages at once. After rolling off the bed, she crossed the room and retrieved her phone. Her best friend, Dani, was the only person she'd consider communicating with right now.

Where are you?! I've called, emailed, tried Voxer and Snapchat … everything. You're MIA. Don't make me call your mother. I heard about what's going on, and I'm so stinkin' worried. You better text me back. I have two more practices then I'm flying home for my brother's wedding and Christmas. Seriously. We HAVE to talk soon.

Alyssa winced. Dani's efforts to reach her must've been buried along with all the other messages clogging her phone. She'd text a quick response, offering just enough detail to ease her BFF's mind. Dani was too kind and considerate to leave hanging like that.

In Alaska. Just collided with a hot skier on my last run. Don't worry. Totally safe here. Merry Christmas!

"Alyssa?" Mrs. Carter's voice filtered through the bedroom door. "I'm sorry to bother you, but I wanted to offer an extra blanket."

She glanced at the door. Ignoring the offer was an option. She could live without an extra blanket.

"Alyssa? Are you in there?"

She sighed and pocketed her phone. "One sec." Pausing to check her reflection in the mirror over the dresser, she dragged her fingertips under her eyes then padded across the room and opened the door.

"Oh dear." Mrs. Carter's brown eyes filled with concern as she surveyed Alyssa's appearance. "Everything okay?"

"Peachy." Alyssa sniffed and tried for a smile.

"Is it your arm? Jeremy mentioned you'd had a collision and asked me to give you some ice. I'm sorry but it slipped my mind." Mrs. Carter pressed the green fleece blanket into Alyssa's arms. "If you'll take this, I'll go make two ice packs."

"My arms are fine. You don't need to bring me any ice." She hugged the blanket to her chest, thoughts of Jeremy pushing past the heartache. He'd cared enough to ask Mrs. Carter to look out for her?

"Are you sure? It's no trouble."

"Positive." She turned away, eager to retreat to her pity party. "Thanks for the blanket."

"Can I interest you in making paper snowflakes? We can use all the help we can get."

Alyssa hesitated. "I—I don't know." She set the blanket on top of the cedar chest beneath the window. Crafts weren't really her thing. And judging by all the squeals and incessant chatter spilling from the kitchen, there were a lot of kids crammed around that kitchen table.

"How about some homemade macaroni and cheese? There's enough to feed an army. The kids were so excited about eating more sugar cookies that they barely touched their dinner."

Now that was an offer she couldn't pass up. Lunch—if you could call it that—had consisted of an energy bar, an apple, and the leftover snacks the flight attendant doled out on the flight from Denver to Seattle yesterday. That felt like it was months ago. Alyssa turned back around. "If it's not too much trouble. I don't want to intrude."

"It's no trouble at all." Mrs. Carter's brown hair, shaped in a stylish bob, skimmed her shoulders as she angled her head toward the kitchen and motioned for Alyssa to follow her. "We treat our guests like family."

Alyssa trailed her down the short hallway toward the kitchen and great room. Hovering on the periphery, she took in the holiday atmosphere emanating from every corner. Evergreen garland with white lights and pine cones adorned the handrail leading up to a balcony and loft. Lights twinkled on the giant Christmas tree that filled one corner beside the massive stone fireplace. An impressive assortment of ornaments, both store-bought and handmade, dangled from the branches. Even the moose sported a few strands of tinsel from its antlers. The fresh boughs on the wooden mantle, tucked around white candles and more pine cones, the spectacular live tree—this is exactly what her mother did for Christmas, too. She heaved a sigh, reeling from the unexpected wave of homesickness.

"Oh, pardon my Christmas decorations. Haven't had a chance to finish yet. We still have about thirty ornaments to hang." Mrs. Carter continued into the kitchen. "I'll get the kids to help, then Matt or Seth can haul those boxes back up to the loft."

More ornaments? Alyssa smiled. Apparently less wasn't more around here. She followed the sound of chatter.

She skirted the long farmhouse-style table covered with scraps of paper, scissors, and several half-eaten sugar cookies coated with generous helpings of frosting and sprinkles. Three pairs of eyes followed her. She was lousy at guessing kids' ages, but the two girls nibbling on their cookies appeared to be in elementary school. The little boy, probably still a preschooler and sporting a giant dollop of frosting on one finger, grinned at her. Alyssa waved at him then quickly claimed one of the stools at the counter, grateful she could observe from a safe distance. Little kids made her nervous.

Mrs. Carter plated a generous helping of macaroni and cheese. "Grab a seat. This is Emmy, Ava, and Gavin. Kids, this is our guest, Alyssa Huard. Please say hello."

"Hello," one of the girls said without looking up, her tongue pressed to one corner of her mouth as she maneuvered her scissors along the edge of a piece of paper.

"Where are you from?" The girl with blonde hair pulled into a side ponytail studied her.

"I like your braids." The other girl, obviously her twin, tilted her head to one side, curling a lock of her blonde hair around one finger. "Can you braid mine?"

"Um, sure." Alyssa glanced at the plate Mrs. Carter set on the granite in front of her. "Maybe after I eat, okay?"

"You don't have to do that. Emmy and Ava can braid each other's hair anytime."

"But not like hers," the little girl objected. "Mommy hasn't taught us the fishtail yet."

Mrs. Carter ignored the protest and passed Alyssa a napkin and silverware. "Can I get you anything to drink? Water? Iced tea? Milk?"

"Water sounds great. Thank you."

"These are my grandchildren, by the way. They have an older brother named Joshua who is probably hiding in my bedroom with the iPad. My son, Matt, and his wife are at a Christmas party tonight."

Alyssa nodded politely. "Cool."

"What brings you to Emerald Cove?" Mrs. Carter brought her a glass of water.

Alyssa chewed slowly, savoring the creamy taste of the cheese-laden pasta. Besides, she needed a minute to formulate her answer.

She dabbed at the corners of her mouth with her napkin. "I'm—"

"Grandma, Gavin's eating another cookie," one of the girls whined.

"Excuse me for a minute." Mrs. Carter crossed to the little boy stuffing a sugar cookie into his mouth with both hands. "Gavin, that's enough, sweetie."

Relieved, Alyssa kept eating her dinner. The less information she offered the better. No one needed to know the real reason she'd come to Emerald Cove.

***

Jeremy propped both elbows on the kitchen table and studied the laptop screen Lauren had angled his direction. She'd pulled up one of the major cable television network's web pages. Under the headline "Troubled Waters Poised for a Fourth Season?", a photo featuring him paddling a kayak near Townsend Glacier twisted his gut in a knot.

"What do you think?" Lauren asked, her eyes filled with concern. "Did you know they were thinking about resurrecting your reality TV show?"

"No."

His former employer hadn't seemed real eager to communicate with him. He couldn't blame them. Nobody wanted a reality television star who'd abandoned his social media following and worked as the hired help at a resort that might not even survive the winter. Not to mention that half of Emerald Cove would run Bo and the rest of his crew out of town if they showed their faces again. *Troubled Waters* had padded his bank account but left nothing but destruction in its wake and the community bitterly divided.

Jeremy kept those comments to himself and stared at his sugar cookie shaped like a Christmas tree. Could they talk about their whitewater rafting and kayaking business instead? Isn't that why he'd stayed for dinner? His downfall should be old news by now. It was hardly worthy of a headline, much less another season of *Troubled Waters*. If Andrew's wife knew—

"Have they contacted you yet?" Lauren pulled the laptop back in front of her.

"Nope." Jeremy reached for the cookie. Never mind that he paid very little attention to his email and avoided social media most of the time. "What's on the agenda for tonight?"

Blake cleared his throat but said nothing. Not that he needed to. His one-word answers to Lauren's attempts at conversation over dinner and frosty glances pretty much said it all.

Her fingers hovered over her keyboard. "I want to ask Jeremy about an idea I had for diversifying our business."

Blake scrubbed his hand over his face. Yep, big brother was running out of patience. Jeremy gave Lauren the side eye. *You'd better not.*

"It won't take long. Promise." Lauren pulled up another website with a picture of climbers scaling a frozen waterfall.

"Are you taking up ice climbing?" Jeremy asked around a mouthful of cookie.

"No." Blake crossed his arms at his chest. "She's not."

"I've had a couple of inquiries since I've been working on marketing.

You guys have done a great job with the rafting and kayaking, but we also need to think about taking advantage of winter tourism, too. I know we can't compete with the Cody Ice Festival. They're big time now. We could offer our more adventurous clients a similar opportunity, especially if they are already here to heli-ski or snowboard. *If* we had enough interest."

"What all's involved?" Blake asked.

"For a basic four-hour outing, the minimal provisions include boots, crampons, ropes for belaying, sunglasses, and layers of clothing, including fleece jackets or vests. Most people would probably have a lot of that equipment already." Lauren sat back in her chair, her expression hopeful. "What do you think?"

"Sounds reasonable. When do we start?" Jeremy grinned. His adrenaline surged just thinking about trying to climb a wall of frozen ice.

"Whoa. Not so fast." Blake's forehead wrinkled. "How about children? Will they be able to participate in these excursions?"

"Of course," Lauren said. "Why couldn't they?"

"Honey, you'd have to consult the insurance provider," Blake said. "There could be some liability involved."

Jeremy drained the rest of his Sprite. *Valid point.*

Blake reached over and rubbed Lauren's arm. "Maybe this is an option for us in a year or so. With this year's numbers like they are, I don't think we can afford to take on any additional expenses right now."

Jeremy caught the disappointment flashing in Lauren's eyes before she dipped her head. Wait. What about this year's numbers? Sure, business had dropped off toward the end of August, but was it really that bad? Everyone said Emerald Cove desperately needed a rebirth. And soon. Before it was too late. They were losing more and more recreational business to other states, and the cruise ship traffic focused mostly on southeastern Alaska, instead of coming to Emerald Cove like they once did.

"If you're getting email from potential clients about winter excursions, why not offer custom trips?" Jeremy asked. "Get a feel for what you're capable of."

Blake smoothed crumbs from the table with the flat of his hand. "I understand you want to capitalize on an inquiry. I'd hate for us to get in over our heads."

Lauren folded her paper napkin into a square. "We won't know until we try."

"But you've never done ice climbing before. Not with paying clients, anyway. Is this a risk worth taking with everything else we've got going on right now?"

Jeremy shifted in his chair. "There's a whole untapped market out there. Once backcountry skiing takes off, we're going to see a new client base."

"Or so Chuck would have you believe." Blake shook his head. "Do you really think extreme skiers will be ice climbers, too?"

"Maybe not." Jeremy kept his tone even. "But they'll tell their friends about how incredible it is here. Why not be ready when the customers call?" He couldn't ignore the snide comment about the resort's new manager. Chuck wasn't the friendliest guy in town, but he wasn't a criminal, either. "That's not the first time you've taken a cheap shot at Chuck. What's up with that?"

Lauren's eyes widened.

"I—nothing. Forget it." Blake pushed back his chair and stood. "I've got papers to grade. Let me know what you both decide." He carried his plate and bowl into the kitchen. A moment later, he disappeared up the stairs.

"Don't worry. I'll talk to him." Lauren offered a wobbly smile. "Blake's got a lot on his mind."

Jeremy swallowed hard. He probably did. "What did the doctor in Seattle say?"

Lauren's chin wobbled. "That there's nothing wrong. No reason why we can't … have a baby." She met Jeremy's gaze, and the hurt reflected in her eyes made his chest ache. "I don't blame Blake for being cautious about growing our business. Last season's numbers were our worst in six years."

Oh. Why didn't she say something sooner? "I—I didn't know. About the doctor or our … numbers. How low are we talking?"

She bit her lip. "Twenty percent drop in revenue."

"Dang. That stinks." He raked his hand through his hair. "No wonder Blake's worried. Listen, if you guys want to shut this thing down, I—"

"What? No." She clutched his arm. "It's going to be fine. Every business has their off years, right?"

"Yeah, right." Her forced optimism didn't fool him, though. Something else was bothering her.

She turned her attention back to the laptop, her eyes flitting over the screen. "Let's see what happens when the resort reopens. Like you said, business will get better for everybody when word spreads."

"I hope so."

"Have you heard anything from Celeste?" Lauren closed her laptop.

His heart lurched at the mention of her name. "Nope."

Lauren's nose scrunched. "I'm sorry."

"I've given up."

"Don't say that. You sounded so crazy about her. I have to believe she felt the same way."

"Yeah, well, apparently not." He lifted one shoulder in a dismissive shrug. "It's been almost a year. Not that I'm counting or anything. Since my celebrity status faded, she's obviously moved on."

The question remained, why couldn't he? How much longer was he supposed to wait for a woman he thought he'd loved to make good on a promise she'd never intended to keep?

3

"Have you lost your mind? What exactly were you thinking, taking off in the middle of a competition?"

Even from a thousand miles away, Lance's words magnified Alyssa's guilt. Which wasn't how this conversation was supposed to go. She stood in the parking lot outside the darkened, supposedly half-finished resort, phone pressed to her ear, while her manager chewed her out.

"Walking off the mountain wasn't cool, either. We were all worried sick."

"It was an exhibition, Lance. Nobody cares who wins those." Okay, so not exactly true. Lots of snowboarders cared. It meant bragging rights heading into the new year. And she had been in first place ahead of Hayley on the leaderboard. That was worth gloating about for sure.

"That's not true and you know it," Lance said.

"You don't understand. There's no way I could stay. They were all—"

"I do understand." Lance cut her off. "But hundreds of thousands of dollars in endorsement deals are at stake. You can't just disappear."

"Easy for you to say. You're not the one plastered all over the internet wearing almost nothing."

"You're overreacting."

So much for sympathy. "Have you seen the pictures?"

"A couple. You don't have anything to worry about. Trust me, I've seen worse."

"Wow. Thanks for that. If this is your idea of helping, I'm touched."

Lance sighed. "Your back is to the camera, and you're in a hot tub. It's a suggestive image, but in the grand scheme of things, it's not exactly scandalous."

"I'm topless. How is that not scandalous?" Despite the chilly air, warmth heated her cheeks. She shouldn't have let Nick talk her into staying at the party. Or accepted the drinks he offered. Alyssa hung her head. How could she have been so naïve to trust him? So weak that she couldn't stand up for herself?

"I don't blame you for being upset, and I know you want to clean this up. Damage control is important. Have you reported the posts as inappropriate?"

"Yes. Nothing's been taken down yet."

"Then the best thing you can do is give people something else to talk about. Catch the next flight out and make an appearance at the Pioneer Outdoor Sports grand opening in Vail."

"Not a chance."

"I don't know how else to say this. Your role in the store's product line is significant. The general manager will want to know why you aren't around to promote it."

"It's one store opening. I'm sure you'll think of a creative excuse." She couldn't bring herself to show her face in Vail. Damage control or not, the mere suggestion turned her stomach.

"It's not just a store opening. There are interviews, photo ops, signing autographs. The whole weekend is about promotion, not to mention a great segue into the X-Games at the end of the month."

"The store has nothing to do with my next competition. Skipping the opening won't impact my rank on the world circuit. At all."

"You're still taking a huge risk."

"I'm staying here. Production begins next week on the Verge commercial. It's stupid to leave when I have to be back in five days."

"If they still want you."

Ouch. She didn't appreciate his caustic tone. "What are you trying to say?"

"People talk, Alyssa. If you're branded as difficult to work with, or someone who doesn't bother to show up, it might be a challenge to land more projects like these. Is that what you want?"

Her heart kicked against her ribcage. Was he bluffing? "I'm not leaving."

Lance mumbled an obscenity. "Fine. I'll think of a way to spin this. In the meantime, don't do anything stupid, okay?"

"Right." She ended the call. *Thanks for nothing.* Didn't he work for her? Wasn't he supposed to offer words of encouragement—maybe even a little empathy? He seemed more concerned about her absence at the stupid store opening than about pictures floating around social media.

Whatever.

Alyssa stared at the horizon, the jagged peaks of the snow-covered mountains like dark centurions lined up against a pink-tinged sky. A cold wind kicked up, making the empty chairs on the rope tow creak. She should've double-checked the hours for the ski hills before coming out. They didn't open until ten—two hours to go. Apparently, they couldn't afford to be open twelve hours a day. Yet.

This had to be the best-kept secret in Alaska. Once word spread, skiers and boarders would flock to Emerald Cove. Until then, she couldn't let powder this glorious remain untouched.

She grabbed her snowboard and trudged through the fresh snow. Her knee was a little stiff and her arms were sore from her collision yesterday, but that wouldn't stop her from carving a few lines down the deserted hillside. For as long as she could remember, snowboarding was the one consistent thing that brought joy to her life. Filled her up. Pushed out the loneliness. Exactly what she needed right now.

***

Jeremy sliced his pocket knife through the packing tape then broke open the shipping carton. The pungent scent of new furniture wafted toward him. Two round bar stools sat inside, their dark brown leather cushions wrapped in several layers of plastic and secured with more tape.

The mindless task of unpacking left plenty of space in his brain for thoughts of a certain snowboarder. Maybe he should've texted Mrs. Carter last night and checked on Alyssa one more time before he went to bed. But hadn't she insisted she could take care of herself?

Still, that intriguing stare of hers had captivated him. Not to mention her feisty attitude. Resting his knife on the new table nearby, he scrubbed a hand over his face and paused to admire the sunrise. Broad windows spanning the wall of the resort's dining area provided a front row seat. Orange and crimson streaked across a baby blue sky as the sun climbed over the snow-covered mountains ringing the community, like an actor bursting onto the stage.

"Oh, good. You're here." Rachel, the resort's new marketing director, walked in, still wearing her parka and a striped scarf knotted around her neck.

"Good morning to you, too." Jeremy turned away from the window. Of course he was here. With the grand opening only twelve days away, none of them could afford to slow their pace. He clocked in before seven a.m. almost every day and accepted minimal financial compensation for his efforts. This was his penance for righting past wrongs. He'd do anything to help and assuage his guilt.

Too bad he couldn't figure out how to gain Blake's approval. Based on last night's tense conversation at dinner, that wasn't happening anytime soon.

"We need to update our social media. New pictures on the Facebook page, tweets about yesterday's snow accumulation, and a teaser on Instagram about opening night."

"Great. Anything else?" He'd known Rachel his whole life. Since the first week of kindergarten, she'd been telling her peers what to do. Her familiar expression and tone of voice told him exactly where this was headed. *We* meant Jeremy going outside in the freezing cold to take those must-have photos.

"Actually, yes." She lifted the flap on her satchel and pulled out her phone. "I need you to respond to an email."

"What's it about?"

Rachel hesitated. "It's someone from one of those entertainment news shows on TV. He's asking questions about you and *Troubled Waters*, your employment history, how long I've known you, if you have a gallery in town where your photos are displayed…" She trailed off, brown eyes scanning the screen, then glanced up at him. "Since when are you opening a gallery?"

Jeremy ignored her question and ripped the plastic off the first stool. The article on Lauren's computer screen the night before resurfaced in his mind. He clenched the edges of the new stool with both hands and fought to take deep, even breaths. Why couldn't they just leave him alone?

"Jeremy?"

"Hmmm?" He leaned over so she couldn't see his expression and examined the new furniture for any damage.

"Are you going to star in another reality TV show?"

Jeremy straightened and offered what he hoped was an expression of disbelief. "C'mon, Rach. How long have we known each other? Three seasons of *Troubled Waters* was more than enough. No, I'm not interviewing for a job or filming another show. Or selling my photos. Anywhere."

"Then why is he emailing the resort?"

"Probably because I never check my email."

Rachel's eyes widened. "Never?"

"Nope."

"Huh. Well, he says he'll follow up with a phone call soon, so you might want to respond."

"Thanks. I'll get right on that."

"I wasn't being bossy." Her phone pinged again, and she studied the screen. "I know you're busy, but I thought I'd mention it, so the call doesn't take you by surprise."

He tried not to fire back with another sarcastic remark, instead moving on to the next cardboard container. He couldn't fault her for mentioning his go-to strategy for avoiding tasks he didn't want to deal with. "A white chocolate mocha can be yours if you'll answer that email for me."

Rachel tilted her head to one side. "How? The espresso machine isn't even here yet."

"I could find a reason to run into town." He unwrapped the second stool and set it next to the first.

"Who will take the pictures for our posts if you go get coffee?"

"I'll take a picture or two before I leave." The words were out of his mouth before he could stop them. What was he saying? He hadn't taken a decent picture, not even with his phone, in months.

His pulse sped. Well, he was here now. Might as well go with it. "We need more light, anyway. Why don't you write the first draft of the message while we're waiting?" Two could play this "delegate responsibility" game.

"Hang on a sec." Rachel craned her neck to look past him. "Your epic photo op is about to happen. Look."

"What?" He turned back toward the window. A petite snowboarder shot down the hill, then launched into the air and pulled off an effortless three-sixty, a flash of pink and black against a stark white background. Alyssa? His heart beat faster. Rachel was right. That would make a great shot. Snagging his jacket from the boxes he still hadn't unpacked yet, he slid his arms into the sleeves while he jogged toward the door, his fingers suddenly itching to get his hands around Chuck's new camera.

"The office is unlocked. Camera's in the closet," Rachel called after him.

"Got it. Thanks." Dodging a painter unfurling a drop cloth in the lobby, Jeremy jogged to the office tucked behind the brand-new front desk. The sharp odor of varnish filled his nostrils as he slipped past, careful not to bump the stained wood in case it hadn't dried overnight. He expected to find Chuck in the office, frowning at his computer screen or pacing like a caged animal, cell phone pressed to his ear. But Chuck's chair and workspace sat empty. Perfect.

Camera in hand, Jeremy left the office and crossed the lobby. When the automatic doors whooshed open, an icy wind greeted him. Hat and gloves might've been a good idea. No turning back now. This would only take a few minutes. He moved beyond the warmth of the building, bracing for the cold air whipping around him. Tucking the lens cap in his pocket, Jeremy scanned the hillside high above the lodge for any sign of the snowboarder. With a click and a beep, the camera's screen lit up. Apparently it didn't take issue with the plunging temperatures. Fingers crossed that it didn't flake out on him before he took at least a couple shots.

Although he hadn't held a camera in months, instinct kicked in. Without hesitation, he quickly adjusted the aperture and shutter speed, then lifted the camera to frame the shot in the viewfinder. A familiar sensation rippled through him—the thrill of capturing a snapshot of nature's beauty. Man, he'd missed that feeling.

He pressed the button and the shutter responded, snapping a clean shot of the vacant rope tow set against the backdrop of the winter sky tinged pink. Not bad. Maybe that one would pass Rachel's scrutiny for Instagram.

Before he could focus on the pink-and-black form rocketing down the slope on a snowboard, the peaceful silence was shattered by the familiar *whup-whup-whup* of an approaching helicopter. Jeremy lowered the camera and turned, scanning the horizon. Sure enough, the helicopter and pilot Chuck had hired to transport heli-skiing clients high into the Chugach Mountains appeared to be headed for the landing pad behind the lodge. Was Chuck on board? Did he expect to be met at the pad? As the helicopter flew overhead, Jeremy lifted the camera and shot a picture of the red underbelly, its rotors slicing through the air.

Determined not to leave the ski hill until he'd taken Alyssa's picture, Jeremy turned back around. He used the camera's lens to zoom in, captivated as she carved a deep swath across the pristine landscape with her snowboard, the lone athlete on the whole run. Her hair cascaded from her knit cap, and she leaned effortlessly into a turn. Jeremy followed her, framing the graceful movement in his viewfinder and clicking the shutter again and again. Even though he stood outside in the middle of winter, his fingers turning to icicles, he couldn't ignore the unmistakable blip in his heart rate as she glided toward him. Another old familiar feeling—one he wasn't sure he was ready for—began chipping away at the wall of protection he'd carefully constructed around his wounded spirit.

Until she skidded to a stop in front of him, yanked off her goggles, and threw a royal hissy fit.

***

"What the heck?" Alyssa jammed her gloved fists on her hips, spots peppering her vision. "Did I say you could take my picture?"

Jeremy's blue eyes widened. He took a step back, fumbling in his pocket until he produced a lens cap. "Uh, no. Did you ask before you snowboarded down my mountain?"

"This isn't your mountain." She fired a quick glance at the shack near the parking lot. "And there isn't a sign that says I can't."

Jeremy's half-smile revealed a dimple she found maddening. "You're right. It's not my mountain. But the hours are posted. The chairlift isn't moving. That's a universal sign for 'closed.'"

"No way." What was his problem? "You're not going to make this my fault. It's not the same thing. Give me the camera."

He arched an eyebrow. "Say what?"

"Give me the camera." She held out her palm. "I want those pictures deleted."

He cradled the camera against his chest. "Sorry, South Lake Tahoe. Not gonna happen."

"Stop calling me that," she said through clenched teeth.

"Okay. But you're still not getting the camera. It belongs to the manager here. He's lousy at sharing." Jeremy gestured over his shoulder with his thumb. "He's probably in that helicopter if you'd like to chat with him."

Alyssa popped her boots from her bindings, then scooped up her board. "Why are you making this so difficult? You took the pictures. I want them deleted. It's quite simple."

"Why don't you come with me and we'll work something out. I've got to see what's up with this helicopter. Besides, it's freezing out here." He walked away, stomping snow from his boots before continuing into the lodge.

Wait. What? There was nothing to work out. She just wanted the stupid pictures removed from the camera. Why wasn't he listening to her? She leaned her board against the wall and followed him inside. "You don't understand. I didn't..." She trailed off. Whoa. The exposed beams, vaulted ceiling, and stone fireplace offered hints of what the finished resort would offer. Hopefully, they would open before she had to leave for the X-Games. This place had real possibilities.

Jeremy scooted past the painters on ladders and disappeared into a larger room.

She hurried after him. "Did you hear anything I said?"

"Every word."

"So you're going to delete the pictures?"

He smiled as he tugged his knit cap over his ears. "Maybe."

Alyssa bit back an obscenity. "That's not good enough."

"Why are you panicking, anyway?"

"I'm not panicking. I just don't like people posting stuff of me online." She didn't have to tell him why. What if he knew why and was just egging her on? A fresh wave of anger roiled her stomach.

"Who said I was going to post it?"

"Why wouldn't you?"

He chuckled. A rich, warm sound coupled with a gleam in his eye that she really wanted to hate but couldn't.

"I'm glad you find this amusing."

His smile faded. "Rules don't apply to you, do they?"

"What's that supposed to mean?"

"I'm pretty sure we've covered this. The run was closed. You ignored the signs and went down anyway. I took a few pictures of you—snowboarding on the closed run—and now you're all fired up because I won't do what you want. Is this how things work in your world?"

Fiddling with the zipper pull on her jacket, she avoided his gaze. "No. I—"

Heavy footsteps thudded into the room. "Jeremy. Let's go." A raspy voice summoned him.

"What's going on, Chuck?"

"Didn't you hear the helo land? Let's make a run up to Lost Lake Gulch and scope things out for next week."

"Now?"

"Yes, now." The odor of stale cigarette smoke and garlic had preceded Chuck's arrival. *Who was this guy, anyway?* He stopped and gave Alyssa a thorough once-over, a knowing grin revealing yellow teeth. "Unless you've got something better to do."

Warmth flushed her cheeks. What a creeper.

Jeremy cleared his throat. "Alyssa, this is Chuck Malone, owner and operator of Chugach Backcountry Adventures and the resort's new manager."

"Nice to meet you." Chuck scratched at the salt-and-pepper stubble on his chin. "You ski?"

"Snowboard."

"Groovy." He shifted his gaze toward some new bar stools nearby. "Did these just come in?"

"Yep." Jeremy zipped up his backpack and slipped his arms through the straps. "I'll unpack the rest when we get back."

Chuck ran his hand over the leather cushions. "Not bad."

"What's happening next week?" Alyssa asked.

"Promo for a snowboard company." Chuck rapped his knuckles on a tall round table. "The crew should be here soon."

"Cool." She feigned ignorance. Maybe she wasn't the only one shooting a commercial here. "Which company?"

"Verge," Chuck said. "Want to come with us?"

So this was her commercial they were talking about. "Sure."

"No." Jeremy shot him a look.

"What?" Chuck's gaze darted from Alyssa to Jeremy. "Don't want your girlfriend tagging along?"

"I'm not his girlfriend."

"She's a professional snowboarder with endorsement contracts and a competitive season coming up." A muscle in Jeremy's jaw twitched. "I'm sure she has a clause in her contract against stuff like this."

"What are you, her agent?" Without waiting for Jeremy's response, Chuck faced her. "Do you have a snowboard?"

"Of course. It's outside."

"Alyssa, this isn't a good idea." Jeremy's eyes clouded with concern. "What if—"

"What's the matter? Don't think I can handle it?"

"That's not what I said."

"It will be a dry run for next week's clients." Chuck grinned. "We'll show you a good time."

"I'll come along on one condition," Alyssa said, linking her arms across her chest.

Chuck's smile faded. "What's that?"

"No pictures. The camera stays behind, and Jeremy deletes whatever photos he took of me just now."

Chuck spun back around. "You took pictures of her without permission?"

Jeremy held up his palm. "Before you freak out, I think she left out one key detail. She was snowboarding before we even opened and without our permission."

"Delete the pictures. No cameras." Chuck growled then moved toward the door. He winked at Alyssa as he passed. "We make special exceptions for professionals."

She flashed Jeremy a victorious smile. "See?"

"That was a hard hit yesterday. Are your arms all right?"

She glanced down at her hands and rotated both wrists in circles, ignoring the slight twinge in her forearms. "Splendid."

He pressed his lips into a thin line then strode toward the door. "C'mon."

Whatever. She'd scored a free trip into the untouched powder of backcountry Alaska. Let him pout if he wanted. She wasn't going to let an epic adventure go to waste.

4

Jeremy claimed the seat behind AJ, the pilot, in the helicopter and slipped on his headphones, palms clammy. He breathed in through his nose, and then out through his mouth, willing his racing pulse to slow.

Alyssa's shoulder brushed against his as she sat beside him. He was grateful that the noise of the blades spinning outside prevented much conversation. It was better if he didn't speak. Chuck was an idiot for inviting her. What if something went wrong? She'd freaked out when he accidentally knocked her down yesterday; imagine what she'd do if a serious injury occurred high in the mountains. He'd filmed an episode of *Troubled Waters* at Lost Lake. The terrain was brutal. Unforgiving. Even with helicopter access and an experienced pilot, the nearest hospital was still an hour away.

"Double-check your seat belts, please. We're ready for takeoff." AJ's voice crackled in his ears. Jeremy grasped the buckle at his waist and tugged the nylon strap a little tighter, wishing his stomach would quit turning somersaults. He'd taken this flight at least a half-dozen times.

Nothing to it.

He shifted his focus toward the windshield and tried to pretend Alyssa's close proximity wasn't getting to him, either. Must've been her shampoo—citrusy with a hint of spice—teasing his senses. Too bad he didn't have the option to bail on this outing.

"Relax. I know what I'm doing." Alyssa nudged him with her elbow.

"Hope so." He stared straight ahead, refusing to engage in this conversation while AJ and Chuck listened in.

The noise outside multiplied, and the helicopter rocked from side to side, then lifted into the air. Snow swirled around them like a sparkling white curtain as they hovered over the lodge. In the distance, the community of Emerald Cove sat nestled between the bay and the mountains. Man, if only Chuck hadn't caved to Alyssa's request and made him leave the camera behind. Now that he'd taken a couple of photos, he didn't want to quit. This was a view worthy of an Instagram post.

"How long is the flight?" Alyssa asked.

"About fifty-five minutes." Chuck glanced over his shoulder. "Pretty sweet, huh? All this fresh powder right in our backyard."

"It's incredible." Alyssa craned her neck to see out the window. "Have you advertised at all? This place will be crawling with snowboarders once word gets out."

"That's the plan." A muscle in Chuck's jaw twitched.

Did he have his doubts, too? Jeremy hoped not. The community's skepticism about a resort catering to extreme outdoor enthusiasts wasn't a surprise. Many had tried before to launch a similar business and failed miserably. Ever since the lodge burned down last year, plenty of residents had encouraged them not to rebuild. But so much was riding on the grand reopening. He couldn't think about what might happen if they didn't succeed. The resort was his lifeline—a place to channel his energy since the crippling anxiety attacks didn't seem to be stopping anytime soon.

"How many inches of new snow in the last twenty-four hours?" Alyssa's voice broke through his concerns, drawing him back into the conversation. "Twelve?"

"We had about sixteen on the ground in town." He'd let the dog out around midnight, amazed to see heavy wet flakes still falling. This morning he'd shoveled a path from his truck to the end of the driveway just so he could get to work.

"Then there's at least that much where we're going?" Her voice tremored with excitement.

"That's right. Probably at least four feet of new stuff on top of the six to ten feet we already had," Chuck weighed in. "The fun never stops in these mountains."

"How long is the season?"

"December to April, hopefully. The weather gets a bit unpredictable so it's tough to book out too far. We'll still have snow while most places are shutting down for the year."

Alyssa nodded. "Right on. You've got an advantage over most of your competitors. Tahoe, BC, probably not even Telluride has this kind of access to untouched terrain."

Telluride. Just hearing the name left a sour taste in his mouth. He'd spent part of last winter in the Colorado resort town—the only place in the country with the training he needed and plenty of people who didn't care about his TV show's epic implosion. He'd picked up some technical skills and convinced himself he could be happy driving a snowcat and working for Chuck. Especially if his relationship with Blake never improved. If they dissolved their white-water rafting and kayaking business, he'd need a back-up plan.

Celeste had been a timely distraction. Their on-again-off-again status over the past four years hadn't bothered him at first. When he'd had the adrenaline rush of the show's fame to keep his spirits high, it was convenient to attribute their shallow relationship to busyness and advancing his career. Then his world came crashing down and he needed her. Wanted her. Craved her companionship to help him cope.

After more than a year of empty promises and waiting for her to visit him in Emerald Cove—Telluride was all a bad dream.

"Hey." Alyssa leaned closer. "Are you okay?"

"He's not a fan of Telluride. Are you, buddy?"

Chuck's laughter set Jeremy even more on edge. No way would he talk about his failures in front of Alyssa Huard. Or admit to the panic attacks.

"Why not?" Alyssa's brows knitted together. "Bad experience?"

He looked away. "Something like that."

"You should give it another go. Maybe in the spring. It's a more laid-back crowd."

Not a chance. He focused on the vast expanse of white sprawling between them. There wouldn't be a return trip. He'd self-medicated with all the wrong vices.

Including Celeste.

Things had moved at a heady pace. She was the daughter of a wealthy real estate developer, accustomed to getting whatever she wanted. Exactly when she wanted it. He'd met her a few years ago in Colorado at a party after a trade show. He should've learned from his initial encounter that he'd need to keep his distance. Then again, he'd never been a quick learner, and playing with fire always offered a taste of the danger and intrigue he found irresistible.

When she found out he was in Telluride for an extended stay, her invitations were harder to decline. At first, when he partied at her family's posh home, their encounters stayed in a zone he could handle. Until their paths crossed late one night at a club. He was weak—unable to walk away—and she had nothing but time.

Or so she led him to believe.

While cuddling by the fire or dancing into the early morning hours with her rowdy friends, his nagging worries about her sincerity evaporated. They spent every possible second together. Life revolved around their intoxicating physical attraction to one another.

He should've realized it was a relationship based on little else.

You knew better.

Shame heated his skin, and he stared out the window. How foolish he'd been to let his emotions trump good sense and the values his parents had instilled in him. Mesmerized by Celeste's attention, he'd turned from his faith, easily swayed by her beauty. But wasn't that the way things went for him? He had the best of intentions, but somehow, the results never quite panned out the way he'd envisioned.

The helicopter followed the ribbon of highway for a little while then banked left, soaring over a few cabins with smoke tendrils rising from their chimneys. A steady climb carried them up into the mountains where saw-toothed peaks blanketed in white formed an imposing ring around a frozen lake.

"Oh my—" Alyssa sucked in a breath. "This is incredible."

"Wait until you take your first run." Jeremy's pulse sped with anticipation. Despite his sullen mood and the simmering anxiety, the view from here always changed his perspective. It was hard to stay bummed out surrounded by miles of jagged peaks and pristine snow.

AJ set the helo down in a bowl-shaped depression. While they waited for the rotors to slow and for the okay to step outside, Jeremy unzipped his backpack again. His chest tightened as he reached in and pulled out two avalanche transceivers. After a quick test to make sure both units worked, he passed one of the yellow devices to Alyssa.

"Here. You need to wear this. Either around your waist or looped over your shoulder."

She frowned. "Why?"

Seriously? He fought to keep his tone even. "On the off chance you're buried in an avalanche, this sends out a radio signal and helps us find you faster."

"I know what it does. I thought avalanches were more prevalent when temperatures fluctuated. Like in the spring and stuff. Do we even need to worry about it today?"

Jeremy bit his lip. Was she always this cantankerous? "Avalanches don't check the weather forecast before they barrel down the hill and take you out."

"Very funny. I thought I had those fancy reflector things sewn into my gear. Aren't they enough?"

"Those reflectors are not a replacement for wearing a transceiver. Think of those as an extra layer of protection imbedded in your jacket. They help us identify your position faster."

"You're being a little overprotective, aren't you? If AJ and Chuck are going to be sitting here with the helicopter, why do we have to wear these, too?"

Oh, good grief. She was jumping on his very last nerve. "Maybe you prefer a slow death by asphyxiation?" He grabbed her hand and pressed the transceiver into her gloved palm. "Just wear it and save me the trouble of worrying about you."

A jolt shot through him as her blue and green eyes flitted from their hands to his face. He let go of her and turned away before that mesmerizing gaze pulled him in. Pushing open the door, he hesitated, her sassy comments still echoing in his head. He leaped to the ground then jogged a few steps away from the helicopter until he'd cleared the rotors. Cold air filled his lungs as he took in his surroundings. His vision tunneled for a moment as the memories nipped at him, filling his head with doubts about his safety. Turning in a slow circle, he assessed the situation.

Dude. Relax. You can't control the weather.

He drew a few deep breaths and quieted his anxious thoughts. *Focus.*

There's work to be done. The decisions about timing, weather systems, fuel provisions—none of that was his responsibility today.

He'd equip Alyssa for this spontaneous run, then make sure she got back in the helicopter safely, but he wouldn't let himself care about her. Celeste had taught him not to let anyone breach the hedge of protection he'd secured around his heart.

***

Alyssa leaned on the edge of her snowboard, calculating the end of her run. With miles of white stretching as far as she could see, it was difficult to tell where the sturdy snow ended and the lake began. While she loved the rush that came from taking chances, she had zero interest in falling through the ice into the frigid waters of a mountain lake.

Chest heaving from exertion, she coasted to a stop and admired the line she'd carved down the pristine hillside. Was this her fourth or fifth run? She'd lost track. Along with all feeling in her fingertips. The pale blue skies that greeted her earlier were blotted out by thick gray clouds. It looked like it could dump more snow any minute.

Every muscle in her body ached but she hated to stop. This was the most fun she'd had in a long time. No cameras. No crowds. Just her and her board and some epic powder on the gnarliest vertical surface ever. If filming that commercial next week meant more of this, she was stoked.

A flash of movement caught her eye. Jeremy skied toward her, arms and legs moving in harmony as he zigzagged across the snow. What a buzzkill. He might be nice to look at, but she'd ignored him ever since that lame speech he'd given her in the helicopter. Was he always so obsessed with safety? Maybe she'd misread him. He struck her as the life-of-the-party type at first. Today? Not so much.

Jeremy snowplowed to a stop a few feet away. "We need to pack up and get ready to go."

His goggles obstructed her view of his eyes. Even though he'd aggravated her, ruddy cheeks and a full mouth still captured her attention. Good thing he couldn't see her eyes, either.

"What's the rush?" she asked.

He tipped his chin heavenward. "Storm's moving in. Chuck and AJ want to get out of here while the visibility's still decent."

"Do I have time for one more run? Please? I promise I'll go fast."

"No." Jeremy jammed his pole in the snow between them. "This isn't up for discussion, Alyssa. We can't take chances out here. If the wind picks up, we're hosed."

"Fine. I'm right behind you." She freed one boot from the binding and used her foot to propel herself through the snow on her board to the waiting helicopter.

Jeremy arrived ahead of her and wasted little time pulling off his skis and stowing his gear. His urgency made her nervous. She stole a quick glance over her shoulder at the sky. It looked even grayer and more determined.

"Here." He reached for her board. "Get in. I'll take care of this."

Too cold to argue, she obeyed and unsnapped the other binding. By the time she gave him her snowboard, Chuck already had the door open for her.

"Well?" He flashed another yellow-toothed smile. "What did you think?"

"Epic." It was all she could manage. Her legs quaked as she climbed in to her seat. There weren't words to describe this day. With the exception of the run that won her an Olympic gold medal, she'd never felt a rush like this.

Jeremy joined her a few minutes later and wedged another backpack at his feet. "We're all good, AJ."

"Roger that." The blades whirred and hummed to life as AJ prepared to leave.

Alyssa's teeth chattered. She clenched her jaw, hoping Jeremy hadn't noticed. That was all she needed—more unsolicited advice about how unprepared she was for extreme outdoor adventures.

"Here." He produced a thermal blanket and spread it across her lap.

"Th-thank you." She clutched it tighter as another shiver wracked her body.

Jeremy reached over and slipped her headphones on her ears, his fingertips brushing her cheekbones.

Her heart blipped in response.

His eyes found hers. "We'll get you warmed up soon."

"There's still coffee in my thermos," AJ said.

Jeremy accepted the silver thermos AJ handed him and unscrewed the cap. "Not exactly Starbucks quality, but it will have to do."

"It's all right." She wasn't in a position to be picky.

He offered the lid filled with coffee. "Sorry. We ran out of cups."

She smiled at his attempt at humor. A nice change from the semi-annoyed vibe he'd given off earlier. "Thank you." Cocooning the metal vessel with both hands, she took a sip. The warm, unsweetened liquid coated her tongue, and she forced herself to choke it down. AJ apparently liked his coffee bitter.

"So the runs were epic today, huh?" Jeremy braced the thermos between his knees.

"Better than anyplace I've been in a long time."

A smile drew one side of his mouth upward. A delicious warmth unfurled inside. The blanket wasn't the only thing warming her up.

"Post that on social media, would you?"

She cringed. "Not happening."

His smile faded. "Why not?"

"I'm thinking about deleting my accounts."

"That's a bold move."

She took another sip, wincing at the acidic taste. Yuck. Still, it was better than nothing and gave her a chance to ignore Jeremy's comment. She'd do anything to avoid this conversation. For a few blissful hours, she'd forgotten all about Nick and those pictures.

Shifting in her seat, she changed the subject. "Is this where the commercial will be filmed?"

"Yep. As far as we know." Chuck ripped open the wrapper on an energy bar. "AJ's confident he can get the crew in and out safely, as long as the weather cooperates."

"Any word on who they're bringing in as the professional snowboarder?" Jeremy asked.

"Nope. They've kept those details—"

Suddenly, the helicopter dropped like a rock, sending coffee sloshing onto her hand.

Chuck's garbled string of profanity was interrupted by AJ's stern instruction.

"Hold on tight, everybody."

Panic knifed at her chest as she dug her fingers into Jeremy's jacket sleeve and tried not to throw up.

"You okay?" Jeremy blotted at her hand with a rag he'd found under his seat. She managed a nod, her eyes riveted on the gray-and-white wall of clouds enveloping the windshield.

No! She wanted to scream. How did this happen? Didn't Chuck look at the forecast before he brought them up here?

If the wind picks up, we're hosed. Jeremy's words echoed in her head. The helicopter bobbed and swayed, the *whump whump whump* of its rotors keeping time with her pounding heart.

"Hey." Jeremy dipped his head and found her gaze with his own, his hand still covering hers. "It's going to be all right."

She swallowed hard and kept her eyes locked on his. Oh, how she wanted to believe him. To trust him. Those blue eyes offered reassurance. A quiet confidence she longed to cling to as AJ fought through the dense fog blanketing the mountains. But she'd learned the hard way that what lurked beneath a calm exterior was often wild. Unpredictable. And just like in a winter storm, those same qualities that drew her in were the first to threaten her and take her down.

***

Thank you, Lord.

Jeremy breathed the prayer as he slid out of the helicopter, his legs wobbly and his stomach still protesting from the ride. A bitter wind greeted him, and he hunched his shoulders against the snow blowing sideways and stinging his cheeks. That was a close call. Too close. And he loved pushing the limits. He reached back and offered Alyssa a hand. She didn't look well with her pasty white complexion. At least she hadn't thrown up. Impressive.

She clasped his hand and climbed down, then quickly let go, avoiding his gaze. He unloaded her snowboard and his gear. While he had plenty to do inside the lodge, he couldn't leave her to fend for herself. Not that they felt like eating yet, but other than a giant container of trail mix and a stash of Chuck's energy bars, there wasn't anything else available inside. She'd shouldered her snowboard, but her fingers trembled as she tugged a windblown strand of hair from her eyes.

Did she plan to buy a lift ticket and spend the rest of the afternoon riding through this fresh snow?

He trudged behind Chuck and AJ toward the lodge, bracing for Alyssa's full-on freak out. She was going to chew them out after a ride like that.

At the entrance, Chuck glanced over his shoulder. "Let's break for some grub then meet back here to work on the dining room. Miles to go before we sleep."

Huh. Not a word from Alyssa. And Chuck pretended like she wasn't even there.

"Got it." Jeremy waited until Chuck went inside then turned to Alyssa. "You hungry? I mean, you're probably not, after that." Shoot. He sounded like an idiot. "Are you? Hungry? I've got to run into town. We could grab a sandwich or something."

Good grief.

"I could eat." She set her snowboard down. "Where are you going?"

"The Fish House. Sandwiches, burgers, awesome fries, and milkshakes. We don't have a ton of culinary options this time of year." Two, actually. The Fish House and Randy's Pizza. He didn't want to admit that, though. She'd already called his hometown "podunk."

"Too bad you guys aren't open yet."

"Yeah. It'd be nice if we could head in and order a burger." His stomach growled in response. "C'mon. My truck is this way."

"Jeremy. Wait." Rachel trotted toward them, her purse bouncing against her hip.

He groaned inwardly. She'd have a few things to say since he never delivered on the coffee promise. He waited for her to catch up. "What's going on, Rach?"

"I'm headed to town. Don't worry about getting the mail at the post office. I'll take care of it." Her gaze flitted to Alyssa. "Since you look like you're busy."

"Alyssa Huard, this is Rachel Teague. Rachel, this is Alyssa."

"Nice to meet you." Rachel offered a tight smile. "Where you from?"

"California." Alyssa tilted her head. "You?"

"Here." Rachel jangled her car keys. "I'd better go." She walked backward a few paces. "I sent that email, too. You owe me coffee."

Jeremy waved. "Thanks."

"What was that all about?" Alyssa asked before climbing inside his truck.

He rounded the front to the driver's side, fishing his own keys from his pocket. Good question. Rachel made it her business to know everyone else's.

"Is she your assistant?" Alyssa asked again when he opened his door. She clicked her seat belt into place, her eyes on him as he sat down and turned the key in the ignition.

"Ha. Can't wait to tell her you said that." Jeremy flicked on the windshield wipers, then shifted into drive and pulled out of the parking lot. "We're co-workers. Sort of. She's doing a little bit of everything until we're up and running. Marketing is her main gig."

"Why does she want you to buy her coffee?"

"We received a weird email message this morning. Lots of strange questions ... There's something about the whole situation that doesn't sit right. Anyway, I promised Rachel coffee if she'd answer it." He left out the part about how it all involved his former career. No need to tell her *everything* in the first twenty-four hours since they'd met.

The ride back to town was the polar opposite of the previous night. She stared straight ahead, one of her long braids threaded through her fingers as she fanned the ends against her cheek. Maybe the mountain took the fight out of her. Not that he was complaining. A subdued Alyssa might be ideal. He watched her continue to play with the end of her braid and smiled. He'd never seen anyone do that before.

She caught him staring and froze. "What?"

"Nothing." He shifted his gaze back to the highway. "Just wondered why you were so quiet."

"Exhausted mostly."

A twinge of sadness in her voice made him give her a second look. "Mostly?"

She released a heavy sigh. "I've got a lot to think about." She touched her chin to her chest, kneading the muscles along the base of her neck with one hand. "Is there a spa around? I could go for a massage."

He bit his lip to keep from smiling. "Nope. Sorry."

She lifted her head. "Seriously? There's no spa? You need to hire a masseuse."

"I'll pass your suggestion along to the management." He tightened his grip on the steering wheel as he imagined Chuck's response. It would be colorful to say the least. Chuck wasn't a hot stone massage or pedicure kind of guy.

"That means you think it's a lame idea, right?"

"It's not lame. A spa would be awesome."

"But it's not going to happen."

He hesitated. "No."

"You should reconsider. If there's no competition, why not? Think about it. Skiers and snowboarders always have a girl tagging along. Usually a girl who doesn't have a clue how to ski. They'd hang out by the fire, go to the spa, get pedicures ... all charged to their room, by the way."

"I like the way you think, South Lake Tahoe. Unfortunately—"

"I thought I asked you to stop calling me that."

"Yeah. You did." He frowned. "Sorry. I'm a slow learner."

He maneuvered his truck into a parking spot in front of The Fish House. There was no way they could add on a spa this late in the game. Besides the added expense, it would push back the grand reopening for days, maybe even weeks.

But that wasn't what bothered him. Alyssa's insights only highlighted the differences between Emerald Cove and the elite ski resorts they were competing against for clients. What if nobody came once the resort opened again? Was their hard work all for nothing?

5

The hum of voices and the occasional burst of casual laughter punctuated the air inside The Fish House. Booths were filled with snowmobilers with their helmets stowed on the floor near their feet, several guys who looked like they might be here to ski, and a handful of locals.

"Wow." Alyssa sucked the last of her diet soda through her straw. Ice rattled as she set the plastic cup on the Formica table. She surveyed the empty french fry containers and sandwich wrappers littering the space between her and Jeremy. "Didn't realize I was so hungry."

He grinned. "Did you save room for a milkshake?"

"No. I can't." She rubbed her upper arms with her palms. "I still haven't warmed up. Just thinking about a milkshake makes me shiver."

His smile faded. "Here. You can borrow my jacket."

"No, don't worry about it. I'm fine."

"Are you sure?" He reached for the parka he'd left on the seat next to him.

"For real. I'm good." She had to stop needing him.

The thought nearly took her breath away. He was kind and sweet and maybe drove her a little crazy pointing out all the ways she should change her behavior to keep safe. But if she was honest, she could get attached. And that wasn't possible. As much as she craved a reprieve from real life, hiding out in Alaska wasn't the solution to her problems. Sooner or later, she'd have to go back to Colorado for the start of the competitive snowboarding season.

"Hello?" Jeremy leaned closer and rapped his knuckles on the table. "Still with me?"

"Yep." She looked down, dragging her finger through droplets of water left behind by her cup.

"Are you…" Jeremy's voice trailed off as he glanced at someone over Alyssa's shoulder.

"Hi, Jeremy. What's up?" A woman with long red curls spilling across the shoulders of her green winter jacket stopped next to Alyssa. A friendly smile accompanied her outstretched hand. "I'm Lauren Carter, Jeremy's sister-in-law."

Alyssa shook her hand. "Nice to meet you. Alyssa Huard."

"Do you want to sit down?" Jeremy scooted over.

"Maybe for a few minutes. I had a major craving for fries and a milkshake."

"See?" Jeremy shot Alyssa a teasing smile. "Everybody's doing it."

"Whatever. Not this girl."

"Not a fan?" Lauren slid onto the bench next to Jeremy, her expression pinched.

"Are you all right?" Alyssa asked.

Lauren squeezed her eyes shut. "Tired. Jet lag, maybe? We were in Seattle for a few days, and I guess my hectic schedule is catching up with me."

Jeremy studied her. "Are you sure that's all it is?"

"I'm sure." She opened her eyes and gave his hand a reassuring pat. "Thanks for looking out for me."

"Anything I can do?" Jeremy pulled his phone from his pocket. "C'mon. Delegate some responsibilities. I can take care of it."

"It's not anything I can hand off, really. But thank you. Between the holidays, getting ready for next summer, and finishing up projects, I've … pushed myself too hard." Lauren massaged her forehead with her fingertips. "This is our first Christmas since my grandmother passed away, and I think it's finally hitting me that she's not here."

Alyssa glanced at the server behind the counter filling cups from the soda fountain dispenser. "Can I get you some water?"

"No, I'm fine. I've got a whole bottle in the car." Lauren offered a tired smile. "Thank you, though."

"Order up." The server set a paper bag and a milkshake next to the register.

"That's me." Lauren pushed to her feet. "Nice to meet you, Alyssa. I'll see you guys later."

"Call if you need anything," Jeremy said.

"'Bye." Alyssa waited until Lauren picked up her order and moved toward the door. "Do you think she's okay?"

"Not sure. I'm texting my brother to let him know. She looked pale. More so than usual."

"Is she pregnant?"

He hesitated. "No. She's had at least two miscarriages, though."

"Oh no. I'm sorry to hear that."

"Yeah, they've had a tough time." He stared at his phone, fingers moving across the screen. She waited while he finished, then tucked the phone in his pocket. "They don't have any other children?"

"They had a child together about fifteen years ago. That's a long story. He lives with his adoptive family someplace in Washington or Oregon. Anyway, Lauren and my brother haven't been able to have any more children." He frowned as he dragged the edge of his palm across the table, swiping away the crumbs and remnants of salt. "Way more than you wanted to know, right?"

"Not at all." Alyssa wished she hadn't finished her drink already. A sip of anything to soothe the dryness in her mouth would be good right about now. *Tell him.* She didn't usually struggle with sharing her own history. It wasn't like it was a secret or anything. But Jeremy's opinion mattered. Already. Even though she wished it didn't. "I—I'm adopted."

Jeremy stilled, and his eyes widened. "Really?"

"Uh-huh. You're looking at a product of California's foster-to-adopt program."

"Cool."

Cool? That wasn't the word she'd used to describe it. She drew a wobbly breath. More like forgettable. So much she'd rather not remember about her past—both the early years and recent life experiences.

"Have you always known you were adopted?"

"Yes. I don't remember my birth parents, but there were other foster homes that didn't go so well." She dipped her head. *Let's not go there today.* Months of therapy hadn't erased the heartache.

"I'm sorry." His voice was laced with kindness. "That sounds like a rough way to grow up."

Alyssa dragged her gaze to meet his. The warmth she found in his cerulean eyes, coupled with his unexpected empathy, sent a tingle zinging to every extremity. She swallowed hard. "Yeah, it was. I mean, more than rough. I can't believe I even mentioned it. I don't usually talk about it with someone I ... just met."

"I have that effect on strangers." Jeremy grinned, releasing the tension. "Do you like basketball?"

She was mortified that she'd been that transparent, so his question threw her for a loop. "What?"

"Basketball. You know, a gym, an orange ball. Two teams defending their baskets?"

She narrowed her gaze. "I know what basketball is. Why are you asking?"

"Pretty much the whole town goes to the games. Would you like to come with me tomorrow night and watch my brother's team play?"

Alyssa lifted one shoulder. "Sure, why not."

"Sweet." He shrugged into his parka. "C'mon. I'll give you a ride back to the inn."

She stood and picked up her tray, her heart thrumming in her chest as she followed him to the trash cans near the door. Doubt crept in. Maybe she should've said no. She hadn't imagined the moment they'd shared a minute ago—that instant connection when she'd been tempted to tell him her whole life story.

Had she?

Her job was to film a commercial, lay low, and figure how to rebrand her tarnished image—not get involved with a local. Even if he was easy on the eyes.

On the other hand, what else was she supposed to do on a Friday night? She couldn't snowboard all the time. It was only one basketball game, right?

***

The familiar aroma of popcorn and hot dogs permeated the cold air as Jeremy held open the door to Emerald Cove High School for Alyssa. She brushed past him, hands jammed in the pockets of her jacket. He followed her inside, noting she'd ditched her knit cap and taken the time to curl her hair in long loose curls. Was that for his benefit?

His chest tightened. He felt like a teenager all over again, giddy with attraction and second-guessing her every gesture and facial expression.

A crowd mingled in the foyer. Moms with young children stood near the trophy case, talking and laughing, while teenagers huddled in small clusters and stared at their phones. The pep band played "Eye of the Tiger," which added to the festive atmosphere.

Jeremy gestured to the line forming at the concession stand. "Would you like anything?"

"No, thank you." She smiled up at him, her lips coated in a rich, glossy pink that made it hard for him to look anywhere else.

But he forced himself to and nodded toward the door to the gym. "We should claim our spots. My mom is good about saving seats, but she can't hold off the masses forever."

"Whoa." Alyssa scanned the bleachers surrounding the court, her eyes wide. "You weren't kidding about the whole town, were you?"

"It's a big game. We have an intense rivalry with Delta's team." His wet boots squeaked on the wood floor as he led the way to the crowded bleachers along the right side of the gym. The boys' teams warming up on the court made the floor vibrate under his feet, and the hum of anticipation in the air sent a familiar wave of nostalgia through him. He loved those sounds. He and Blake had spent hours here, running around together and hiding under the bleachers as little kids, then eventually taking their places on the court and playing countless games. Even winning quite a few and proudly hoisting championship trophies into the air.

The onslaught of memories pricked at him, reminding him of simpler times. Times when half the town didn't resent him for a reality show that wasn't what they'd hoped. Jeremy scanned the gym for his brother.

Blake stood near one end of his team's bench, a clipboard tucked under his arm and eyes riveted on the kids as they went through layup drills. He glanced over his shoulder, worry creasing his brow. Poor guy. He didn't usually look so agitated.

"I should talk to my brother." Jeremy leaned close to Alyssa's ear so she could hear him above the music. "It'll just take a second."

She nodded and followed him toward the line of folding chairs.

Did she sense every pair of eyes in the gym observing her entrance? Hopefully her experience as a world-class athlete prepared her for the unofficial spotlight of walking past most of Emerald Creek and a majority of Delta, too, who had brought a healthy contingent of their own fans.

"Hey." He stepped into Blake's line of sight. "Everything okay?"

Blake slid his fingers along the starched collar of his royal blue dress shirt and tugged at it. "Lauren's not here yet. We had a fight, and I'm worried about her."

Jeremy scanned the bleachers. Dozens of familiar faces stared right back. Except their curious gazes were riveted on Alyssa. Of course. Most people in town wanted very little to do with him these days. Instinctively, he reached out and pressed a protective hand on the small of her back. The fabric of her coat felt cool against his palm. Maybe he should've warned her.

"Blake, this is my friend, Alyssa Huard. Alyssa, my brother Blake."

Recognition flashed in Blake's eyes. He clasped her hand in his. "Nice to meet you. That was a sweet ride at the last Olympics, by the way."

Two red splotches highlighted her cheekbones. "Thanks."

"Good luck tonight." Jeremy bumped fists with Blake. "I'll check on Lauren."

"Thank you," Blake said as his assistant coach gathered the players for a huddle.

"My family's over here." Jeremy pointed, then guided Alyssa toward the bleachers behind the home team's bench.

She hesitated but didn't look at him. "I'm meeting your parents? Right now?"

He grinned. "No worries. They're relatively harmless."

Alyssa made a small noise in the back of her throat.

His parents stared at him, their surprise poorly masked with expectant smiles. He drew a deep breath. *Here goes.* It had been ages since he'd introduced his parents to a girl. He led the way as they climbed up the metal steps, then stopped beside his parents at the end of the third row. "Alyssa, this is my mom, Sandy Tully."

Mom slid over to make room. Her silver hoop earrings dangled as she flipped her ash blonde ponytail over her shoulder and motioned for Alyssa to come closer. "Hi. Please sit down."

"Thanks." Alyssa eased into the space. She had that deer-in-the-headlights expression already. Maybe sitting right next to his parents was too much to ask. Mom did get a little worked up if Emerald Cove fell behind.

Dad leaned forward and reached across Mom, blue eyes twinkling and his beefy hand outstretched. "Ben Tully. It's great to meet you."

"Alyssa Huard." Her hand almost disappeared in Dad's giant grasp.

Jeremy sat down beside Alyssa and glanced back. Mrs. Carter's usual spot next to Lauren's remained empty. "Did the Carters say if they were coming or not?" He leaned close to Alyssa again, relishing the opportunity to breathe in the sweet scent of her perfume.

She shook her head. "They said they were having dinner with their son—Seth? He and his wife are leaving tomorrow for the holidays."

Seth and Molly Carter. Maybe Lauren wanted to say goodbye to her brother and sister-in-law, too?

He reached for his phone to text Lauren and check on her. When he was finished, he caught Alyssa giving him a sidelong glance through dark lashes. A slow heat worked its way up his neck. If it weren't for the obnoxious stares of almost everyone he knew, he would have slipped his arm around her shoulders and pulled her in for a reassuring hug.

But he couldn't.

Not when he wasn't even certain she was single. He'd meant to wander around her Instagram account before he picked her up. Chuck had kept him busy most of the day, and then he'd rushed to get ready so he wasn't late. She said she'd planned to delete her social media accounts anyway, so he'd have to find another way to figure out if she had a boyfriend. *Ask her.* He squirmed in his seat. That could get awkward.

The opening notes of the team's favorite song blared from the loudspeaker and applause erupted as the starting lineups were introduced.

He'd ask later.

He snuck another peek at Alyssa. She stood next to him, her expression unreadable. She'd pulled off her jacket, revealing an aqua blue sweater that accentuated her curves and almost matched one of her eyes. *Mercy.* Before she caught him staring, he forced his attention back to the court.

They remained standing for the national anthem then took their seats.

Mom leaned forward and caught his gaze. "Have you heard from Lauren?"

He fished his phone from his pocket and checked it. "Not yet."

"She's always here by now." Mom frowned. "I'm worried something happened."

"Maybe she stayed for dinner with Seth and Molly," Jeremy said.

"I hope she's okay." Mom shifted, the concerned expression not quite fading from her features.

The opening jump ball led to a quick offensive play and an easy basket for Emerald Cove. More applause erupted, and Jeremy watched Blake pump the air with his fist. Good. Maybe the adrenaline rush of a first quarter lead would keep him from noticing his wife hadn't arrived yet.

A loose ball, players hustling, then a nice pass by one of Delta's players led to the opposing team scoring a three-pointer at the opposite end and claiming the lead.

"This is intense," Alyssa said, eyes gleaming.

"It's not quite as exciting as a backside seven-twenty for a gold medal win, but it'll do." He was proud of himself for mentioning her signature snowboarding trick.

A wide grin stretched across her face—the biggest smile he'd seen since they met. His heart responded with a noticeable kick in his chest. Whatever it took to make her look at him like that, he wanted to keep doing it.

"Oh no. Jeremy, did you know about this?" Mom held up her phone, brow furrowed, sucking the magic right out of the moment. "Lauren and Blake had a fight. She's not coming to the game."

His breath caught. "Blake told me about the fight, but I didn't know she wasn't coming."

"She just can't let it go," Mom said and jammed her phone back in her purse. "It's killing Blake."

Jeremy exchanged worried glances with Dad, then shifted his focus back to the court.

"Is everything okay?" Alyssa asked, her face clouded with concern.

"Not sure." Jeremy kept his voice low, determined to shield their conversation from curious listeners nearby. "My sister-in-law wants to adopt a little girl from China, but my brother's not on board with the idea. I think they might've had another fight about it."

His heart ached. Blake and Lauren had been through so much. It didn't seem fair that their inability to have another child had driven a wedge into their relationship. Dinner the other night was rough. Who was he kidding? Things between he and Blake had been strained for months. And he felt powerless to help.

***

Alyssa sat on the edge of the plastic bleacher, picking at a hangnail on her thumb. The music played through the time-out, and the basketball team gathered around their assistant coach and his dry erase board. She hadn't anticipated getting into the game, but the fact that Emerald Cove trailed by six points with two minutes to go in the first half made her nervous.

"Excuse me." A middle-aged woman wearing an Emerald Cove sweatshirt tapped Alyssa on the shoulder. "Have we met?"

Alyssa hesitated. Always a challenging question to navigate. "I—I don't think so."

The woman leaned forward and glanced toward Jeremy, her blue eyes narrowed. "You look familiar. Thought maybe you were one of those girls from Jeremy's program."

What program? Alyssa shot Jeremy a questioning glance.

He avoided her gaze. His cheeks looked more ruddy than usual, though. "Mrs. Lindstrom, this is my friend, Alyssa."

"Nice to meet you," Alyssa murmured.

"What brings you to Emerald Cove, honey?" Mrs. Lindstrom's gaze traveled over Alyssa, making her link her arms across her chest in an effort to shield herself from the nosy woman's probing stare.

"I'm just here to snowboard." The fib rolled right off Alyssa's tongue. She could lie to a total stranger, right? It's not like she'd be sticking around.

The time-out had ended, and Emerald Cove quickly scored a basket. Enthusiastic applause and loud cheers made any further conversation impossible.

She stole another glance at Jeremy from the corner of her eye. While he put his fingers to his lips and let out a loud whistle, she took the opportunity to admire his clean-shaven, boyish good looks and the way his forest green Henley clung to his muscular arms and broad chest. The dude was ripped.

I could fall hard for you, Jeremy Tully.

The random thought alarmed her. It was laughable, really. She couldn't fit into his world. And he couldn't fit into hers either.

Her phone vibrated in her pocket, pulling her from her Jeremy-filled daydream. Out of habit, she reached for her phone and checked the screen.

Where are you, baby? Beaver Creek is epic. Everyone is asking about you.

Every word from Nick carved a deeper wound.

I need you. Don't be like this.

She gritted her teeth. How could he be so selfish? Not even a hint of remorse. Didn't he realize he'd wrecked her?

A buzzer on the scoreboard summoned the players off the court for halftime. Conversation hummed around her, bits and pieces like background noise as she tried to formulate a response.

"Lauren's not here?"

"That's weird. She doesn't usually miss a game, does she?"

"—I bet it's a scheduling conflict. She's probably at a Christmas party—"

"—Isn't tonight the youth group thing at the church? That means..."

Her fingers trembled as she put her phone away without answering Nick's texts.

"Are you okay?" Jeremy's eyes scanned her face.

"Of course." She forced a smile. If she mentioned Nick, she'd have to explain the whole story. Did Jeremy already see the pictures? Her throat tightened. He hadn't said a word. Or maybe he'd seen them and was too classy to say anything. Either way, she couldn't bring herself to mention the fiasco right now.

Jeremy studied her, as though weighing her answer. Before she could say anything to reassure him, her phone hummed again. Nick refused to be ignored.

She didn't respond. Did Nick even mean what he said? Or was he irritated she hadn't come back yet? Did he miss her, or did he miss the fringe benefits of being with her?

The sickening twist in her gut confirmed it was the latter. Regret washed over her in a hot flush.

Drawing a deep breath, she turned her attention back to the game. Jeremy didn't press her for any more information. Relieved, she tried to enjoy being close to him. He was kind, generous, and dedicated to his family—not to mention incredibly nice to look at.

She hated herself for not telling him everything. She'd offered up fragments of her life story in the last couple of days, pieces of herself she could share risk-free. Despite the nagging tug in her gut to come clean, she justified her choices the same way she always did—in the end, it wouldn't matter. She'd be gone before he ever found out. Back to the World Tour, a new city, and a new mountain every weekend. He'd never leave everything he loved here. Why offer up the tender, vulnerable places? She owed him nothing.

***

Jeremy parked his truck in the Carter's driveway, the engine still running.

He glanced at Alyssa from the corner of his eye. Both the porch lights and a light in the yard reflected off the snow, bathing her face in a silver-blue glow. A crease marred her smooth brow. Should he offer to walk her in? Maybe stick around for a while? She'd remained quiet on the ride back from the game. Ever since she'd looked at her phone, something seemed off. Like a deflated balloon, her spunky demeanor had vanished. He'd tried to ask, but she'd shut down right away.

"Do you have a key?" He shifted into park. "I'm not sure the Carters are home."

"Oh, right." She dug into her pocket and came up with a key dangling on a plastic fob. "Got it."

"Are you sure everything's okay? You look worried."

"Some people aren't too happy with me for coming here."

"To a basketball game?"

"No. Here. Alaska."

"Why? Did you blow off a hot endorsement deal?"

Her head shot up. "How did you know?"

"Just a guess."

She heaved a sigh. "It's only a new store's grand opening. Not a big deal. At all. I launched a new product line that they carry. My manager wanted me there, but ... it's not my scene."

"I for one am glad you decided to stay here."

She ducked her head and fiddled with the key. "Thanks."

"Can I walk—"

"No." She cut him off. "I mean, thanks for the offer, but I'm good."

Oh. Disappointment curled in his gut. He let his hand slide from the door handle. "Thanks for coming with me. I hope you had fun."

A shy smile pushed her lips up on one side.

He let his eyes linger there for a second longer than they should. Man, he wanted to tunnel his hand through those honey-brown locks and pull her in for a kiss. Or three.

"It was fun. Thanks for the ride." She opened the door and slid to the ground, dousing any possibility of something more. "I hope your brother and his wife work things out."

"Thanks. Me, too. Good night."

"See you around." She slammed the door and walked up to the porch.

Hope so. He waited until she disappeared inside before he backed out of the driveway and steered his truck down the hill. Maybe he'd grab a quick bite to eat, give the dog a chance to run around in the yard, and then binge watch more episodes of *Blue Bloods*. Anything to avoid sitting by himself and overanalyzing where he went wrong tonight. Had he misread their flirty banter? Her eyes had locked on him when she thought he wasn't watching. He'd snuck his fair share of glances her way, too. But she'd shut him down when he offered to walk her to the door.

He eased to a stop at the intersection and scraped his palm across his jaw. Her story about skipping the store's grand opening sounded legit. Was that all, though? She'd seemed on edge—checking her phone, frowning. Despite her initial feistiness the night they'd met, she guarded a deep wound—something way more serious than sore arms. He recognized the hurt in her eyes because he saw the same emotion in his own reflection every day.

Careful. She's … complicated.

He tapped the accelerator, gritting his teeth as the doubt niggled its way in. She was gorgeous. Talented. Could call dibs on any guy she wanted. Why would she bother with an anxious, washed-up reality TV star from Alaska who barely even had a high school diploma?

A few minutes later, he parked in front of his duplex, still wrestling with thoughts of Alyssa. He couldn't deny his attraction. Sure, her skittishness waved a few red flags. But everybody had issues, right?

Wyatt Madsen, one of his best friends from childhood and now his new neighbor in the duplex's other half, stood in the driveway, unloading a suitcase from the back of his SUV. He paused when Jeremy got out of his truck.

"Hey, man. What's up?" Wyatt rested the suitcase on the ground. "Did we win?"

"No." Jeremy slammed the door and then joined Wyatt in his driveway. "Delta beat us by a three-pointer at the buzzer."

"That stinks." Wyatt frowned. "Is your brother still coaching?"

"Yeah." Jeremy didn't want to think about how this loss would impact Blake. Or his issues with Lauren. He forced a smile and clapped Wyatt's shoulder. "It's good to see you. Welcome back."

"Thanks." Wyatt grinned. "It's great to be home."

"Congrats on the new job," Jeremy said. "When do you start?"

"January 1st." Wyatt shrugged. "The new guy gets the holiday shift."

"I'm sorry to see Sergeant Grant retire, but we're all glad they picked you to replace him." Jeremy gestured toward the remaining luggage behind the SUV's back seat. "Is this everything?"

"For now. I shipped the rest from Sitka."

"Let me give you a hand." Jeremy grabbed a suitcase and followed Wyatt up the driveway toward the front door. Wyatt had spent the last four years with the police department in Sitka, waiting for a position to open in Emerald Cove. There wasn't a more thoughtful or conscientious guy than Wyatt. It was going to be awesome having him around again.

"How's your family?" Wyatt called back over his shoulder. "Megan home for Christmas yet?"

Jeremy stared at the back of Wyatt's head. Why was he asking? Mom hadn't mentioned anything about Megan tonight, and he admittedly hadn't kept up with his younger sister while she'd been away at college like he should. "Not yet," he said. "Hopefully soon."

Wyatt nodded then pulled his keys from his pocket.

A muffled barking cut through the air. His dog Hazel must've seen him from the window or else heard him talking. Patience wasn't her strong suit. "I'd better let her out."

"Go ahead. I've got the rest." Wyatt opened the door and heaved his backpack and suitcase into the entryway. "Thanks for your help."

"No problem. See you later." Jeremy set the suitcase down then hurried toward his place, thoughts of Alyssa temporarily upstaged by Wyatt's question. When *was* Megan coming home? And why did Wyatt care? Sure, she'd followed him and Wyatt around like a shadow when they were kids, but—Jeremy shook his head. He couldn't quite wrap his mind around her hanging with his best friend. At least not like *that*. Besides, she probably had her pick of the guys at the university, plus a volleyball scholarship and classes to worry about. Wyatt was nothing more to her than a family friend.

6

Alyssa swiped the sleeve of her T-shirt across her sweaty brow then leaned forward on the exercise bike's handlebars, forcing herself to pedal through the burning sensation in her quadriceps. How she loathed indoor workouts. The bike's seat felt like she was riding on a cement slab.

No quitting.

She kept peddling as she battled back mental images of Hayley McFadden, somewhere out there, working just as hard, if not harder. Allowing one of her competitors to gain an edge was out of the question. Using an app on her phone, Alyssa'd set up a punishing interval workout, determined to force the negative thoughts from her mind. As her heart pounded and every leg muscle screamed in protest, she concentrated on the television across the room, streaming an upbeat hip hop music channel.

She half-expected Mrs. Carter to come in and ask her to turn it down or tell her the exercise bike wasn't included with her stay, but nobody came. Lauren, the girl she'd met at lunch yesterday who had been the center of all the gossip in the bleachers last night, showed up at the inn before Alyssa hopped on the bike.

Alyssa had grabbed coffee and a carton of yogurt, then left Lauren and Mrs. Carter alone in the kitchen. Judging by Lauren's red-rimmed eyes, she needed a few minutes with her mom.

Thoughts of family only took Alyssa's mind to places she couldn't afford to go. If she narrowed her focus to her body's performance, then she wouldn't have to think about anything else. Not the basketball game, or Jeremy, or even her evasive maneuver to get out of the truck last night before something happened they'd both regret.

Or would they?

Don't do it. Don't even allow yourself the possibility.

The workout called for thirty seconds of less intensity, so she slowed her pace and sat up straight, sucking in deep breaths. Cross-training was her least favorite method of staying fit. Give her a mountain and a snowboard any day over sweating it out on dry land.

But heading out to the resort meant an encounter with Jeremy. She couldn't trust herself not to do something foolish.

He was kind. Thoughtful. Attentive. Unless she'd imagined those stolen glances and flirty banter, he was clearly interested in her.

And she was a train wreck.

It wasn't fair to lead him on, not when she had every intention of leaving once the commercial was filmed and she could risk being seen in public again. Before Nick humiliated her, she might not have thought twice about a casual fling. She'd hooked up with a guy she'd met in Zurich for a competition once. Charlie. What an epic week that was. He was hot. And available. She'd landed a new trick on her board, earning the attention of every guy on the mountain. It was intoxicating—the way every head turned when she walked into the bar after the competition, the way girls glared at her and tugged their guys away from her.

All that power and control was an illusion, though.

She'd given little thought to the physical or emotional consequences. Even though three years had passed, her heart fisted at the memory. They'd used each other. Pretending not to care when they'd parted ways was easy, but if she was honest, it hurt to think about how quickly she'd disposed of the relationship. How little respect he had for her.

It wasn't right.

But if it was wrong, why did she fall into the same old habits with Nick? Why was the bad-boy type always her kryptonite? She straightened and clasped her hands behind her head, chest heaving as she sprinted on the bike, forcing her body to comply with her demands.

While she'd toyed with Charlie and then done whatever she needed to capture Nick's attention, she wouldn't use Jeremy to assuage her heartache.

He deserved better.

Besides, as soon as he saw the pictures of her online, he'd distance himself. He was too good for someone like her.

Her phone chimed, notifying her of a social media update, and her fingers itched to jab at the screen and read the latest posts. Apparently her vow to delete her accounts was just a bunch of talk. She wasn't strong enough to follow through on that, either.

Why was she so weak?

Sweat trickled into her eyes, and she swiped it away with the hem of her T-shirt. The phone chimed again, alerting her to change up her pace for the next interval. The physical pain ramped up, yet she refused to yield. Because physical pain was way better than the emotional wounds she couldn't escape.

★★★

Should've kissed her.

Jeremy dipped his shovel in the fresh snow piled on the hood of his truck and knocked it to the ground. Spontaneity had never been a problem. Leap first and ask questions later—that had been an effective strategy for most of his life. Until Celeste. Her careless actions had left him wounded. Afraid to fall again. Then last night happened. Or maybe it all started with a collision on the ski hill. Something about this girl with the mismatched piercing stare made him want to put himself out there.

And it scared him to death.

He tightened his grip on the shovel, his breath leaving a white contrail in the inky darkness as he rounded the truck and started clearing a path toward the street. A headlamp mounted over his knit cap gave him enough light to work with. It was just after six—way too early to fire up the snowblower—but still at least two hours before the sun made a brief appearance. He needed the physical exertion anyway, something to do while his thoughts were stuck on an instant replay of the previous night. The same old questions spinning in an endless loop. Why was Alyssa here? Hiding out in Alaska was a drastic measure just to avoid a store opening, especially so close to Christmas. There had to be another reason a star like her walked away from a snowboarding season before it barely started.

Why do I even care?

It wasn't like a serious relationship with her was an option. She didn't strike him as the kind of girl who'd want to get married and settle down. He couldn't see her moving into his condo in the off-season and making Emerald Cove her second home.

Whoa. Take it easy. His gut tightened. He'd been here before. And he hadn't learned his lesson, either. Women like Alyssa loved his free-spirited outlook and willingness to be the life of the party.

Despite the single-digit temperatures, warmth flooded his cheeks. He was almost thirty, for Pete's sake. There wasn't much he was proud of in the last decade. He'd partied way too much. Got caught up in the rush of fleeting fame and forgot all about the faith he barely clung to now. Treated women as objects. Made poor choices without regard for consequences. Until the consequences proved deadly for one of his closest friends. Was the anxiety plaguing him now a punishment for his wrongdoing? The God he served and believed in didn't seem like He operated like that. Rain fell on the just and the unjust, didn't it?

Jeremy shook his head and finished clearing the driveway so he could leave for the resort. In his heart, he didn't believe the God of the universe operated on a merit-based system. Otherwise there wasn't any room for radical grace. But the longer he struggled to make sense of his heartache, the more he doubted. Would the fear and the regret ever go away?

He put away his shovel and trudged toward his front door. He'd have to keep working hard, that's all. Prove to himself and his family—the town—that he could bounce back. Soon the lodge would reopen, and he'd finally be able to put the unfortunate events of that devastating night behind him. Inside his comfortable two-bedroom bachelor pad, Hazel jumped up from her usual spot by the gas fireplace and stretched, tail wagging.

"Must be nice, Hazel girl, lying by the fire while somebody else does all the work." Jeremy unlaced his boots and tugged them off.

The yellow Labrador trotted over, a tennis ball wedged in her mouth.

"Three tosses, all right? Drop it."

She complied, the faded green ball bouncing at his feet as he stood in his entryway.

"Good girl." He lobbed it across the living room and she scampered after the ball, barking with delight as it bounced off the wall beside the couch. Jeremy hung his jacket on one of the hooks by the door and rolled up the cuffs of his jeans. Hazel returned, proudly depositing her slobber-coated prize in front of him. They repeated the process again and again—exceeding his mandate of three tosses—until his phone chimed from where it charged on the kitchen counter.

"Good job, girl. That's enough for now." He gave her a solid pat on the head and stepped around her. She'd retrieve that thing all day if he let her.

She followed him into the kitchen and paused at her bowl to lap up some water.

He reached for his phone. A voice mail, an overwhelming number of email messages, and a text waited for him. He checked the text message first. Blake.

Lauren's staying at her parents' place for a couple of days. We need space. No ice climbing clients scheduled.

"Dang it." He stared at the screen, rereading the message. "That stinks." Not the part about the ice climbing clients. Booking new customers was the least of his worries now. His stomach clenched. Lauren and Blake had slayed their demons in recent years. Despite the tension bubbling between he and his brother, Jeremy only wanted the best for Blake. For Lauren, too. A broken relationship after all they'd been through seemed completely unfair.

Jeremy texted back a quick response.

I'm sorry. Let me know if you want to hang out.

Hazel splayed on the floor at his feet and released an empathetic whimper.

Blake must be flipping out.

Jeremy wished he'd known sooner about their marital struggles and the challenges of starting a family. Maybe if he'd paid attention to somebody other than himself, he wouldn't have been so feisty at dinner the other night. Blowing out a long breath, he silently prayed for protection for Blake and Lauren's marriage. Apart from his plea of thanks when the helicopter had landed, this was the first time he'd prayed in quite a while. Guilt swept in again, reminding him of yet another way he'd fallen short.

Shoving the guilty feelings aside, Jeremy went into the kitchen.

While he scrambled eggs for breakfast, his phone buzzed again. Those email messages couldn't be avoided forever.

He hesitated, letting his finger hover over the inbox. Nothing wrong with glancing at a couple. Heck, he'd waited so long to read any of his email, most of it was probably old news and required no action on his part. Gnawing on his lower lip, he tapped the screen and scanned the first message.

A short note from one of his former co-workers. Producers in California were meeting to talk about reviving the show. Was he interested?

Not a chance.

He closed the message without reading the rest. Didn't she get it? Starring in *Troubled Waters* had nearly ruined him. Divided his community and his friends and made it impossible for him to even go the grocery store without getting dirty looks. Not to mention the cameraman who'd lost his life. How could they even think of filming another season?

Emerald Cove wasn't the town it had once been, and he'd never get over the guilt for playing a huge role in its downfall. People had warned him not to get involved in the show. But he'd brushed off the advice—arguing that the success of other shows like *Deadliest Catch* proved that not all reality television shows were bad. For three seasons, he'd made sure that *Troubled Waters* was the best thing that ever happened to his hometown.

Then he'd invited the whole cast and crew to the new resort—it had just opened—to celebrate the production of the last episode. And everything went up in flames. Literally.

He plated his scrambled eggs and carried them to the table, stopping to grab a fork from the drawer and his medication. The production company must be desperate, chasing after a wounded has-been like him. *Maybe they'd contacted the wrong person. Maybe that message was meant for someone else—someone who didn't depend on pharmaceuticals to keep him afloat.*

The second-guessing seeped in, twisting its ornery tentacles around his heart and filling his head with ugly thoughts. Jeremy squeezed his eyes shut. *Stop.* He wasn't healthy and maybe never would be. Hadn't he learned that wanting the impossible was futile?

While he ate, he glanced at a new email message in his inbox from someone at *Explore* magazine. No, thank you, Doug Kelton from *Explore* magazine. Not interested. He ignored the message and opened the phone's web browser instead. What could it hurt to Google Alyssa Huard? Maybe a little sleuthing would shed some light on the growing list of questions he couldn't ignore.

The first link to an article from a popular entertainment magazine caught his attention. "Olympic snowboarder and Aspen resident Alyssa Huard vanishes after scandalous photos go viral."

What? He scrolled down, goosebumps pebbling his skin.

He whisper-read the headline. "Olympic snowboarder walks away from competition. Is a viral social media post to blame?" He'd never heard of the website, but every word was still like a punch in the gut.

Who wrote this?

I'm thinking about deleting my social media accounts.

Her comment from the helicopter replayed in his mind, and he scrolled down to an Instagram post included in the story. Instead of snow-capped mountains, a picture of Lake Tahoe, or an awesome shot of a snowboarder laying down a trick on a Colorado mountainside, the image on his screen sent his stomach plummeting to his toes. That was Alyssa all right. He'd recognize those eyes anywhere. But this shot had nothing to do with snowboarding.

Jeremy gritted his teeth. She wasn't completely topless, but close enough. While the temptation to let his eyes linger tugged at him, he jabbed at the screen then pushed his phone away. Sighing, he pinched the bridge of his nose with his fingertips. Who posted the picture? Based on her facial expression, she didn't seem surprised by the camera. Had she opted to pose like that? It sure looked intentional. He scrubbed his palm across his face, struggling to make sense of what he'd seen. What kind of girl was this who'd managed to capture his heart so easily?

***

Alyssa rode the lift to the top of the ski hill, heavy metal music blasting from the earbuds she'd jammed in her ears. A guy named

Wyatt had been kind enough to give her a ride out to the mountain. He'd dropped off some Christmas gifts at the inn, said he was a friend of the Carters. No sense passing up a free ride, right? Cabs in this town were crazy expensive, and Uber wasn't available.

When she reached the top of the hill, she slid off the seat and dropped to the snow, scooting her board across the hard-packed surface with her free leg. Adrenaline pulsed through her veins as she stared down the run. That killer workout on the bike had done a number on her legs, and her knee still ached if she turned too quickly. But the longer she lounged around her room, alone, the more she wanted to climb right out of her skin. Wyatt's offer gave her the perfect opportunity to get outside. To forget all her worries.

Unfortunately, the snowcat crossing her field of vision reminded her of Jeremy—for at least the twentieth time today. Not a problem. She adjusted her goggles then drew a cleansing breath. She could avoid the giant trail groomer. And Jeremy at the controls.

Alyssa locked her other foot in the snowboard's bindings then straightened. Out of habit, she tapped her helmet, readjusted her gloves one more time, rocked forward on the edge, and cruised down the mountain. The gray clouds overhead and a crisp bite in the air hinted at more snow. Fine with her. Another ten to twelve inches meant even more afternoons of shredding fresh powder.

This ride was unbelievable. Leaving Colorado was spontaneous and maybe even a little risky, but at least she'd landed in a place with incredible opportunities. Too bad she didn't have anyone to tell about her latest discovery. Lying low still proved to be her best coping strategy, though. She'd ride the proverbial storm out like she always did, just her and her board.

Pushing aside the loneliness threatening to engulf her, she leaned back and cut a wide berth around two guys skiing down the center of the hill. The resort had drawn a crowd today—quite a big change from her weekday visits. As she picked up speed, Alyssa bent her knees, propelled her body into the air with a grunt, then pulled off a three-hundred-sixty-degree turn. Her stomach dipped and weaved, the now-familiar high of pulling off a trick making her crave it more.

She landed with a satisfying thud and couldn't resist pumping her fist in the air.

Several skiers stopped and watched her zoom by. *That's the way it's done, peeps.* Despite her resolve not to draw a lot of attention to herself, she couldn't resist lifting her chin a little higher. The spotlight still offered its own kind of addictive thrill.

At the bottom of the run, she lifted her goggles and rested them on top of her helmet. Looking uphill, a smile pulled at the corners of her mouth. *Man, what a rush.* Even though her legs trembled in protest, she couldn't wait to give it another go.

She didn't see Jeremy until he stood next to her.

She stifled an obscenity. Her smile faded. Where did he come from? She'd been so impressed with her run she'd lost track of the snowcat.

"Hey." She tugged her earbuds free. "What's up?"

"Nice run." A hesitant smile formed on his lips. He searched her face with those amazing eyes of his.

She warmed under his appraisal. "Thanks."

Stubble clung to his jaw. He definitely had that rugged outdoorsy thing going on. All resolve to ignore him melted away. His presence rivaled the rush she'd just experienced on her last ride.

He tipped his head toward the chairlift. "Are you going again?"

Alyssa shrugged. "Maybe. Why?"

"Just wondered. I've got a few minutes free. I'd like to stick around and watch. It's fun to see you do your thing."

Her heart flip-flopped in her chest. Oh, boy. Resistance might be futile. She quickly changed the subject. "How's your sister-in-law? She looked pretty upset when I saw her this morning."

A crease formed between his brows. "They're taking some time apart. You'll probably see her staying at the inn for a while."

She winced. "I hope everything works out."

"Yeah, me, too."

The kindness in his expression, his almost palpable concern for the people he loved, slayed her. What she wouldn't give to be the center of his world. The thought rammed its way in and took up residence before she could chase it away with straight logic.

He reached up and tugged on a lock of her hair, his eyes glinting and that dimple of his threatening to make another appearance. "Wish I had time to play in the snow with you."

Her pulse jumped at his innocent gesture. Despite the freezing temperatures, all her senses were on high alert. Honed in on his face, his voice, his gloved hand still toying with her hair. "I wish you did, too."

The words slipped out before the harsh reality rained down on her like sleet in a mid-winter storm. *What am I thinking?* Jeremy seemed like a good guy. The best kind. Why would he want to be with a girl like her?

She cleared her throat and reached down to free her boot from her binding. "I'm sure you have work to do. Maybe I'll see you around."

"Alyssa, wait."

She pretended not to hear him and popped her earbuds back in as she cruised toward the lift. *Keep moving.* She didn't need him to rescue her. Even if he could. But as she waited at the back of the line, hot tears pricked her eyes. Add that to the half-dozen other lies she'd told herself about him.

***

Jeremy's heart ached as Alyssa took off. He should've said something—told her he'd seen the pictures. That he wanted to help. But the indecipherable emotion flickering in her eyes when he touched her hair and the wall she'd instantly erected made her feelings clear. She didn't want his help. How could he show her he cared? That he didn't have an ulterior motive?

He blew out a long breath and trekked toward the lodge. All the grooming was finished. At least until another storm hit or the Saturday crowd carved up the mountain. This had to be record attendance. Chuck was probably stoked. Without another glance in the direction of the line waiting for the lift, Jeremy picked up his pace. Rachel had texted twice while he was driving the snowcat to let him know she needed his help. Were they ever going to be finished?

Inside the lodge, he pulled off his hat and gloves then stomped the snow from his boots on the mat. The painters had finished, and the fireplace only needed a mantel. Judging by the plastic-wrapped furniture jammed in the center of the lobby, more sofas and chairs had arrived. Good grief. Every time he turned around, he found something else to add to the to-do list.

The sound of Michael Bublé's Christmas album played from a wireless speaker at the front desk, reminding him he had limited time to buy gifts. While a last-minute run to Anchorage wasn't out of the question, online shopping was a better option at this point. Unless Chuck sent him, he'd better stick close to the resort or they'd never make their New Year's Eve deadline.

Rachel sat behind the desk, holding a paper coffee cup in one hand while she pressed the phone to her ear with the other. "Uh-huh ... absolutely ... yes, of course." She rolled her eyes and gestured to the drink carton sitting in front of her. She mouthed, "For you. From Megan."

He gave her a thumbs up. That was an unexpected surprise. So his little sister was home. He frowned. What was she doing making coffee runs, though? Did she get her old job back as a barista at the Copper Kettle Coffee Company? He made a mental note to go by their parents' house and see her. Not to mention that Wyatt's cryptic interest in her was too intriguing to ignore.

After lifting the cup from the carrier, he grabbed an empty seat across from Rachel. She'd abandoned her coffee and had the phone pinched between her shoulder and her ear, both hands on the computer keyboard, fingernails clicking as she plugged data into the system. This might take a while. He sipped his mocha, enjoying the warmth and sweetness. His phone vibrated in his pocket, but he refused to respond.

Rachel had ended the call. "Oh my word." She pressed her palms to her cheeks. "This is insane."

"What's wrong?"

She adjusted the red scarf draped around her neck. "Chuck wants me to keep accepting reservations for New Year's Eve. So I did. We're four rooms away from being sold out."

"Whoa." Jeremy almost dropped his coffee. "He knows there isn't a bed in the whole place, right?"

"I've mentioned that. He assures me the delivery will be here any day."

"Great." His voice dripped with sarcasm. The combination of

shoveling snow and unpacking furniture was taking its toll on his weary muscles. Imagine how he'd feel after unloading a tractor-trailer full of beds and dressers.

Rachel glanced at the computer screen again and her eyes widened. "Oh no."

"More reservations?"

"No." She spun the laptop around so he could see the screen.

He squinted and leaned closer, pretending to study the information. "What's up?"

She released a pent-up breath. "More emails from clients expecting things we can't deliver. This guy says they have a room booked the first week of January. Now he's mentioned an ice climbing excursion and a snowmobile ride. Do you know anything about this?"

A dull ache formed near his temple. Was it too late to spend Christmas in Cozumel? "I don't think that's anything you need to worry about. Lauren asked me about the ice climbing thing. She wanted to offer it as a custom excursion, even though we've never done that before. I didn't realize she'd confirmed the details. I thought Blake said to—never mind. I'll try to follow up."

Rachel frowned. "Don't forget."

Jeremy stood to leave. "I won't." If Rachel had heard about Blake and Lauren's issues, she was smart enough not to ask.

"Wait. Don't go. We also need four rooms ready for the film crew." Rachel picked up her pen and scribbled on a notepad. "They'll be here Monday."

He hesitated. "This Monday? That's a nice thing to tell me on a Friday afternoon."

"Don't shoot the messenger, okay?"

He shook his head and flopped down in the chair. Ridiculous. "There's no way."

"Supposedly, we'll have a skeleton crew in place."

"I hope you like waiting tables."

"Ha. You're hilarious. I hope you like making beds."

"Not on your life."

Chuck's voice echoed from the lobby.

"Here we go." Rachel reached for her coffee. "Brace for impact."

Jeremy stifled a laugh with his hand.

"Jeremy, my man." Chuck clapped him on the shoulder. "I heard your sister is looking for work. Is she any good at waiting tables?"

Rachel choked on her coffee.

Jeremy fumbled for words. Was he serious? "Megan? I—I don't know. She used to wait tables part-time."

"Sweet. If she's twenty-one, she's hired."

"She won't be twenty-one until August."

"Oh." Chuck shrugged. "She looks older. Maybe she can make beds. Or work the morning shift when the bar's not open."

Jeremy bit his tongue. What was up with Chuck pushing to hire Megan? Nothing about that sounded like a smart idea, especially if she'd be going back to school after the holidays.

"C'mon. The truck's here. Help me unload the freight."

Jeremy trailed after Chuck, dreading what they'd find in the back of that truck. Any hope of hanging out with Alyssa faded fast, obliterated by the pressure to stay on task and get the resort opened in time for New Year's Eve.

7

On Monday morning, Alyssa paced outside the lodge, her snowboard and gear piled beside the front door. She stopped and checked her phone. Lance and the film crew's chartered flight should've landed at the airport twenty minutes ago. Why hadn't he called? What if he'd missed his connection? They'd had limited communication since their terse discussion about her absence at the store's grand opening. Maybe ignoring his messages was a lousy decision after all.

She glanced up and scanned the semi-dark parking lot again. Still no sign of any headlights coming up the hill. Facing this commercial shoot without Lance as a buffer had her insides tied in knots. While she talked a big game, handling an all-male film crew in the rugged Alaskan mountains was more than she could take. Especially now. They'd probably all seen the pictures online. She didn't want to think about the horrible things they'd say to her.

"Do you want to wait inside?"

Jeremy's voice sent her pulse skittering. A whole weekend had passed since their conversation at the bottom of the ski hill. It was two days too long. She'd spent most of it moping at the Carter's and alternating between hating herself for wanting him and wishing he'd find a reason to come by or they'd run into each other. Nope. *But he's here now.*

She turned around. Big mistake. Any clever words she'd formulated died on her lips. He'd closed the distance between them, and those blue eyes locked on hers made her heart beat faster. Oh, for the love of—

He grinned. "There's a fire going. We've even unpacked the furniture."

The mental picture of those muscular arms of his wrapped around her teased her senses. *If only.* She bit her lip, and he arched his brow, then stepped closer. A delicious tingle arced down her spine.

The rumble of a car engine caught her attention.

She quickly turned away, severing the connection. An SUV wound its way up the hill from the highway, as her phone chimed in her pocket. Finally. That had better be Lance calling. She yanked it free. Perfect timing—before her heart got the better of her and made her say things she shouldn't. "I've got to take this." She answered the call without giving the caller ID a second thought. "Hello?"

"Sweetheart? Thank God you're okay." Mom's voice broke. "I've called and called. Didn't you get my messages?"

"Mom?" Alyssa whirled away from Jeremy's inquisitive stare. "Um, hi."

"I finally spoke to Lance yesterday. We've been worried sick. What are you doing in Alaska?"

Her heart fisted. "I know. I'm sorry. Things got kind of crazy."

"Kind of crazy? More like unreal. Why did you leave the competition? You were doing so well." Mom sniffed. "Your dad and I couldn't believe it when you … vanished."

"I just … needed to get out of there. I'll explain some other time." The SUV cruised to a stop in front of her. "Can I call you later? I'm late for an appointment."

"Alyssa, wait."

The desperate plea kept Alyssa from ending the call. "What? I'm still here." The back door swung open and Lance stepped out, his messenger bag slung over one shoulder of his traffic-cone orange North Face jacket. They wouldn't lose him in a blizzard, that was for sure.

"Are you coming home for Christmas?" Mom asked. "We'll all be here this year. It won't be the same if you're not."

Emotion clogged her throat. Lance raised an eyebrow, and she ducked her head. "I—I don't know. I'll keep you posted."

The film crew spilled out of the Suburban, deep voices, gear, and luggage adding to the chaos as they encroached on the lodge's entrance.

"Alyssa, honey, Christmas is less than a week away. It might be nice if—"

"I'll call you soon, Mom. Love ya." She ended the call, stuffed her phone in her pocket, and pasted on a smile for Lance before she turned and faced him. "Hey. It's about time you showed up."

"That's quite the welcome. Thanks, I guess." Lance pulled her in for a quick hug.

Over his shoulder, she caught Jeremy watching them, a muscle in his jaw tightening. A twinge of satisfaction deep inside caught her off guard. She liked that he cared. Averting her gaze, she refocused her attention on Lance. "Nice flight?"

Lance stepped back, blowing air into his bare fists. "It's really cold around here. Can we move this party inside?"

"Absolutely." Chuck had emerged from the lodge, looking surprisingly well put-together. He'd shaved and perhaps even washed his hair. A broad grin stretched across his weathered features as Chuck shook hands with each of the four guys from the production company.

Chuck hesitated when he saw Alyssa. "Hello again, sweetheart. What brings you out so early?"

She narrowed her gaze. "Trust me, I'm not a fan of mornings. Aren't we leaving as soon as it's light?"

Chuck shot a questioning look around the semicircle. "Leaving?"

Lance came to her rescue. "Alyssa's our featured snowboarder for the commercial shoot. With Verge? Remember? She'll need to be a part of our production meeting. Is there a conference room free? We've got logistics to work out before the helicopter lands. I believe your assistant offered to have brunch available."

The color drained from Chuck's face. "Brunch. Right. I'll have Rachel, uh, fill you in. C'mon. The fire's going in the lobby. Maybe you could just meet there?" He led the way inside.

Alyssa bit back a smile. Chuck didn't have a clue what he'd signed up for. This could be fun.

Lance motioned for her to go ahead of him. "Why do I get the feeling he's not prepared for us?"

"Hang on. He kind of flies by the seat of his pants." She stepped inside, surveying the lobby.

A fire crackled and popped in the giant stone fireplace, casting an inviting glow over the leather sofas arranged in a U-formation. In the corner, an artificial Christmas tree stood barren, while Rachel—the young woman who worked with Jeremy—balanced on a ladder, an impressive string of white lights spilling from her arms. Alyssa let her gaze ping around the room. Where was Jeremy, anyway? Outside unloading the luggage? She peeked through the glass doors. Nope. She turned and scanned the lobby again. He wasn't behind the tree or near the front desk either. She tried to pretend his absence didn't bother her. *Focus. You can't afford any distractions.*

***

Jeremy heaved the last duffel bag into the back of the Super Cub airplane. "Slight change of plans," he mumbled under his breath. More like a complete one-eighty. Somehow Chuck had convinced them at the last second to charter another plane, in addition to the helicopter, so they could get to Lost Lake Gulch sooner. Over a hearty breakfast prepared by the resort's new chef and short order cook, he'd also convinced them that filming for more than a few hours during the limited December daylight required an overnight stay. On the side of a mountain, in sub-zero temps. And he'd appointed Jeremy as their unofficial Sherpa.

He shook his head. How did Chuck get away with stuff like this? Either these film people were idiots, or they wanted to get the job done and get home for Christmas.

"All set?" Dale, the plane's pilot, stood next to him, eyeing the weight calculated on the scale. Judging by his expression, he didn't think they'd come in under the limit, either.

"How about that. Five pounds to spare," Jeremy said.

Dale nodded his approval and tugged his knit cap lower. "The weather's changing. Let's get this bird in the air."

Jeremy didn't even want to think about what might happen if they got stuck up at Lost Lake. One thing was for sure—Alyssa's behavior set him on edge. He hadn't imagined the sparks arcing between them outside the lodge this morning.

Had he?

But she'd blown him off for a phone call and hadn't spoken to him since. And why hadn't she admitted she was in town to film the Verge commercial?

Maybe he was jealous—especially after she'd smiled and hugged that smooth-talking dude in the orange jacket. He didn't trust him.

Against his better judgement, he took his place in the back seat of the plane, debating if he should speak up about the ominous forecast. Dale was right. The weather forecast for the next two days was questionable at best. What if Dale couldn't take off tomorrow and they had to spend more than one night on the mountain? Were they prepared for the conditions?

Alyssa and Mr. Wonderful sat in the two seats in front of him, their heads close together and voices low. She didn't acknowledge Jeremy's existence. *Whatever.* He fastened his safety belt and settled in for the short flight. His gut twisted. Why did he even bother to care?

The whine of the aircraft's propeller filled the small cabin, and two cameramen exchanged nervous smiles. The rest of their team had left earlier in the helicopter with AJ.

As the plane picked up speed and left the ground, soaring into the clouds, Jeremy dug his fingers into the seat's arm rests and breathed in for three counts. The best way to handle turbulence was to try to concentrate on something else. He exhaled slowly, steeling himself for the onslaught of flashbacks.

Relax.

Despite his efforts to stare straight ahead and focus on the horizon, Alyssa's laughter floated through the enclosed space, keeping him distracted. When they hit an air pocket and the plane's altitude dropped, the collective gasp rippling through the cabin forced him to glance ahead and make sure she was okay.

She looked at him over her shoulder, eyes wide, her cheeks lacking their usual rosy glow.

He held her gaze, willing her to remain calm, despite her obvious unease. While a healthy fear was good for her because it meant she'd respect the elements and avoid foolish mistakes, he wanted to spare her the anxiety that plagued him. She may have snowboarded around the world and even been an Olympic athlete, but that didn't mean she was prepared for this. He'd lived here most of his life, and Alaska still never ceased to amaze him.

Less than an hour later, Dale brought the plane down on a flat stretch of compacted snow not far from Lost Lake. Jeremy breathed a sigh of relief as they cruised to a stop. The helicopter, a bright splash of red against a monochromatic white backdrop, sat with its rotors still. Judging by the guys huddled near the door, packs at their feet and cameras on tripods already, they didn't want to waste much time out here, either.

Jeremy got out of the plane last, wincing at the noticeable drop in temperature. It had to be well below zero up here. He made short work of unloading all the equipment, mentally checking off his list of essentials as he piled it in the snow at his feet. Tents. Lanterns. Cook stove. Ready-to-eat meals. Sleeping bags. Extra—

"Nice work," Dale said, giving Jeremy a tight smile. "Is that everything?"

"Yep." Jeremy nodded. "See you tomorrow?"

A look of uncertainty flashed in Dale's eyes. "I'll try. It might not be tomorrow, though, not with the way that front is moving in."

Jeremy's mouth went dry. "You're joking."

"Nope." Dale brushed past him, headed for the cockpit. "I told Chuck and his people before we left this was a long shot. They threw plenty of money at me, but Mother Nature has a mind of her own. Besides, I've gotta make a run to Cordova and pick up my parents." He stopped, one hand on the open door. "They want to be at our house in time for Christmas."

Jeremy swallowed hard. They all wanted to be home for Christmas. He stole a quick glance at Alyssa. She stood nearby, examining the bindings on her snowboard. Did she know what she'd signed up for?

The thought of spending more than a night out here planted an icy ball in his gut. "Safe travels, Dale."

"Thanks. Catch you on the flip side."

A few minutes later, Dale fired up the plane and taxied down the makeshift runway formed by Mother Nature's whims.

Alyssa wedged the end of her board in the snow and jogged over. "Where's he going?"

"Back to town," Jeremy said. "Didn't they tell you?"

Her chin dropped as the plane disappeared into the clouds, the engine noise fading. "N-no. He's coming back, right?"

"Not today." Maybe not tomorrow either. He couldn't bring himself to tell her that part.

"But…" She looked at the helicopter. "We'll never fit in the helicopter. Not in one trip, anyway."

"We might be here for … a while. The weather's unpredictable, and it's too expensive to fly back and forth. Better to get in, hunker down, and film as much footage as possible." He surveyed her face, the worry creasing her features tugging at him. Didn't her team bother to explain the challenges of shooting a commercial in Alaska in the middle of winter? Wasn't there a contract negotiated or anything?

"Alyssa." Lance motioned for her to come closer.

Still staring at the empty sky in disbelief, Alyssa sighed.

"Hey." Jeremy reached for her, grasping her upper arm in his gloved hand. "It's going to be all right. I promise. You can do this."

She bit her lip, a sheen of moisture turning one of her eyes a brilliant shade of aquamarine. Tugging her arm free, she moved away, just like the first time they met. She snatched her board and joined the rest of the crew circled up nearby.

Jeremy's chest tightened. He didn't want to care. He'd tried so hard not to. Yet standing out here in the wilderness, freezing his tail off, reality set in. She'd worked her way into his heart. There was no turning back. And he'd do everything he could to protect her.

8

Dang, it was cold. A numb-all-the-way-to-your-bones kind of cold. An icy wind howled off the mountain, stinging Alyssa's cheeks and blowing snow sideways. She slogged toward what she hoped was her tent, every muscle in her body aching with fatigue. Why had she ever agreed to this? Three intense rides down the mountain coupled with the hike back up had wiped her out. What she wouldn't give for a hot bath, warm bed, and a three-course meal.

Lit up like jack-o'-lanterns, four tents glowed orange in a dug-out area. An impressive man-made wall of snow encircled the impromptu village. Had Jeremy done all this? She hadn't seen him since they'd witnessed the plane's departure. Wow. He'd been busy.

Moving closer, she identified a familiar shape filling the entrance of the tent to her right.

Jeremy held the flap open. "Here. Get inside." He took her snowboard. She didn't bother to argue. It could blow away in the middle of the night for all she cared. Then she wouldn't have to perform for the cameras while a storm raged around her. These film people were insane. Sure, it was money in the bank, but hardly worth it at this point.

She hesitated in the tent's entrance. Two blue sleeping bags that had been spread across a double layer of foam pads occupied most of the space. Cozy arrangement. Her stomach tightened. Jeremy hunched over a gas stove in the tent's vestibule, pouring hot water from a kettle into a thermos.

"Hurry." He glanced over his shoulder. "Zip up the tent flaps and take off your gear."

"Not happening, dude." She fisted her hands inside her gloves. Did he think she'd just strip down in front of him? She trembled, her body quivering all over.

"Only your boots and any wet layers. We have to keep you dry." His brow furrowed. "Are you shivering?"

She didn't want to confess that her body's reaction had more to do with what she'd found inside the tent than her exposure to the elements. On the other hand, he made a valid point. Wet clothes and sub-zero temperatures posed a dangerous combination.

He sprang into action, twisting the cap back on the silver container. "I have an idea." He pulled a bivvy sack from his supplies stored at his feet. "If you leave your boots exposed, they'll be frozen tomorrow. We'll stash them at the bottom of your sleeping bag."

Too tired to debate, she gritted her teeth to stop the chattering. How could anything *not* be frozen by morning? She tugged off her mittens and liners, followed by both of her boots.

"Are your socks wet?"

"No."

Jeremy collected her boots then shoved the sack deep inside the first sleeping bag. "There. Your body heat will keep them warm overnight."

It was a backcountry survival tip she'd read about in magazines and blog posts. Still, she had her doubts.

"Sit down. I'll have chili ready in two minutes."

Alyssa lowered her aching, half-frozen body to the tent floor. The cold seeped through her layers of long underwear, microfleece, and snow pants. She tucked her knees up under her chin and wrapped her arms around her legs, determined not to panic.

Jeremy examined the contents of a ready-made meal. A tendril of steam curled into the air. He dipped a spoon inside and offered it to her. "Here. Dinner is served."

"Thank you." She cupped the warm pouch between her palms. The spicy aroma teased her senses. "Did you already eat?"

"Not yet. Mine's almost ready."

She took a bite of the beef and bean concoction, bracing for an unsavory experience. Dehydrated meals had a reputation for tasting like mush. While the flavor impressed her, the chili scalded her mouth. She cringed and forced herself to swallow.

"Careful. It's hot."

"No kidding." She regretted snapping at him. It wasn't his fault the storm had blown in, trapping them on the side of a mountain.

"Maybe this will help." Jeremy set a water bottle at her feet then sank down opposite her on the end of his sleeping bag.

She took a few sips of water, letting the cool liquid soothe the stinging sensation on her tongue.

"I'm sure you're well aware that the best defense against hypothermia—after staying warm and dry—is to keep drinking fluids."

She blew on the soup this time before taking a bite. Another shiver wracked her body, and the chili dribbled off the spoon. Shoot. Was she battling hypothermia?

He shook his head. "I knew this was a bad idea."

"What's a bad idea?"

"Bringing you up here." He yanked a down jacket, wool hat, and microfleece pants from his pack.

"What are you doing?"

"Getting warm clothes for you. I'm guessing you don't have any extra layers in your duffle?"

"Extra wool long underwear and lots of socks."

"You can borrow these." He stacked the clothing beside him. "Why don't you finish eating first."

"What are you going to wear?"

"Don't worry about me." His gentle gaze captured hers. "You're my first priority."

She ducked her head, pretending to focus on finishing her dinner. His words warmed her, more than a hot meal ever could. His first priority? Other than her adoptive parents, nobody had ever said anything like that before. She'd grown accustomed to being a commodity. An asset. The headlining snowboarder at an event. Somewhere in her quest to be the best in the world, she'd forgotten her value. Her own worth.

The familiar zing of a zipper pulled her back to reality. Jeremy had unzipped both sleeping bags and now maneuvered them into one giant bag, with the bivvy sack shoved in the end.

Her pulse ramped up. Wait. What? "You're joking, right?" She scraped the last of the chili from the pouch. "It's early. Too early to …

sleep." Her chattering teeth prevented her from saying more. Was this how he rolled? Had this all been a ploy to get her alone?

Loud male voices, followed by boisterous laughter, erupted from one of the other tents. Of course. Lance had forgotten all about her. Maybe Jeremy had conveniently orchestrated this setup.

"See? You're freezing." He unfolded the fleece pants. "I'll shield my eyes or whatever, but I need you to get out of that jacket and snow pants and put these on over your base layers."

She set the empty pouch aside and pushed to her feet. As promised, Jeremy turned his back while she stripped off her outer layer and added the fleece, then tugged her snow pants back on.

"Better?" he asked, facing her again.

She nodded, not trusting herself to speak. A lump formed in her throat. This couldn't be happening. Stranded in the remote mountains of Alaska four days before Christmas. What if the storm didn't subside by tomorrow? Visions of search and rescue recovering their frozen, lifeless bodies flashed in her head. A dam burst inside. Tears blurred her vision as she sucked in a ragged breath.

"Hey, what's wrong?" He let the sleeping bag fall to the foam pad and moved closer. His eyes searched her face, forehead creased with worry. "Talk to me. Why are you crying?"

His warm hands cupped her cheeks.

She tensed.

"Are you worried?"

Alyssa managed a quick nod. *You have no idea.*

"Scared we'll be stuck here a while?"

Another nod. Then a pathetic sniffle.

"Yeah, me, too." He thumbed away a tear. "I'm not going to let anything happen to you. Winter camping is possible out here. We need to make smart choices, though. Can you do that?"

"Maybe." She swallowed hard. This whole arrangement still made her uneasy. Slightly less so the longer he caressed her cheek and spoke in a soothing voice. Was she wrong to assume this wasn't what it looked like?

"If you'll put on this extra jacket and get in the sleeping bag, I'll put a hot water bottle by your feet and tuck you in. The shivering has to stop. Agreed?"

"I—I know."

His hands dropped to his sides, and he crossed to the stove in two long strides. She stared down at the sleeping bags, now combined into one. Her pulse kicked against her rib cage. The wind howled outside, rippling the walls of the tent. This was a matter of life and death, right? Jeremy had given her no reason not to trust him.

Dragging the back of her hand across her nose to staunch the drips, she reached for the down jacket and slipped her arms inside. Then she dropped to the floor and crawled inside the sleeping bag, avoiding the bivvy sack jammed in the bottom.

"Here." Jeremy knelt beside her, holding a lantern and the silver thermos he'd filled earlier. "Put this between your feet. Do you need extra socks?"

"No. Thank you." She took the container and slid it down. The warmth against her soles felt like heaven.

"Alyssa, I know this is hard, but if you're going to have to ride again tomorrow we need to do everything we can to stay warm tonight." The lantern light illuminated his features, including the tightness in his jaw. Her chest ached. He was genuinely worried. About her.

She lifted the top flap of the sleeping bag. "Get in."

A half-smile turned up one corner of his mouth. "Music to my ears." He set the lantern down and slipped in next to her.

She rolled onto her side and faced him, propping up on one elbow and supporting her head with her hand. His leg brushed against hers as his muscular frame filled the space beside her. She stared at his profile, admiring the planes and curves. The strands of blond hair sticking out of his gray wool cap added to his boyish good looks. Despite the Arctic-like temperatures inside the tent, warmth flooded through her. What if she snuggled up?

He turned his head, his gaze capturing hers. "Better?"

She managed a hesitant smile. "Much. Thank you. I'd be in serious trouble if you weren't here."

"Whatever. These guys know what they're doing."

"Lance doesn't."

"That's why he's bunking with Chuck."

Another round of hearty laughter punctured the silence.

Jeremy smirked. "See? It sounds like they're doing just fine."

"I hope so. If anything happened to Lance, I'd feel awful."

Jeremy fumbled through his backpack nearby and pulled out a plastic Ziploc bag filled with chocolate. "Does he always come with you when you shoot commercials?"

"No. I think he came this time to make sure I didn't blow them off." She eyed the bag. "What is that?"

"My mom's fudge. This stuff is legendary. She only makes it for Christmas."

"Wow. That's impressive. Dinner and homemade treats. Remind me to get stranded with you more often."

Her words hung between them. Shoot. Did she really just say that? He arched one brow, eyes gleaming. "Deal."

She sat up and held out her hand. "Better let me try some first. Just to make sure it's okay."

He hugged the coveted dessert to his chest. "Not until you tell me your favorite Christmas memory."

She rolled her eyes. "Seriously?"

"Seriously. Tell me about the best Christmas you've ever had."

"That's easy. I was eight—old enough to think maybe a real Christmas wasn't ever going to happen for me. Then the Huards adopted me. Finally. No more waiting and worrying that I'd have to leave. They did it up big, too. Presents everywhere, a huge tree, three sisters. It was everything I dreamed it would be." She stared at him. "I got what I'd wished for—my forever family."

"You win." Jeremy offered the fudge. "Best Christmas memory of all time."

"Sweet. Thanks." Alyssa broke off a chunk and popped it in her mouth, the rich chocolaty flavor exploding on her taste buds. "Oh my."

"I know, right?" He took a generous portion for himself then offered the rest. "Have more. We need to have plenty of energy for tonight."

She coughed, cupping her palm over her mouth.

His cheeks reddened. "Energy to keep warm, silly. Our bodies will be working hard—"

Her cough transitioned to a self-conscious giggle.

It was Jeremy's turn to roll his eyes. "Oh, please. Get your mind out of the gutter. You know what I meant."

Her laughter faded, and they consumed the last of the fudge. Another chill wracked her body. She cocooned inside the sleeping bag once again, the reality of their situation weighing heavy on her mind. Proper hydration, replenishing energy stores, and keeping each other warm were all essential in battling hypothermia. But would it be enough? Could they survive another twelve, twenty, or even thirty-six hours up here?

***

"Your turn." Alyssa's voice was muffled against the collar of the down jacket as she burrowed deeper inside the sleeping bag. "Tell me about your favorite Christmas."

Her body trembled next to his. Jeremy gritted his teeth. He couldn't let her lie there and freeze. "Alyssa, what can I do? I know you're still cold. Want some hot chocolate?"

"No. I—I'm fine."

"Yeah? You're not a very good liar. I can feel you shaking." He mustered his courage. "Let me hold you. I promise, it'll be warmer."

She didn't respond.

Great. She probably thought he only had one thing on his mind.

Then the fabric swished together as she moved closer, her eyes downcast. She rested her head against his chest. He curled his arm around her shoulders. Slowly, her gloved hand slid across his abdomen and encircled his waist.

"There. Better?"

She nodded, her wool cap scratching his jaw. Small price to pay. Despite his silent vow to behave, it would take every ounce of self-control he possessed not to tip her chin up and kiss her. Warmth unfurled in his gut. He might be cold, but he wasn't dead. What normal American male wouldn't enjoy holding a beautiful girl like her in his arms?

Dude. Seriously. This was a matter of life and death. They had to find a way to make it through the storm. Dale and AJ wouldn't let them down. Dale had flown in the most rugged parts of Alaska, Idaho, and

Montana for almost two decades. There wasn't anybody more skilled at landing a plane in a snowbank. If AJ thought he could get the helo off the mountain, he'd give it his best effort as soon as the weather broke.

"I'm still waiting." Alyssa lifted her head to study him, her breath warm on his cheek.

He trained his focus on those beautiful eyes. If he let his gaze travel toward those perfect, bow-shaped lips, he was a goner.

"Waiting?" His mouth went dry. "For what?"

"We were talking about Christmas, remember?" She nestled in the crook of his arm. "Tell me about the Tully family traditions."

He hoped she couldn't hear his heart thrumming in his chest. Her long hair spilled across his arm and hand. He yearned to pull off his gloves and run his fingers through the silky ends. The exposure to the cold air would be worth it. Instead, he stared at the tent's ceiling and envisioned his parents' house decked out for the holidays. "We're pretty stereotypical, I suppose. Stockings above the fireplace, candlelight service on Christmas Eve … a big breakfast after we open presents. When I was a kid, the community talent show and Christmas tree lighting were a big deal. Santa always made an appearance. I haven't been in a while."

"Is that your favorite memory? The tree lighting?"

"No. My favorite Christmas was five years ago. Blake and Lauren were married, and we were all finally together for Christmas, and nobody was holding any grudges or missing someone they … loved. That was before the show started filming, and—"

"What show?"

His chest tightened at the memory. Could he tell her about all of it? "It's a long story. Blake and Lauren were childhood sweethearts. Like I told you before, they had a baby together, but Blake didn't know about him, so that was tough for all of us. Blake was a mess, moved away for a while, and then Lauren came back. Eventually, it all worked out, and that Christmas, the brother I remembered was finally home. Lauren, too. It was awesome."

"That's a beautiful story, but you still didn't mention anything about a show."

He hesitated. "I started posting photos—just scenery, and animals, and people out on the water with us when we were kayaking—stuff that caught my eye. Someone at a production company saw them, and that morphed into a reality show that was filmed in Emerald Cove for three seasons."

"Really? What was it called?"

His heart hammered at the trajectory of her questions. He didn't want to talk about this. Not tonight. Not ever. "Troubled Waters."

"Huh. I've never watched it. Why did the show end?"

The tent walls suddenly felt much closer. His breathing increased, and he wanted to climb right out of his skin. Please, please, not another attack.

Alyssa pushed up on one elbow, her concerned gaze searching his face. "Jeremy?" She pressed her gloved hand to his chest. "Are you all right?"

He squeezed his eyes shut and swallowed hard, fighting for control. He couldn't come undone. Not here. She needed him to be strong.

Drawing a ragged breath, he opened his eyes and forced himself to look at her. "I—I'm fine."

"What happened?"

"We'd just finished filming season three. Ratings were at an all-time high, and most other shows filmed in Alaska had tanked." He paused and looked away. *Keep going.* "The cast and crew decided to celebrate, so I suggested they stay at the new resort. It had just opened. The weather changed quickly—kind of like right now—and flights were canceled. Even the road was closed. The whole crew was stranded."

The unwanted memories roared back, and his throat constricted. "Things got out of hand as the party stretched into a second day. My buddy Andrew and I had argued about him leaving. He had a new baby at home and promised his wife he'd be back in California as soon as the show wrapped. I—I told him to quit being a pansy and live in the moment."

Hating the regret tinging his voice, he ploughed on, determined to reveal the worst. No sense holding back now. "A fire broke out at the resort, and Andrew ... he, uh, didn't make it."

He stole a glance at Alyssa, expecting to see judgment and

condemnation in her expression. Instead, moisture gleamed in her eyes, deepening them to brilliant shades of turquoise and emerald.

"I'm so sorry," she whispered, tracing a small circle on his jacket with her gloved palm. "That must've been awful."

His heart somersaulted at her tender response.

"It wasn't your fault. You know that, right?" She sniffed. "I've seen how attentive you are to details and protocols. Accidents happen."

He scoffed. "I appreciate you saying that, but that doesn't change what happened. If I hadn't convinced Andrew to stick around, he'd probably still be here."

She lowered back down and snuggled against him. His body responded to her nearness. His shallow breaths deepened, and the tightness in his chest dissolved. Anxiety was no match for Alyssa's warmth.

"Maybe the best thing you could do to honor your friend's memory is to get back out there and take more pictures."

That was advice he'd heard countless times already. Too bad he didn't believe for one second it was true. Sure, he'd listened to physicians and the counsel of mental health professionals. But he'd put his camera away, since he couldn't bear to share his art with the world, knowing he was a liability to himself and others.

Nothing about that had changed.

"The town was already pretty divided about filming a reality show here. Lots of Alaskans will tell you it only leads to trouble. Selfishly, though, I'd persuaded everyone to take a chance on the show, because I was the one local with a large, consistent role. But what they worried about came true, and now Blake's on my case, and people haven't forgiven me for burning down the lodge. I'm just ... I don't know." He pressed his lips together, searching for the word that best described his tangled emotions. "Starting to wonder if I'll ever stop feeling like a total loser."

"Wait. You burned down the lodge?"

He groaned inwardly. "I didn't light the match. One of the production crew fell asleep with a cigarette in his hand. Since I'm the one who invited them to stay at the lodge, I feel responsible."

"Were you staying there, too?"

"No. I'd partied with them for most of the day, but then I left for my parents' place before the fire started."

"So it wasn't your fault."

He shifted, his breath vaporizing in the frigid air. Why was he telling her all of this? Probably because she made it so easy. He liked that she asked. Genuinely cared. "I'm—I wish things were different. I hate that Blake thinks I'm a total screw-up. I wish I'd made better choices. If we'd been more responsible, maybe the fire would've never happened, and maybe I ... wouldn't feel like I'd failed the whole town."

There. He hadn't said that out loud to anyone. Ever. Not even his parents whom he suspected shared his feelings. He'd always been a tiny bit jealous of Blake's success. In the classroom. On the high school basketball court. They'd been super competitive growing up, and he'd dreamed of besting Blake's achievements. Starring in the show and building his social media following had finally set him apart. Foisted him out of his brother's shadow. Now, thanks to his mishaps, he'd ruined that opportunity, too.

"I've wasted a lot of time and energy wrestling with all the baggage that comes from being a foster kid." Regret laced Alyssa's voice. "I have tons of questions about my birth parents and almost no answers. We can't change the past or erase bad decisions that other people made. Some things just are what they are."

Jeremy's chest tightened. She'd lived a complicated life. And there he was, going on and on about his stupid problems to someone who'd survived the foster care system. He ran his hand up and down her sleeve. "I'm sorry."

She tipped her face up, eyes wide. "For what?"

"For whining—when overall I've lived a pretty great life—right after you finished telling me how awesome it was to finally have a family of your own. I must've sounded pretty selfish."

"It's not selfish to have regrets or worry about your relationship with your brother. This is your family. They mean everything to you. That's both beautiful and excruciating, all at the same time."

Yes. Emotion clogged his throat. Those were the words he couldn't verbalize on his own.

Her raw vulnerability captivated him. The urge to protect this fierce yet wounded soul overwhelmed him. He wanted to know so much more about her. Would she share if he asked? Was there any harm in trying? "Did your birth parents try to find you?"

"After the Olympics and all the media coverage, ten different people tried to claim me. There's just one who I believe was legitimately related."

"How do you know?"

"He's the only one who brought me a gift and didn't ask for money."

His breath caught. "People claimed to be your parents and then asked for money?"

"Uh-huh. Except for one. He thought he might be my dad—said he recognized me on TV because I looked like my mother. We had a nice breakfast at a diner in Tahoe. He's a truck driver."

She said it all so matter-of-fact, like they were discussing the latest snowboard gear or favorite Christmas songs. "Unreal. What did he bring you?"

"A postcard from every state. He's seen them all, keeps the cards in an album. And my mother's earrings."

"Whoa. What did you say?"

Alyssa released a heavy sigh. "What was I supposed to say to this person who allegedly gave me life? Thank you? How could you? Where's my mother? No, thank you. I told him to keep the gifts."

She trembled again. Instinctively, Jeremy dipped his chin and pressed a tender kiss to the top of her hat.

She stiffened. "What was that for?" she whispered.

"You're an incredible girl. Tough. Independent. It makes my heart hurt that you've been through so much. I—"

She sat up, eyes blazing. "Don't."

Oh no. What did he say? "Don't what?"

"Pretend to feel sorry for me so you can get what you want." She pulled the edge of the sleeping bag against her, like a shield. "How stupid do you think I am?"

Her words knifed at him. "What? No. I would never—"

She scrambled to put more distance between them, flopping on her opposite side, her back a rigid wall.

"Alyssa—"

"Just—stop talking."

He clamped his mouth shut. Man, where did that come from? One innocent kiss on her forehead and she assumed he expected... He shook his head and turned off the lantern. Staring into the darkness, he berated himself for being so impulsive. *Again.* When would he ever learn?

9

Alyssa awoke with a start. Male voices orbited the tent, growing louder as they moved closer. Her pulse accelerated. Darkness surrounded her, yet the soft muted glow of lanterns bobbing outside the tent wall indicated it might be morning. Had the storm passed? Would they shoot more footage once it was light?

Too cold to move, she let her eyes take in her surroundings. Yesterday was like a pleasant autumn evening compared to the current temperature. She wiggled her toes to make sure they were still there. Icicles clung to the walls overhead. Slowly, she raised the top layer of the sleeping bag and peeked inside. Jeremy shifted, his arm looping tighter around her abdomen as he nestled closer, his body spooned against hers.

She lay still and squeezed her eyes shut. Last night's conversation replayed in her mind. Why had she reacted like that? He'd been so kind and empathetic, and she'd shut him down. Again.

So stupid.

As usual, negative self-talk prevailed, her old demons reminding her that she had issues—ones she'd probably never resolve. The Huards may have loved her as their own and equipped her to chase her dreams, but they couldn't fill the void in her heart. She was beginning to think nothing would. Hadn't she tried it all? Drugs, hot guys, stomping epic tricks, an Olympic gold medal.

The zipper on their tent jerked upward. Alyssa sucked in a breath. Great. Just what she needed—somebody finding her wrapped in Jeremy's arms.

A man cleared his throat.

She didn't move an inch. *Please go away. Please go away. Please—*

"Alyssa," Lance said in a harsh whisper. "Wake up."

Jeremy grunted.

"Hey, it's morning." Louder this time. "We started a fire. C'mon."

A fire? The thought of hot flames dancing was enough motivation to end her charade. She opened her eyes and popped her head up, squinting against the light from Lance's lantern spilling across their sleeping bag. "Give me a sec, okay?"

Lance's disapproving gaze flitted from her to Jeremy and back. "Two minutes."

"Whatever."

Lance ducked out of sight and zipped the tent flaps shut, taking his light with him. Snow crunched under his boots as he moved away. More muffled conversation ensued, but she couldn't make out the words.

The raw cold in the air made her think twice about getting out of the sleeping bag. Alyssa eased back down, careful not to disturb Jeremy. What was so wrong with wanting to lie here and savor the warmth of his embrace? To ignore, for a few more minutes, the demands of the outside world.

She let her eyes wander, taking in the stubble clinging to his jaw. He was a beautiful human—the kind that came along once in a blue moon. He worked hard. Loved the outdoors. And the way his eyes lit up when he talked about his friends and family proved his devotion. He'd lived the life of a professional outdoorsman—but gave up his career to preserve his mental health, and the good of this community he obviously loved. Her chest ached. What she wouldn't give to be the reason behind that amazing smile.

But she couldn't give in to her fickle emotions. And hadn't she proven last night with her outburst that she was ridiculously fickle? She squeezed her eyes shut. *Why* had she accused him of trying to take advantage of her?

He deserved better.

She wouldn't ask him to give up his life here, not when he'd just told her how much it meant to him to be close to the people he loved. Nothing about her lifestyle was stable or predictable. For all her desperate longings to get away from the chaos of her life, she couldn't blow off her professional commitments in the new year—endorsements, competitions, the world tour. Her meetings with designers about her new line of fitness wear were already scheduled. None of it could be ignored for much longer.

Jeremy's smooth brow furrowed, and his eyelids fluttered.

Alyssa's pulse quickened. She needed to get up and go outside before he woke up. Last night's conversation begged for a follow-up, and she didn't trust herself to wrestle her true feelings into submission.

Maybe he'd go back to sleep.

Then his eyes opened, and his gaze searched her face. A sleepy smile dimpled his cheek, his mouth inches from hers.

"Hey."

His morning voice, gravelly and rich, sent her heart into a swan dive. She moistened her dry lips and forced herself to avoid eye contact. "Hey." What she wouldn't do for a breath mint.

"How did you sleep?"

"Okay, I guess."

"You cried out a few times." He didn't bother to put any space between them. "Bad dream?"

"I—I don't remember." Her determination to do the right thing and hustle outside slipped away the longer he held her close.

"What time is it?" Jeremy asked.

"I have no idea. Lance came in a few minutes ago and said they'd built a fire."

"Sweet. I hope that means they're working on breakfast."

"Define breakfast."

He chuckled, his breath tickling her cheek. "It will be edible, I promise."

"Good to know." Food was the last thing on her mind. Jeremy's laugh coupled with his close proximity made it difficult to think at all.

"Alyssa, about last night. I—"

She sat up and threw back the sleeping bag. "You know what, if I don't find someplace to pee in the next two minutes, I'm going to have a serious problem."

"Right. Of course." He sat up, pulled off his gloves, then rifled through his pack. "Here." He handed her a large Ziploc bag filled with unidentifiable contents.

"What's this?"

"A sanitation kit. Everything you need to … take care of business."
She felt her cheeks warm. How embarrassing. Reason number six
hundred and seventy-three why she despised being the only woman
on this misadventure.

"Perfect." Alyssa tossed her own gloves aside and fumbled around
for her headlamp. Her fingers hooked around the elastic strap, and she
tugged it on over her hat. Then she emptied the bivvy sack and pulled
on her boots in record time. Thank goodness for Jeremy's winter
camping hack. The insoles weren't frozen solid. Her toes might not
freeze off after all.

"Do you need another pair of socks?"

"Nope. I'm good." She traded the down jacket he'd loaned her for
her own. Once she zipped it up, she put her gloves back on and
grabbed the kit.

"Are you sure you know what you're doing?"

She hesitated. "I'm not waiting for one of you guys to show me, if
that's what you're asking."

"Very funny. Do you know you're supposed to hike at least two
hundred feet from the campsite? There's a small shovel in the kit. You'll
need to—"

"Whoa. Dude. TMI." She unzipped the tent flap and stepped out,
then quickly zipped it shut again. An icy wind smacked her cheeks,
making her wish she'd put on her goggles. At least it wasn't snowing.
Yet.

The guys huddled around a fire nearby. Conversation stopped, and
every head swiveled her direction. Even in the semi-darkness, she felt
the weight of their curious stares.

Lance moved toward her. She turned away, the light from her
headlamp bouncing across her path.

"Wait a sec." Lance snagged the sleeve of her jacket.

"Let go." She pulled away. "I have to pee."

"In a minute." He stepped in front of her and blocked her path, eyes
flashing. "What in the world is going on in there?"

"In where?"

"Don't play dumb with me. I know what I saw."

"That's not fair. You didn't see—"

He barked out a laugh. "Oh, please. Next you'll tell me you were just cuddling."

"We're trying to survive, Lance." She fought to keep her voice even. "In case you hadn't noticed, it's about sixty-five below zero. Unlike some people I know, we didn't rely on Jack Daniel's to keep us warm."

"Don't try to make this about me. At least I wasn't hooking up." He linked his arms across his chest. "Does Nick know you've found someone new?"

A tent zipper opened behind her. Her heart lurched. "Shut up, Lance." She brushed past him, intentionally clipping him with her shoulder. She traipsed through the snow. Thanks to Lance's big mouth, Jeremy had probably heard every word.

***

Jeremy hovered inside the tent, his fists clenching and unclenching at his sides. *So she wasn't single.* When—if ever—was she planning on mentioning Nick? It might've been nice to know about him before Jeremy spent the night with Alyssa wrapped in his arms. Hypothermia or not, snuggling with somebody else's girl wasn't cool. Although it wasn't like he could just let her lie there and freeze to death, either. Good grief. What a mess.

He tugged on his gear then went outside to warm up by the fire. Tripp, the cameraman, shot him a knowing look as he joined the guys huddled around the meager flame.

"Did you have a good night?" Chuck grinned at him over the rim of his thermos lid.

"We survived." Jeremy held out his gloved hands, hoping to soak up a little bit of warmth before the hard work began. He needed to be standing here when Alyssa came back, anyway. No telling what they'd already said about her. He gritted his teeth. Better that he hadn't heard it.

Chuck fished a lighter and pack of cigarettes from his pocket then studied the sky. "We've got about three, maybe four hours, until this thing closes back up, boys. Don't know about you, but I don't want to spend another night on this mountain."

"Three hours?" Lance scanned the faces around circle. "That's not much time. You think you'll get enough shots for a whole commercial?"

"Better tell your girl to get it right the first time." Tripp's gaze swung from Lance to Jeremy. "Unless you'd rather spend another night up here. Kind of romantic, don't you think?"

Laughter broke out, sending adrenaline pulsing through Jeremy's veins. If this kept up, he'd slug somebody before breakfast. Especially if they said anything like that in front of her.

"What's so funny?" Alyssa's voice cut through the conversation. An awkward silence fell over the group.

Chuck's lighter clicked, and a flame licked the end of the cigarette dangling from his lips. He pinched it between two fingers, drew in a deep breath, then blew smoke into the air. "Coffee's hot. Want some?"

"Please." Alyssa filled the gap in the circle next to Lance, her eyes downcast. Tripp passed her a cup of coffee and then conversation turned to their game plan for the day. Alyssa listened, nodding at Tripp's and the others' comments about taking advantage of natural light, nailing an airborne shot with the mountains in the background.

Jeremy grew impatient. The longer they talked, the deeper the cold seeped into his bones. He helped himself to a cup of coffee then went back inside the tent and fixed a packet of oatmeal.

The hum of male voices wafted in, followed by Alyssa's laughter ringing in the air. The musical sound made his heart somersault in his chest. See? She didn't need him hovering out there, refereeing their juvenile banter. Wasn't she proving she could hang with the guys?

His gaze landed on their sleeping bags—make that one sleeping bag—still in a rumpled pile from her hasty exit. When she came back in to grab breakfast, he'd ask her about Lance's comments. If he could muster a little more confidence, maybe he'd even ask why she'd gotten upset with him last night. What could it hurt? Then he'd know the truth, and they could both move on. So what if last night felt like the beginning of something … meaningful. He was stupid to think she'd actually be single, anyway.

He'd downed the last spoonful of oatmeal when the tent flaps opened, and she stepped in, cheeks red from the cold.

"Hey." He tipped his head toward the stove. "The water's hot if you'd like some oatmeal."

"No, thanks. I'm good. Tripp gave me a breakfast burrito thing. Not too bad."

Oh, he did, did he? Imagine that. Jeremy bit his lip as she avoided his gaze and knelt beside her bag, fumbling with the zipper. "Listen, about this—"

She stood and looked around, a panicked expression on her face. "Have you seen my goggles?"

He glanced around the tiny space. "No."

She picked up a microfleece jacket she'd discarded the day before. "There they are." She grabbed them then slid them on over her hat. "I've got to go. They're already threatening to keep me here past Christmas if we don't finish the shoot today."

And that would be a bad thing? He cleared his throat. "Right. We'll talk later then."

She stepped out with little more than a non-committal *yep* tossed over her shoulder.

He stared after her, confusion swirling around him. That hadn't gone at all like he'd planned.

He shook his head then got to work cleaning up the stove and stowing their gear. It wasn't long before the familiar drone of a Super Cub coming in for a landing sent him outside in the bitter cold.

While Dale set the plane down between their campsite and the lake, Jeremy scanned the higher elevations for any sign of Alyssa on her snowboard. Tripp and the rest of the Verge people were huddled in a tight-knit semicircle, cameras angled toward a snow-covered ridge in the distance.

A flash of pink soared into the air.

Jeremy held his breath. *Easy.*

She spun three-hundred-sixty degrees, did some kind of fancy board grab, then landed flawlessly and cruised the rest of the way down the mountainside. Jeremy exhaled as she eased to a stop, snow spraying behind her like a rooster tail.

Dale turned off the engine then hopped out of the plane and jogged toward him.

"Hey." Jeremy clapped him on the shoulder. "Didn't expect to see you today."

"I almost didn't make it." Dale released a low whistle. "We've got to get you guys out of here, man. Mother Nature's whipping up another doozy."

"Tell that to the guys in charge. They aren't sure they have enough footage to finish the commercial."

"Unless they want Santa to deliver their Christmas presents up here, they'd better figure out a way to wrap things up. Fast."

"Is AJ bringing the helicopter, too?"

"Supposed to be." Dale pulled the hood of his parka up over his knit beanie then strode toward the producer speaking with Tripp. Dale didn't waste any time making his feelings known.

There was a fair amount of swearing and raised voices, Jeremy kept his head down and stayed focused, directing the guys to break down their tents quickly while Lance stomped around complaining this whole thing had been a huge mistake.

By the time AJ landed the helicopter, Jeremy could barely feel his toes. They were more than ready to load everything up and get home. The wind had picked up, blowing snow in vicious circles as they scrambled to take their seats.

Jeremy threw the last duffle bag inside the metal cage bolted to the helicopter's skis then secured the door. Shielding his face with his hand, he squinted into the icy flakes pelting his cheeks as he made his way to the side door and climbed in. Dale was right. If they didn't get out of here soon, they might be forced to spend another night—or two—here.

He'd claimed a space on the helicopter with AJ, intentionally avoiding a ride home in the Super Cub's cramped quarters with Alyssa. Had that decision cost him an opportunity to see her one more time? What if their brief conversation in the tent this morning was their last? She probably had a flight out of Emerald Cove first thing tomorrow. Bound for Colorado or California or maybe someplace even better—wherever that Nick fella waited.

He gritted his teeth. Enough. If he'd learned anything about Alyssa in the short time he'd known her, it was that she was as unpredictable as a winter storm.

And maybe just as dangerous.

10

The next day, Alyssa stood outside the resort, hands jammed in the pockets of her jacket as Lance stowed his luggage in the back of the waiting Suburban.

He moved toward her, his forehead creased. "Wheels up in less than two hours. You can still make the flight if you hurry."

She shook her head. "I'm staying here."

Lance groaned and tipped his head back. "You are so stubborn. Christmas is two days away. Go home to your folks and your sisters. Spend the holidays with people who love you. Then we'll hit it hard in the new year."

She bit her lip and looked down, scraping the toe of her boot against an icy patch on the ground. "I—I can't."

"Can't or won't?"

Tripp honked the Suburban's horn, making her flinch. She tipped her chin up and met Lance's critical gaze. "Just let me do this my way. Please? I promise I won't do anything stupid."

His jaw tightened. "No attachments. Do you hear me?"

"What's that supposed to mean?"

"I don't know what your status is with Nick. As far as I'm concerned, you need to kick that guy to the curb. But a rebound relationship is never a good idea. Just sayin'."

"Who said anything about a relationship?"

Lance snorted. "Please. I saw the way he looks at you. He's—"

"We're just friends. You don't need to worry." She forced a casual smile. "I'll be back in Colorado before you know it."

"What else can I say to change your mind?"

"Nothing." She gave him a quick hug then steered him toward the passenger door. "Have a safe trip. Merry Christmas."

"Merry Christmas." Lance shot her one last look before he got in. "Be careful."

"Goodbye, Lance." She waved until they drove away, an ache settling in her chest. She'd brushed off his concerns, but as usual, his words hit close to home. Good thing Lance couldn't see the dozens of ways Jeremy had filled her thoughts since they'd left Lost Lake. The way he looked at her across the fire when he thought she wasn't paying attention. His tireless efforts to load them all up before the weather made it impossible to fly. She might not have made it off the mountain if it weren't for him. Shivers raked her spine at the thought of how badly that whole trip might've ended.

She stared at the shed in the distance. The door was shut, and the snowcat wasn't grooming the runs—at least not that she could see. Was Jeremy even at work this morning? He deserved a day or two off after their ordeal. But this hectic season probably wouldn't allow for that.

She scanned the parking lot. Her heart sped up at the familiar sight of his truck in its usual space. Now that Lance and the Verge people were gone, she needed to talk to him—really talk to him and both apologize for how she'd spoken to him and offer a genuine thank you for all he'd done.

At the entrance to the lodge, the automatic doors parted, and she stepped inside, wiping her boots on the mat. A twenty-something guy glanced up from the new coffee bar in the corner where he was stocking the disposable cups. Was the espresso machine finally up and running? Flames crackled in the fireplace, tempting her to linger on one of the new sofas and order a coffee—

No. She'd mustered the courage to find Jeremy. Now she needed to follow through.

Rachel stood behind the front desk, eyes riveted on the computer in front of her. She looked up as Alyssa moved closer and offered a polite smile. "Are you looking for Jeremy?"

Was she that obvious? "Is he here?"

"Down the hall and take a right. He should be around that first corner hanging artwork for me."

"Thank you."

Alyssa kept moving, following the muffled sound of a hammer tapping on a nail. Her heart thrummed in her chest, and she licked her suddenly dry lips, hoping he'd be willing to listen to her.

When she reached the end of the corridor, an unfamiliar female voice slowed Alyssa's steps.

"So you spent the night with her?"

"It's not what you think." Jeremy's low voice held an edge of impatience. "She was freezing cold."

"Uh-huh," the girl teased. "I bet she was. What's her name?"

Alyssa flattened her back against the wall. Who was he talking to?

"None of your business."

Yes! Alyssa pumped her fist in the air. He was going to put this nosy little thing in her place.

"We're all worried about you, Jer."

"Why?" he asked.

"Because you tend to fall for people who hurt you."

Alyssa winced.

"That's not fair," he said.

"But it's true. Mom said you've moped around for months, waiting for some—"

"I'm not moping."

"Okay, fine. You're not moping. But she hurt you, right?"

Alyssa's breath hitched in her throat. She should go. Eavesdropping wasn't cool. But she couldn't make herself walk away. Instead, she strained to catch Jeremy's response.

"It's not going to happen again."

"Because you're not going to get involved or—"

He hesitated. "Look, I'll be the first to admit I've overlooked some pretty important things when it comes to women. Honesty, shared values—all that stuff gets pushed aside when I'm caught up in the moment. Physical attraction trumps logic, you know?"

Heat crawled up Alyssa's neck.

"I'm determined not to make the same mistake again," he said.

The girl chuckled.

"What's so funny about that? I'm serious, Megan. My player days are over. I want to be with someone who loves living here as much as I do. Someone who appreciates having a close-knit family and maybe wants to settle down, raise kids…"

Alyssa eased away from the wall, raw emotion forming a lump in her throat. She'd heard way more than she should've. Careful to keep her jacket from rustling and drawing attention to herself, she tiptoed back toward the lobby, his words echoing in her head.

Honesty. Shared values. Small-town living. *Marriage?*

Well, that pretty much put her out of the running, didn't it? Once Jeremy saw the pictures online, he'd want nothing to do with her. She definitely wasn't a poster child for family values, and marriage wasn't even on her radar.

***

"Are you saying that Celeste girl didn't want any of those things?"

Not even close. Jeremy set down the hammer and reached for a framed photograph of Denali, willing his sister to find something else to do. This was a long hallway with lots of empty walls. At the rate he was going, he'd be hanging pictures right up until they opened next week. He eased the frame onto the hook then stepped back to assess his work. "Isn't there someplace you're supposed to be? I have a lot to do, and I'm really not in the mood for any more questions."

"Sorry," Megan said. "I've got nothing but time. That's not straight, by the way."

He glared at her over his shoulder.

She nudged him with her hand. "Relax. You know I'm only trying to help."

"Yeah? Then make yourself useful and straighten the picture."

"Don't mind if I do." She brushed past him. "Step aside. Let me show you how it's done."

"Feel free." He sighed and rolled his shoulders back in slow circles. Every muscle still ached from the exertion of his misadventures at Lost Lake. He didn't have the patience to hang pictures. Megan's pointed questions had burrowed under his skin, too. All he wanted to do was find Alyssa and see her one more time before it was too late.

"There. That's better." She turned, tossing her long blonde hair over her shoulder. A wide smile emphasized her white teeth, and why did she spend so much time on her makeup? When had his baby sister morphed into a beautiful young woman?

"Thanks. I guess." He grabbed his hammer and measuring tape. "As much as I love seeing you, I know you didn't come out here to hang pictures and discuss my personal life. What's up?"

"Nice to see you, too." She scanned his face then patted the beard growing on his chin. "What's this?"

He swatted her hand away. "Knock it off."

Her teasing smile faded. "I came to apply for a job."

"What? Why? Doesn't second semester start next month?"

"I'm thinking about taking some time off."

"No way."

Her eyes flashed as she tipped her chin up. "What do you mean, 'no way'?"

"You can't take a semester off. You'll never go back."

"Says the one who dropped out."

Sheesh. Thanks for that. "So take my advice. You'll wish you hadn't."

"Ironic, isn't it?"

He glared at her. "What's that supposed to mean?"

"In case you hadn't noticed, there aren't many places to work around here. A lot of the shops downtown look abandoned. From what I've heard, the resort is the best option—if not the only option. If you're working here, why isn't it good enough for me?"

He hoisted the picture of a stunning waterfall onto the nail. No need to tell his baby sister that his anxiety kept him tethered close to home. That he wanted her to finish school so working at the local resort *wasn't* her only option.

She gestured toward the next framed photo propped against the wall. "Shouldn't you be taking photos instead of hanging up somebody else's? When are you going to open a gallery of your own?"

"How about never." He hammered the nail home with more force than necessary. She always did know how to aggravate him.

"Then spare me the lecture, okay?" Her tone softened. "If we're not going to talk about your issues, no fair bringing up mine. Besides, nothing's for sure yet."

"Will you at least tell me what happened? You seemed happy in Seattle." He turned and studied her. She'd spent hours in high school daydreaming about getting out of Emerald Cove, applying to colleges up and down the West Coast and even a couple in North Carolina. Why the sudden urge to stick around?

She lifted one shoulder. "I—I just don't know what I want to do when I'm finished."

The hairs on his neck stood on end. Likely story. "You're only a sophomore. Isn't there still plenty of time to declare a major? What about your volleyball scholarship?"

"Now who's asking too many questions." She narrowed her gaze. "Can we talk about this later? Like over dinner? I need a date to the play tonight."

He shook his head. "I'm not going to the play."

"Awww, c'mon. Why not?"

There weren't any more pictures unpacked, so Jeremy headed down the hall toward Chuck's office. "I've hardly been home. There are a zillion things to do, none of which include watching a bunch of little kids perform onstage."

Megan trailed after him. "Matt and Angela's kids have most of the starring roles. They'll be sad when they find out you're not there."

He snorted. "They won't even notice."

"Not true." Meg hovered beside him as he stowed his tools in the closet. "Please? I don't want to go by myself."

"Whatever. You'll know everybody there." All their parents' friends, former teachers, and high school classmates would want to talk to her. They'd want to hear all about how her classes were going. She didn't need him to... *Oh.*

"That's the problem, isn't it?" He squeezed her arm gently. "You don't want to talk to anybody."

"No." She shook her head, her voice barely audible and eyes brimming with fresh tears.

His chest ached. Poor girl. What was going on with her? "Fine. I'll go. I'm about finished here, anyway. Chuck owes me at least a half day off. Give me a couple of hours to take care of Hazel and shower. Then I'll come by the house."

"Perfect." Her expression brightened. "I'll have dinner ready."

Jeremy shrugged into his jacket and resisted the urge to pepper her with more questions. Based on the tears threatening to fall, Meg was struggling. It hurt that she didn't want to reveal what was really going on, but at least she'd made an effort to connect with him. How had he and his siblings grown so distant? And what could he do to bridge the gap that seemed to be widening every day?

***

"Baby, don't do this."

Nick's voice was smooth like melted chocolate. Huddled outside Emerald Cove's community center, her phone pressed to her ear, Alyssa stamped her feet on the ground, partly to keep warm and also to stop the quaking in her limbs. He could talk her into—or out of—anything. And he knew it.

But not this time.

"It's over, Nick. You had no right to post those pictures."

"Whatevs. You know you love the attention. Have you checked my Instagram lately? Sweet mother, that's a ton of 'likes'."

Her stomach soured. Easy for him to say. That wasn't his half-naked body accessible to millions of viewers. "I don't love the attention. That's the thing. Have you read the comments? People are horrible. I want you to delete the posts. I've already reported you."

Nick laughed. "Aw, baby, you can't let that stuff bother you. It's probably just a bunch of bored dudes trying to get a reaction."

They'd succeeded. Hot tears pricked her eyelids. How could he dismiss her hurt so carelessly? "You shouldn't have posted those pictures, Nick. Heck, you shouldn't have taken them. How about an apology?"

Silence saturated the air. "Nobody forced you to take off your bikini top. A few sips of rum and Coke and you were putting on a show. I had to make you put on one of my T-shirts to get you to stop."

She swallowed back the bile rising in her throat. That wasn't true.

Was it?

She'd never strip down or perform in front of an audience. Who kept refilling her glass, anyway? If he really cared about her, why didn't he help instead of mocking her?

"We're good together, you and me. Don't let a little misunderstanding come between us, all right?"

"A misunderstanding?" Her voice climbed an octave. People rushing to get into the community center before the play began paused at the door, their curious stares angled her direction. She spun away, hoping they'd leave before she let loose and spewed the pent-up anger simmering inside. "You don't get it, do you? You could've ruined me with those pictures. I'm so done with you. It's over, Nick. Don't text, don't call. Ever. Take the posts down. *Now.* You disgust me." She finished her verbal tirade with a string of words that would make a sailor blush. Her heart pounded in her chest as she jabbed the screen with her trembling finger and ended the call.

There. Message delivered. She sniffed and wiped the back of her hand at the moisture trailing down her cheek. Telling him off didn't feel nearly as satisfying as she'd imagined. All those hurtful words had sounded much better in her head. Here she stood, crying on the outskirts of a community gathering, with Christmas looming. Too mortified to fly home and too stubborn to ask Lance to let her spend the holiday with him and his family. Maybe she should've listened and boarded the plane with him this morning.

She turned in a slow circle, staring at the cars jammed in every available space in the parking lot. The Carters had driven her. Bless them. They'd been kind enough to invite her to the play. Their grandkids apparently were pretty involved in the whole thing. She'd opted to wait outside and call Nick, knowing she wouldn't enjoy the program until she'd said what she'd rehearsed all afternoon.

Snow flurries teased the night air, dancing in the street lights surrounding the community center. Alyssa shivered and plunged her bare hands deep into her coat pockets. Her phone vibrated against her palm. She ignored it. Probably Nick or one of her frenemies texting to plead his case. That would be like him to get somebody else to persuade her to change her mind.

It was too cold to wait out here much longer. She could probably find her way back to the inn, but she'd be frozen solid by the time she got there. Maybe little kids onstage singing Christmas songs would distract her from the disaster that was her life. Mustering up her courage to face more curious stares, she turned and slipped inside the door then eased it closed behind her.

A beautiful Christmas tree adorned with white lights and satiny red ribbon took up an entire corner of the lobby. Piles of toys sat beneath the lowest branches, probably for a holiday toy drive. Several long tables lined the wall, filled with every kind of cookie and scrumptious treat imaginable. A white, pedestal cake stand full of fudge served as the centerpiece of the table closest to the door. Tempting. Was it the same fudge Jeremy had shared with her?

Jeremy. Her breath hitched in her chest. Was he in the audience tonight? After the conversation she'd overheard earlier, she wasn't sure she could face him. After the things Lance said outside the tent, he probably thought she was a player, too. *Imagine what he'd think if he saw those pictures.* She hung her head. Despite his declaration that she wasn't exactly girlfriend material, she couldn't leave Emerald Cove without seeing him one more time. Even if it was only to say goodbye.

11

Jeremy curled the play program like a scroll, tapping it against his palm as he scanned the auditorium for Lauren's brother, Matt, and his wife, Angela. Their kids had done a great job tonight. He wanted to congratulate them and ask if they knew how Blake and Lauren were doing. Neither had showed up tonight.

"Who is that?" Megan's elbow jabbed Jeremy's ribs.

"Who?"

"The girl in the pink hat." Megan directed a purposeful glance toward the back of the room. "She looks familiar."

He turned around.

Alyssa lingered alone near the back row, shifting her weight from one leg to the other. She wore a navy wool coat belted at the waist and a pink knit hat. Her brown hair glinted in the overhead light, and his chest tightened. *So she hadn't left town.* He needed to go talk to her before somebody recognized her and monopolized her attention.

"Hello?" Megan tugged on his shirt sleeve. "Do you know her?"

"Alyssa Huard."

"The snowboarder?" Her jaw dropped. "You're joking."

"Nope. I thought you knew."

"Mom said you were with a snowboarder. She didn't say *that* one. Can you—"

"Hey, guys." Shannon Ferguson worked her way along a row of empty chairs, a smile on her face and a weary preschooler draped over her shoulder. "I'm so glad you came."

"Hi, Shannon. Merry Christmas." Jeremy leaned closer and patted the little boy's back. "What's up, Marcus? Rough night?"

"He's out. Missed his nap this afternoon." Shannon pressed a tender kiss against his hair. "It's tough being four sometimes."

Marcus stirred but didn't lift his head.

"It's tough being twenty-nine. I could've used a nap today myself."

"I heard you were stuck overnight at Lost Lake." Shannon arched an eyebrow. "Didn't get much sleep?"

Thoughts of Alyssa snuggled next to him sent warmth creeping up his neck. Had Shannon heard about her, too? If she had, how did he respond without provoking more questions?

"Shannon, did you see the pictures yet?" Megan pulled out her phone and tapped the screen.

"No. Did you?"

"Yep." Megan grinned. "She's precious."

Shannon stretched out her free hand. "Let me see."

"What pictures?" Jeremy craned his neck to see as they huddled around Meg's phone and admired the image on the screen. "What are you talking about?"

Shannon sent Megan a nervous glance. "Lauren wants to adopt from China. Someone at the agency sent her a picture of a little girl who might be an option." Shannon bit her lip, as though she'd said too much.

"And Blake's okay with this?" Jeremy asked.

Megan shook her head. "Mom says he refuses to sign any papers."

Jeremy scrubbed his hand along his jaw, then glanced at Shannon again. "Do you think they'll be able to work this out?"

She hesitated. "I hope so."

Her response made him uneasy. Shannon was Lauren's best friend, and her expression looked anything but hopeful. Despite his rift with Blake, he couldn't blame his brother for being unsupportive. Blake seemed to have dealt with the hurt and regret over Lauren secretly placing their first—and only—child together with an adoptive family. Was adopting another child, even one who needed a loving home, the right decision?

Man, he needed to talk to Blake. Offer a listening ear or something. But Blake would probably tell him to get lost.

"I hope they call a truce before Christmas," Megan said, pulling Jeremy back to the present.

"Yeah, me, too." Jeremy glanced around the auditorium again. Alyssa had disappeared from sight. He needed to get to the lobby and see if she'd stuck around. While her appearance tonight pleased him, the pained expression on her face left him feeling unsettled.

Shannon angled her head to one side. "Who are you looking for?"

"Who said I was looking for anyone?"

"Alyssa Huard," Megan said, blowing his attempt to play it off. "Did you know she was here?"

"Yeah, she's staying at the inn with the Carters." Shannon flashed a knowing smile. "I'm sure Jeremy can tell you more."

"Thanks for that." Jeremy pretended to glare at her. "'Tis the season for gossip to spread like wildfire."

"How long has she been here?" Megan smacked him on the arm. "Are you seeing each other?"

Whoa. "If you want me to introduce you, I suggest you back off on the personal questions."

"That's a yes." Shannon high-fived Megan. "I knew it."

Shoot. He was no match for these two. "I didn't say yes."

"You didn't say no, either." Megan craned her neck. "Wait. Where'd she go?"

"She's probably gone. Who would want to stick around here and listen to people whisper and stare?"

"Why is she here, anyway?" Megan's questions flew rapid-fire. "Did you get to see her snowboard? Is she staying in town for Christmas?"

"You guys have fun." Shannon shifted Marcus in her arms. "I'm going to go find the rest of my family."

"Merry Christmas, Shannon," Jeremy said.

Megan waved to Shannon and Marcus then prodded Jeremy again. "C'mon, hurry."

He sighed then slowly worked his way through the crowd toward the exit, Megan at his heels like an overanxious puppy. This was probably a mistake. After spending the night in a tent on a mountain, he hated that their next conversation had to be so … public.

"Do you think she'd give me an autograph? It wouldn't hurt to ask, right? Except I didn't bring anything cool for her sign."

"Trust me, she doesn't need you asking for autographs," Jeremy said. "Back off and let her be."

"Jeremy. Wait up." A familiar male voice called from behind.

He turned.

Wyatt sidestepped a cluster of people chatting then jogged toward them. "Hey, Megan. Welcome home. How's Seattle?" He gave her a quick hug.

She returned his hug then pulled back. Pain flashed in her eyes before she forced a smile for Jeremy's best friend. "Merry Christmas, Wyatt. Seattle's all right, but there's no place like home."

"I hear that." Wyatt glanced at Jeremy. "Congratulations, man. I hear you saved the day up at Lost Lake."

"Thanks. It was pretty crazy. I'm glad we made it back safely." Jeremy shifted his gaze to Megan, eager to steer the conversation away from himself. While he didn't have anything to hide, his sister's masked expression coupled with her comment about loving being home didn't sit well. Something didn't add up. Next time they were alone, he'd press her for more details. For a girl who couldn't wait to get to Seattle and start the next chapter, she certainly didn't seem to be in a hurry to go back.

"Any word on whether or not we're all getting together for Christmas?" Wyatt asked.

Jeremy shrugged. "I have no idea. We'll probably hear more from my mom soon."

"Sweet." Wyatt pulled his hat and gloves from his pocket, then focused all his attention on Megan. "I'm going to ride with my dad and help him do a few last-minute things for Christmas, but I'd love to catch up with you sometime. Maybe grab coffee or whatever?"

The uncertainty in Megan's eyes was unmistakable. She swallowed hard. "Um, yeah. Maybe."

Wyatt looked like she'd slapped him. He nodded slowly, tugging his gloves into place. "See you around."

"Take it easy," Jeremy said, secretly willing his sister not to break his friend's heart. And vice versa.

"Yeah, you, too." Wyatt turned and walked away, moving quickly toward the auditorium's double doors.

Why did Megan blow him off like that? Before he could ask, he saw Alyssa standing along the wall in the lobby, a plate balanced on one

hand while she nibbled on a cookie. Nate Adams, one of Jeremy's high
school classmates, stood beside her wearing his usual cocky grin.

"He must have about half a tube of gel in that nasty hair," Jeremy
muttered.

Megan chuckled. "Jealous much?"

Jeremy shot her a glare. "Do you want to meet her or not?"

Her amusement faded. "Absolutely. We'd better hustle, too. Nate's
about to put on the moves."

"Whatever." Jeremy moved quickly, his pulse accelerating as he cut
through the crowd. Alyssa might not be his to defend, but there was
no way he'd stand by while the town's biggest loser tried to hit on her.

***

Somebody save me. Alyssa nibbled on an iced sugar cookie and
pretended she was still listening to the guy standing uncomfortably
close to her ramble on about his new snowmobile. He smelled like
cheap cologne and marijuana, a combination all too familiar given her
profession and usual hangouts. Why was she such a magnet for the
bad-boy type?

"Are you here by yourself?" He pressed his palm against the wall
beside her head and leaned in, his bloodshot eyes boring into her.

Alyssa faked a coughing fit and doubled over, the paper plate sliding
from her hand. The last cookie hit the floor and crumbled into pieces
next to a familiar pair of boots.

Her heart leaped in her throat. *Jeremy.* Thank goodness.

"Way to go, Adams," Jeremy said. "She's so repulsed by your
presence that she's tossed her cookies."

"Why don't you go back to your bunny hill, dude. I've got
everything under control."

"Is that so?" Jeremy's icy tone made Alyssa straighten. A stunning
blonde hovered near his elbow, her gaze darting between the two men.

Alyssa cleared her throat. "I—I'm fine. Must've swallowed the wrong
way."

"Need some water?" Nate pushed off from the wall. "I could
probably find some."

"No, thanks." She angled her head toward Jeremy and flashed a bright smile. Fingers crossed that wasn't a girlfriend he'd failed to mention standing beside him. "Are you ready to go?"

He shot Nate a victorious grin. "Whatever you want to do, baby."

Baby. Her breath hitched.

"Wait. You're with him?" Nate shook his head, eyes narrowed. "Bad decision, princess. You're wasting your time. Not too bright, that one. Too many knocks to the head."

Jeremy's fists clenched, and his eyes flashed.

Alyssa linked her arm through Jeremy's and steered him away. "Don't," she whispered. "He's not worth it."

A muscle in Jeremy's jaw twitched as they moved deeper into the crowd milling around the food. It wasn't until they'd garnered the attention of several people around them that she realized the blonde had followed. Ugh. This could get messy.

Alyssa released her grip on Jeremy and stepped back. "Thank you for helping me. I—I'm sorry if I interrupted…" She stole a quick glance at the girl.

"What?" Jeremy turned. "Oh, right. This is my sister, Megan Tully." He slung his arm around her shoulders and pulled her closer. "She's a huge fan."

The tense muscles in her neck uncoiled a fraction. His *sister.* Duh. She should've known. They had the same nose and mouth. Alyssa offered a relieved smile. "It's nice to meet you. I'm Alyssa Huard."

"I know." Megan pressed her palms to her cheeks. "I can't believe this. Would it be okay if we took a picture? I mean, I know it's kinda crowded. Maybe we could go—"

"Megan." Jeremy shook his head. "Seriously. If you take a picture now, this place will go crazy. She'll be signing autographs and posing for selfies all night."

"And that's a bad thing?" Alyssa shrugged. "It's no trouble."

"Are you sure?" Megan dropped her hands to her sides then glanced around. "He's right. There are still a lot of people here. What if everyone wants to take a picture?"

"Then I guess I'll need you to get me some more cookies." Alyssa grinned. "Just kidding. We probably should find a better place to pose. Unless you like the backs of people and their winter jackets as a background."

"Not really." Megan wrinkled her nose. "How about over by the Christmas tree?"

"Sounds good. Let's do it." Alyssa followed her through the crowd, grateful for the distraction. Now she could procrastinate going back to the inn for at least a little while longer. If she smiled and hammed it up with a few fans, she wouldn't have to think about how the guy she thought she'd loved had cleaved her heart wide open. Or that she was too embarrassed to go home for Christmas and confess to her parents they'd been right about him.

But Jeremy had saved her for now. And while he might not be willing to step in and be her rescuer in the future, this moment was enough for her.

***

The musical sound of Alyssa's laughter planted an ache in Jeremy's chest. He sat nearby in a folding chair he'd snagged from the auditorium, taking it all in.

She was a natural at working a crowd and clearly reveled in the attention. Yet she took her time chatting with each person, as if there was nowhere else she'd rather be. One family took their picture with her in front of the Christmas tree. She scrawled another autograph on a napkin then plopped a Santa hat that someone had found onto a little boy's head. More laughter bubbled from her lips as the white faux fur slid down over his nose. He pushed it back with his chubby fingers and gave her a tired smile.

Jeremy smiled. Finally, he'd had a role—admittedly a small one—in doing something that benefited the community. He didn't care who got the credit. At least no one was shooting him dirty looks, which had often been the case after his show had wrapped.

His phone chimed in his pocket, and he pulled it out to read his text messages. Megan had found a ride home with a friend, and Mrs. Carter texted a reminder that Alyssa might need a ride, because she and Mike had left already.

Not a problem. Even if he had to down another cup of the tepid coffee left in the pots nearby, he'd do it. Sheer exhaustion wouldn't keep him from spending a few more minutes with her. Too bad the drive back to the inn was so short. It was hardly enough time to tell her how he really felt.

Rachel had said Lance and the rest of the snowboard people left without her. Surely she had a seat on the first flight out in the morning. If the planes flew. Was it wrong to wish for another blizzard to blow through? He'd already checked the forecast, and it wasn't completely out of the question. If the flights were canceled and the roads closed, maybe he'd get a second chance to ask her to stay.

To spend Christmas with him and his family.

Seriously. Get a grip, man. Hadn't he learned the hard way how much it hurt to ask a woman to choose him?

The familiar clutches of anxiety closed in, like an avalanche barreling down the mountainside, just as Alyssa walked toward him, her eyes gleaming. "That was fun."

He offered the coat and hat she'd discarded earlier and rubbed his knuckles against the tightness squeezing his chest. "Thank you for doing that."

"No problem. I never expected so many people to stick around, though."

"We don't see too many Olympic gold medalists in Emerald Cove."

"Stop." She slipped into her coat then pulled a pair of gloves from the pocket. "As soon as the resort officially reopens and word gets out, this place will be crawling with ski bums."

"I hope you're right." He rocked back on his heels. There was no hurry to leave. Goodbye was only moments away. *Nice knowing you. Have a great life. See you...*

Where? He'd never be in Colorado, Park City, or Tahoe—any of the places the tour took her. He couldn't leave Emerald Cove now. Not until the lodge was reopened and he knew for sure that the town was thriving again.

Desperate to spend even one more hour with her, he pulled his phone from his pocket, his mind working quickly to come up with an idea. "Are you hungry?"

"A little."

He glanced at the screen. "It's almost ten. If we hurry, we can grab pizza at Randy's."

"Deal." She put on her hat as they walked toward the door. "Did your sister leave?"

Jeremy fell in step beside her. "She went with a friend, and Mrs. Carter texted me, too. She said they'll be home late—helping Angela and Matt finish a dollhouse for one of the girls or something."

"Is your sister-in-law okay?"

"I—I'm really not sure. She and Blake didn't show up tonight."

Alyssa's expression filled with sympathy. "I'm sorry."

"Yeah, me, too. I'm hoping they'll work things out and we can all celebrate Christmas together." He zipped up his jacket and fitted his gloves in place before pushing open the door and stepping outside.

Ask her.

His pulse accelerated as a hint of her perfume teased his senses. What if she laughed off his invitation to stay? That would make dinner super awkward.

Coward.

The streetlights along the community center's perimeter cast a bluish-white glow on the remaining cars in the parking lot. A thin layer of fresh snow coated every surface, but the flurries had stopped, and now stars dotted the inky black sky. So much for a blizzard.

"Brrr." Alyssa shivered. "It's too cold here. I'm ready for warmer weather."

Say you won't go.

His stomach clenched at the thought of her lying on a beach without him. "Aren't you a professional snowboarder? It's not like you haven't spent a million hours on a snowboard, in the dead of winter, year after year. How in the world did you ever survive?"

She reached down and scooped up some snow, formed it into a ball, then launched it at him.

He tried to duck, but it was too late. The snowball smacked him in the chest. "Hey. What was that for?"

"For being such a smarty-pants." A smile played at the corners of her mouth as she quickly reloaded.

"Is this any way to treat your driver?" He took refuge on the other side of a sedan. "I'm your direct line to a food source, remember?"

"Whatever. I'm resourceful."

"Humble, too, I see." He swiped snow from the roof of the car, shaped it quickly, then lobbed it her way.

It collapsed on the ground near her feet. "Is that all you've got?" she taunted.

"I'm trying to take the high road and not retaliate for this senseless attack."

"Oh, please." She wound up and chucked another snowball at him. It flew past his ear. "That sounds like something you'd say if you think you can't win."

"Define win."

"Hitting me with a snowball. Duh." She splayed her fingers on either side of her head and waved them back and forth. "Betcha can't do it."

"Those are fighting words, woman. I never back down from a challenge."

"Is that so?" Alyssa knelt and scooped up more snow. "I'll just be over here, building a snowman."

Jeremy pulled back and zinged the ball her way.

She chose that exact moment to straighten to her full height. A wide-open target.

The snowball pegged her on the cheek. She yelped and pressed her glove to her face.

His breath caught in his chest. *Oh no.* "Shoot." He raced around the sedan. "Alyssa, I'm so sorry. Let me see."

Her shoulders trembled, and she twisted away.

"Please. Just let me take a look."

In one deft move she turned back toward him, tugged on the hem of his jacket and shirt, then shoved a gloveful of snow up inside.

He gasped and jumped back as the snow chilled his skin. "No way!"

Alyssa laughed with glee, thrusting both fists heavenward. "Yes! Gotcha. Can't believe you fell for that."

Jeremy shook his head as he tried in vain to shake the rest of the snow from inside his clothing. "You're wicked, you know that?"

"I've been called worse." She brushed the last of the snow from her gloves. "Does this mean I have to walk to the pizza place?"

That grin of hers. Man, it did crazy things to his insides. "I suppose I'll take pity on you, since it's your last night in town."

Her smile wavered. "How thoughtful. Let's go. It's freezing out here."

He stifled a groan. That flicker of something just now. Doubt? Regret? Did she want to leave or not? Alyssa jogged to the passenger side of his truck. With his key fob, he unlocked the door then reached past her to grab the handle.

He scanned her face, his pulse pounding. A droplet of water glistened on her cheek and clung to the curve of her cheekbone. He longed to reach up and wipe the moisture away. Any excuse to touch her again. Their breath mingled in the air, puffs of white filling the mere inches between them. His gaze slid to her lips, full and perfect. It would be so easy to dip his head and capture her mouth with his own.

Logic sang its warning loud and clear. *Don't.*

He forced himself to meet her gaze. Those blue and green pools might just be his downfall—fueling his desire and sending reasonable thought into a tailspin.

She cleared her throat and stepped back. "We should go."

"Right." He opened the door, waited for her to climb inside, and then closed it gently. Lame. Why put the moves on a girl who would be gone in less than a day? Talk about desperate.

As usual, his impulsiveness had almost led him down a dangerous path. Saying goodbye to Alyssa was already going to be difficult. Acting on his physical attraction would make it even more painful.

***

The familiar aroma of pepperoni and tomato sauce wafted toward Alyssa. Under normal circumstances, she'd have inhaled her meal.

But tonight was anything but normal. She picked off a black olive from her pizza and slipped it into her mouth, barely tasting it.

Jeremy sat across from her, devouring his second slice. Between her phone call with Nick then the almost-kiss in the parking lot, her insides twisted in knots. What was she *doing?* Who breaks up with their boyfriend and is almost lip-locked with another guy before the night is through?

Not just any guy, though. The one who'd been kind and thoughtful and … wrapped up in her sleeping bag less than twenty-four hours ago. Her cheeks grew warm. She couldn't think straight with Jeremy sitting there, clean-shaven, hair tousled in the perfect combination of messy.

The waitress stopped at their table. "Can I get you guys anything else?"

"No, we're all set," Jeremy said. "Thank you."

"You're welcome." She pulled a small black folder from the front pocket of her apron and set it on the red-and-white checked tablecloth. "I'm your cashier whenever you're ready."

"I guess we should eat fast. I'm pretty sure they close at eleven." Jeremy plated a third slice for himself. "Do you want more?"

Alyssa glanced around.

Almost every table was still full. The familiar hum of conversation and laughter filled the air. At the far end of the restaurant a raucous game of darts was underway. Nobody seemed in a big hurry to leave.

Least of all her. She envisioned lots of dates spent here. With him. Maybe one day they'd walk past this table and exchange knowing smiles, remembering their first meal shared…

"Alyssa?"

She shifted in her seat. "I'm sorry, what?"

"Do you want more pizza?"

She glanced down at her half-eaten slice then shook her head. "No, I—I'm good."

"Are you okay?"

No! Her fingernails dug into her palm. *Can't you see I'm falling for you?* Boy, how things had changed since their collision on the ski hill. She'd wanted nothing to do with him that night—convinced he'd sprained both her wrists. Now she couldn't stay away. Starting a snowball fight. Flirting. Posing for a picture with his sister and then half the town so he'd think well of her. His feelings for her seemed to have changed, too. She could see it in the way he looked at her.

"Are you all packed for your flight tomorrow?"

She reached for her drink and took a long sip through the straw. Her stomach coiled in a tighter knot. This game she'd played—darting away from meaningful relationships, always morphing to be what she thought the other person wanted—was exhausting. For once in her life—just once—she wanted to put herself out there. To be as fearless with her heart as she was on a snowboard.

What's the worst that could happen?

Adrenaline hummed through her veins. She set the glass down and tipped her chin up, hoping he didn't see how her hands were shaking. "I don't have a flight tomorrow. I—I'm thinking about staying."

There. She'd said it.

His eyes widened. "Here?"

That reaction rattled her. Did he want her to stay? She wanted him to want her to stay. More than she'd wanted anything in a long time. She bit her lip. "Yes, I'm thinking about staying here. In Emerald Cove."

"What about Christmas? Won't your family miss you?"

"Probably not."

"Alyssa." He cocked his head to one side. "C'mon. Be serious. Your family won't be upset if you aren't with them for the holidays?"

She lifted one shoulder. "Doubt it."

"I find that hard to believe."

"You can believe what you want, I guess." Alyssa pushed her plate aside. Even though she'd ignored her instincts and allowed him in, she felt herself shutting down—falling back into her default mode of self-protection. Being honest and vulnerable was just too hard.

Jeremy leaned toward her, bracing his elbows on the table and locking his eyes on hers. "Alyssa."

Oh, the sound of her name on his lips. Her heart blipped, but she willed herself to be strong. *Quick!* Her brain roared. *Bail out while you still can.*

Silence hung between them. She drew a ragged breath. "Have you … there's a…" She willed the tears not to fall. "Never mind."

Confusion flashed in his eyes. "Are you sure?"

Won't make the same mistake again.

The conversation she'd overheard echoed in her mind, and her confidence waned. She already didn't meet his standards. Why tell him about the pictures and give him more evidence to prove his point? "It's nothing. Forget it."

"I can't. You look miserable. Does this have anything to do with that Nick guy?"

She winced. "You heard what Lance said outside the tent, didn't you?"

He nodded.

She squirmed in her chair. Could she tell him about Nick and not mention the pictures? "We're not together anymore, if that's what you're wondering."

"His loss."

She outlined the checked squares on the tablecloth with her fingernail. "That's sweet of you to say." *If you only knew the whole story … if I only had the guts to tell you.*

"Do you want to talk about it?"

She forced herself to meet his gaze. "Not really."

"I'm sorry you're hurting." His eyes darkened like the depths of Lake Tahoe on a hot summer day. "Breakups totally bite."

"Is this the Telluride thing Chuck was teasing you about the other day?"

"Maybe." He pulled his wallet from his back pocket then extracted a few bills.

"Would you care to elaborate?"

"No. But I like how you tried to change the subject. Well played."

See? He didn't want to be vulnerable either. She'd been so stupid to think this would go well. She sighed and fumbled in her jacket pocket for the twenty-dollar bill she'd shoved in earlier with her phone. "You don't have to pay for dinner."

"It's the least I can do." He refused her money and slid his own inside the leather folder with the bill then placed it back on the edge of the table. "Have you told your family?"

"About Nick? They wouldn't understand."

"I meant about not going home. Do they know you're not coming?"

"Trying to get rid of me, huh?" She forced a smile, moisture still blurring her vision.

A mixture of emotions she couldn't quite interpret washed across his face. Hurt? Frustration? "That's not what I said. I'd hate for you to wake up here on Christmas morning and regret your decision."

She toyed with her straw wrapper. Regret was an emotion she'd grown quite familiar with in recent months. Far easier to handle than the disappointment she'd see in her parents' eyes. "Here's the thing. It will be all fun and festive at home for about ten minutes. They'll make a big deal about me being there. Then the questions will start. Followed by the 'I told you so's'. No thanks."

"Why would they say that? I bet they'd just be happy to have you home."

Alyssa's gut cinched tight. He sounded like Lance. Hadn't they had some version of this conversation already? How dumb of her to think Jeremy might understand. Or that he wanted her. "Can we go? I'm worn out."

"Sure." He signaled the busboy clearing a table nearby. "May we have a box, please?"

"Yep. Hang on a sec." The boy picked up his loaded plastic bin and carried it toward the kitchen.

"As soon as he boxes this up, I'll drive you back," Jeremy said.

"Thank you." She'd opened up, hoping that by pushing through her fear of being vulnerable she'd find acceptance. A lot of good that did. He was wrong. Running home to Mom and Dad wouldn't solve anything. How could she make him see she just didn't have it in her?

Maybe she shouldn't bother trying. Forget the almost-kiss in the parking lot and the comfort she'd found wrapped in his arms in the tent. Like most of the relationships in her life, she'd somehow managed to mess this one up, too.

***

Back at the inn, Jeremy climbed out of the truck, shut the door, then jogged after Alyssa as she hurried up the driveway. The porch light clicked on when her boots thumped up the steps. He caught up with her, longing to reach out and touch her arm before she took refuge inside. Her hair fell forward like a curtain, obscuring his view of her profile while she dug the key out of her pocket.

He rubbed his hand across the back of his neck. "I'm sorry if I upset you."

She stilled, the key halfway to the lock. "Don't worry about it."

That's the thing. He was worried. She'd stared out the window and said almost nothing during the ride back from Randy's. Where had he gone wrong? "I don't want this to be goodbye."

"It's not." She tipped her chin up, eyes like glittering orbs. "I told you I'm staying."

"Good." He tried for a smile. "Then I respect your decision."

"Do you?"

"Of course."

"Because that conversation at dinner felt like you wanted me to go."

At least five different responses flitted through his brain. Which to choose? She was as prickly as a porcupine, so no matter what he said, it'd probably be the wrong thing. "I want you to be happy. You know that, right?"

She scraped one palm across her face then dropped her hand to her side. Staring out into the night, she whispered, "That's not your responsibility."

Oh, how he wanted it to be. He'd captured glimpses of the carefree, I'm-on-top-of-the-world Alyssa in the little time they'd spent together. He wanted more. Her zest for life was intoxicating.

But this broken, wounded version of her pained him. The urge to pull her into his arms and chase away the hurt hadn't lessened, despite her rapid inward retreat. Powerless to stop her spiral into self-pity, here he stood, making a last-ditch effort to rescue her. "Take care of yourself, okay?"

She nodded.

"If you change your mind, let me know. I can drive you to the airport."

"I'm not going to change my mind." Without a backward glance, she turned the key in the lock. Then she pushed the door open and went inside. The hurt in her eyes was the last thing he saw before she closed the wreath-adorned door.

The decoration's piney scent filled his nostrils, another reminder of

Christmas's imminent arrival. Tonight, he felt anything but festive. Maybe he should go in. Tell her he'd somehow messed things up.

Glancing over his shoulder, he surveyed the driveway. The only tire tracks in the snow were his own. The Carters must still be at Matt and Angela's house. Not that it mattered if they found him here. He was practically family anyway.

He reached for the doorknob, then pulled back, jamming his hands in his coat pockets. He could totally relate to trusting someone only to have them turn on you. Hadn't Celeste's inability to commit left him strung out emotionally, too? He'd been a wreck for weeks. Months. Okay, most of the last year. And a few years before that in their crazy on-again-off-again relationship.

Alyssa's words echoed in his head and stopped him from going after her. She was right. Her happiness wasn't his responsibility, no matter how badly he longed to play that role. Maybe this wasn't his door to open. Alyssa seemed determined to cope with this heartache on her own.

"Have it your way."

Turning around, he walked down the stairs and back to his truck. Somewhere in the forest beyond the house, a coyote released a mournful howl. Jeremy paused and tipped his head back, staring at the dark sky. Why did making the responsible choice and taking the moral high road make everything seem so stinking complicated? He'd looked out for her—made sure she got off that mountain without hypothermia or frostbite. Risked his own safety so she'd have a chance of getting home for Christmas. Tried to be there for her when her world came apart. He'd even had the decency not to ask her about what he'd seen online. So why had it all backfired? Had someone mentioned the pictures while she signed autographs?

He shook his head and got back in his truck. Hands clenched on the steering wheel, he blew out a long breath. Maybe he'd made it worse by almost kissing her in the parking lot and then telling her she should leave.

Mixed signals, man. Not cool.

"Dude, I'm not…" He trailed off, biting his lip. He was obviously delirious and in desperate need of sleep. How else to explain arguing with a voice in his head? He turned the key in the ignition, and the engine roared to life.

He shifted into reverse, his headlights shining on the snowbank lining the driveway. Ever since she'd arrived in Emerald Cove, he'd tried to help her. Keep her safe. Encourage her to make smart choices. If anyone knew the heartache wrought from an impulsive decision gone wrong, it was him. Yeah, he wanted her to stay, but only for the right reasons.

She doesn't want my help.

"Why not?" He drove slowly down the hill toward town.

She wants to be loved.

The realization hit him like a sucker punch.

"Oh."

He sat idling at the stop sign. Love. His heart beat faster just thinking the word. Sure, he loved his family. Hazel. Romping through the great outdoors. But *love.* That had messy and hard and scary written all over it. He'd thought he loved Celeste and that imploded.

Man, he had to talk to somebody. Pulling his phone from his pocket, he scrolled to Blake's number. If anybody knew about messy and complicated, it was Blake. But he was knee-deep in his own personal heartache right now. Not to mention barely speaking to him.

Dropping the phone in the truck's console, Jeremy blew out a breath. He'd done it again—fallen hard for a woman who was completely wrong for him, yet she'd worked her way into his life and now his heart.

12

Alyssa guided the scissors through the wrapping paper, working to make a straight cut. Christmas music streamed from her phone to the wireless speaker she'd set on the coffee table. If she focused on the music and the festive vibe in the air, she could almost forget she was spending the holiday with total strangers.

Almost.

She grabbed a box of Legos from the stack of gifts Mrs. Carter had deposited on the couch, placed it in the center of the paper, then reached for the tape dispenser. Once these were wrapped and tagged, she'd help wash the dishes still covering the kitchen counter. Then torture her body with another go on that vintage exercise bike. Anything to keep busy and her mind occupied.

"Oh, look at you." Mrs. Carter came in, carrying yet another plastic shopping bag. "Thank you for your help. I'm really cutting it close here, aren't I?"

"Not really. Lots of people leave the wrapping until Christmas Eve."

"That's sweet of you to say. The holidays come at the same time every year, and every year I'm surprised by how much there is to do on Christmas Eve. I'm so glad I didn't miss the Christmas program last night, though. Wasn't that amazing?"

"It was. Your grandkids were great." Alyssa attached a tag to the gift and passed it to Mrs. Carter. "There's the Lego set."

"Thanks." She perched on the edge of the couch and grabbed a pen. "I think I went a bit overboard this year. I just—just want everything to be perfect, you know? I'm old enough to know that the gifts aren't what Christmas is all about…" She offered a wobbly smile. "Listen to me, getting all sentimental. If I'm honest, what I really want is for Blake and Lauren to make amends."

Alyssa hesitated. It wasn't really any of her business, but she didn't want to ignore Mrs. Carter, either. "Do you think they will?"

"Hard to know what they're going to do. Lauren has always had a mind of her own. This time her strong will might be her demise."

Alyssa bit her lip. Ouch. Those words pricked at her.

Mrs. Carter sniffed and pulled clothes from the bag in her lap. Classic two-piece kids' pajamas. "I couldn't resist. Look at those penguins. They're sledding. Isn't that adorable?"

"Very cute," Alyssa said. "Would you like me to wrap them, too?"

"I hate to ask you to do that."

Alyssa shrugged. "I don't mind."

Folding the pajamas tenderly, Mrs. Carter placed them on the sofa. "Angela will tease me for buying her kids matching pajamas, but they're only young once, you know?"

Before Alyssa could respond, Mrs. Carter's eyes glistened with moisture. "Good grief, I'm a mess. You're probably wishing you hadn't volunteered for this assignment. This is our first Christmas without my mother, and I just—I really thought this would be the year Blake and Lauren would have a baby." She sighed and dabbed at her cheeks with a tissue. "Sometimes this season magnifies the hurt and broken places, doesn't it? Thank goodness we have a Savior who wipes away every tear."

Alyssa said nothing as a lump formed in her throat. Even if it was Christmas Eve, she wasn't in the mood for a mini-sermon. But Mrs. Carter's words touched something deep inside, something she'd been trying to avoid since she got here.

Belonging.

This trip to Emerald Cove was supposed to be an escape—a work commitment conveniently packaged as a hiatus from reality. Yet here she was, wrapping presents for people she barely knew and getting all emotional about strangers' marital problems. That was the thing, though. Jeremy's family and friends didn't feel like strangers. She'd never cared this much about people she'd just met—which was kind of frightening. When she'd bounced from one foster home to another, helpless to provide for herself and in desperate want of a family to call her own, she'd learned not to form attachments quickly. She'd cried into her pillow countless nights, with nobody to wipe her tears away. Although the Huards had loved her unconditionally, she'd never fully understood why. Despite her vow to not trust anyone, now she was smitten with this town—these people.

What was *happening?*

She cleared her throat and forced a smile. "What should I wrap next? The dolls?"

Mrs. Carter reached for a cardboard box with a clear plastic front revealing an almost life-like baby doll. "Isn't this adorable? Emmy is going to love it. I had to get an identical one for Ava. Do you think they're too old to get these for Christmas? I said…"

Listening to Mrs. Carter's misgivings about the appropriate age to still receive dolls, Alyssa suddenly felt six years old again. Another Christmas, another temporary placement. This time in Modesto, California. The whole placed reeked of cat pee. She'd desperately wanted a doll and a stroller, even went so far as to scribble a letter to Santa.

There *were* presents for her on Christmas morning. Her hopes were quickly dashed, though, when she ripped off the paper to find socks, underwear, a Bible, and a stuffed animal. No doll. The stroller under the tree was destined for the family's biological daughter.

That was the last time she ever bothered to make a wish list for Santa. Even after the Huards adopted her, Mom had to beg her to say what she desperately wanted.

"Alyssa?" Mrs. Carter pressed her hand to Alyssa's arm. "Are you okay?"

She looked up. "Sorry. Zoned out for a second. What were you saying?"

"Let me finish wrapping those. Angela and Matt will be by to pick you up in a few minutes."

The gift slipped from her hand and landed on the table. "Why?"

Mrs. Carter's scissors hovered over the wrapping paper. "Didn't we tell you? Snowshoeing with the Tully's is our Christmas Eve tradition, usually followed by hot cocoa and plenty of treats. Then we go to the candlelight service at church."

"I don't know. I haven't snowshoed in years."

"It's like riding a bike. You never forget." She chuckled. "If you can win a gold medal in snowboarding, I'm sure this won't be much of a challenge."

Alyssa crumpled up the extra pieces of wrapping paper scattered at her feet. She hadn't seen Jeremy today. After last night's drama, she'd popped a sleeping pill and disappeared into a blissful state of unawareness. She'd done her best to pretend he didn't exist.

If she saw him today, even in a group, she'd have to deal with the mess she'd made. Snowshoeing wasn't like snowboarding. She couldn't shoot down the side of a mountain and leave everyone else behind. They'd be in close proximity, trekking along a trail. Just the thought of those blue eyes searching her face made her heart beat faster. Last night's conversation might have ended, but it still felt half-finished. And now she'd have to face him. Try and pretend she didn't care about him. Hadn't fallen in love with him, these people, and this place he called home.

***

"Meg? Do you know where your snowshoes are?" Jeremy came up the stairs from his parents' basement, a pair of snowshoes in his arms. "I only found one extra pair."

No answer.

Impatience niggled its way into his gut. They'd agreed she'd pack snacks while he finished his Christmas shopping and gathered their gear. Had she changed her mind? "Megan?" He followed the sound of somebody sniffling in the kitchen.

Megan stood in the middle of the hardwood floor, wiping away tears with the cuff of her long-sleeved shirt. In her other hand, she held a small card. An impressive bouquet of red roses sat in a vase on the counter.

"Wow. Who sent those?"

"Nobody." She crumpled up the card, stomped to the cabinet under the sink, then stuffed it in the garbage can.

"Really?" He counted the blooms. Two, four, six, eight, ten, twelve, fourteen, sixteen, eighteen, twenty, twenty-two, twenty-four ... Holy cow. "*Nobody* doesn't send two-dozen roses on Christmas Eve."

She reached for the vase. "Pretend you never saw them."

"Wait." Jeremy lurched toward her, clamping his hand on her forearm. "You're not going to throw them away, are you?"

Her eyes flashed. "Let go."

"Meg, talk to me. Are you in some kind of trouble?"

"Not exactly." She whirled away, escaping his grasp.

That didn't sound convincing. Leaning against the counter, he linked his arms across his chest while she shoved the flowers in the trash then poured the water from the vase into the sink. He wracked his brain for any details about her time in Seattle that might provide a clue. Had she mentioned dating anyone? They hadn't texted very much while she was away. He'd figured that meant she was doing well. Man, he'd been way off on that one.

She pulled the bag from the can, cinched the drawstrings, and tied them in a knot. The red rose petals pressed against the inside of the plastic, crushed. Bummer. Whoever sent these … well, this probably wasn't the effect the guy was hoping for.

Megan tossed the bag at his feet. "Will you take this out on your way to the garage?"

"What's in the garage?"

"More snowshoes." She crossed to the pantry and pulled out a box of granola bars. "Will eight be enough? How many people are coming?"

"You, me, Angela, Matt, Wyatt, and possibly Alyssa. The kids are coming, too, but Matt said they have their own stuff packed." The mental image of Alyssa trekking along the trail beside him, her hair in braids and that adorable beanie perched on the crown of her head, made his heart beat faster. Despite the slammed door last night, he still hadn't been able to get her out of his mind. He'd never been so relieved to not get a text on his phone. She'd kept her word and stayed after all.

Megan shot him a look before she knelt and pulled a cutting board from the cabinet near his legs.

"What?"

"Nothing." She stood and smacked the board against the granite.

He inched over, giving her space. She grabbed an apple from the fruit bowl and a knife from the block nearby. The tight line of her mouth and the way she carved up that poor apple told him it wasn't nothing. Just like those beautiful flowers weren't from nobody.

"Your body language says it's something. What's wrong?"

The knife hovered in the air for an instant then cracked against the plastic again. "I see the way you look at Alyssa, and I'm worried."

Wait a minute. So they could talk about his struggles but not hers? "You didn't seem too worried when you went all fangirl after the play."

"I didn't go all fangirl."

"Really."

She dragged the back of her hand across her nose. "I'd hate to see a repeat of last winter, that's all."

Oh-kay. He knew how that poor apple felt under her knife blade. He pushed off from the edge of the counter and grabbed the trash bag. "I'd better go look for those snowshoes. They'll all be here in a few minutes."

He went out the back door, across the deck, and down the steps. Megan's comment bounced around in his head. Alyssa was nothing like Celeste. Hadn't she proved that by staying in Emerald Cove for Christmas? Circling around the corner of the house, he shivered in the crisp air. Surely he hadn't fallen into the same trap that ensnared him so often in the past—a woman who only wanted him when it was convenient for her.

His gut twisted in knots. He punched the buttons on the keypad then waited for the garage door to open. Why give Megan's insights credit, anyway? She obviously had a few issues of her own when it came to romance. He lifted the lid on the large bin then chucked the bag inside. Nope. Not letting the doubt take up residence. He'd wasted too much time feeling sorry for himself. If Alyssa showed up today, he'd do everything he could to make the most of another opportunity to spend time with her.

Moving deeper into the garage, he examined the equipment hanging neatly on hooks. Dad must've moved all their outdoor gear here. Since Mom and Dad were still out shopping, he'd loan Alyssa a pair of Mom's boots and trekking poles.

A pair of crampons and a harness dangled next to the cross-country skis. Jeremy ran his hand along the nylon straps. Maybe Alyssa would stick around long enough to try ice climbing. Lance would freak if he found out. Jeremy smiled. That probably hadn't ever stopped her before, though. He'd love to see her in a harness, to conquer a frozen waterfall.

The sound of a car in the driveway made h⁚ below the open passenger door as people climᵤ. the pair he wanted to see the most. Black with pink aᵤ Alyssa's gaze met his, making his pulse stutter. Whether he . hours or six weeks with her, he was determined to savor every minute.

He tipped his chin in a casual nod, flashing a grin that he hoped concealed his nervousness. "Morning. You all ready for some exercise?"

***

Alyssa stood in the Tully's driveway, examining the Sorel boots she'd borrowed from Jeremy's mom. Now that she'd added an extra pair of socks, they felt good. Snug but not too tight.

"Are you sure they fit? I'd hate to give a professional snowboarder a blister for Christmas." Jeremy's eyes crinkled at the corners as he smiled.

Her insides flip-flopped. She'd miss that grin of his when she was gone. Okay, maybe she'd miss a lot about him. The sound of his voice when he teased her…

"Alyssa? Do you want to try a different pair of boots?"

He'd caught her daydreaming. She shook her head. "The boots are fine. It's these things I'm worried about." She pointed at the wood and leather teardrop shaped contraptions on the snow at her feet.

"You don't have snowshoes in Lake Tahoe?"

"Not like these."

"Let me guess. Yours are metal and sleek, probably came from a chain sporting goods store."

"And what's wrong with that?"

"Nothing." He shrugged. "We're purists around here, though. The natives knew what they were doing. Not everything has to be modernized. Why mess with a good thing?"

His piercing gaze held hers.

She looked away. The weight of his words made her insides dip and sway.

"You guys coming?" Angela called from the end of the driveway.

and the rest of their group were ahead of her, already on their
y down the trail.

"Yep. Go on. We'll catch up." Jeremy squatted beside Alyssa and
nudged the snowshoes closer. "Here. Slide your toes in and I'll buckle
the strap."

Standing on her right leg, she tucked her left toe into the leather
binding. Her balance wavered, and her hand shot out, clasping
Jeremy's shoulder.

He glanced up. "Don't worry. I got you."

Her heart fluttered in response. If only that were true. Or even
possible. After the way she'd reacted last night, he and his friends were
probably including her out of obligation.

"There." He buckled her other foot into the second snowshoe then
reached for his own. "Let me put these on and we'll catch up with the
others."

She pointed to the metal poles lying in the driveway. "Do I need to
use those?"

"If you want. Might help with your confidence."

"What are you trying to say?"

"Nothing." He straightened. "Walking with snowshoes is a different
experience. Sometimes people get frustrated because it isn't like
anything else they've tried. Then they get tired, and the poles can
diffuse some of the fatigue."

"I'll try it without."

"Suit yourself."

She turned too quickly, trying to catch Angela before she
disappeared out of sight. The long tails on the back of her snowshoes
tangled. Her arms flailed, and her stomach sank as she fought to stay
upright.

Laughter erupted behind her.

Glad he finds this so amusing. She glanced over her shoulder and
glared at Jeremy.

He held up a set of poles in one hand. "Sure you don't want these?"

"No." Determined to get it right, without the poles, she took another
tentative step. This time the frames of the snowshoes knocked together.

Seriously?

"Here." Jeremy came alongside her. "Watch me. If you can walk, you can snowshoe."

"Thanks so much. I feel super confident now."

"Easy. I'm here to help, remember?"

She clamped her mouth shut and stared at his feet, studying his stride.

"Widen your stance so you aren't stepping on the frames. The snowshoes are designed to support your weight, so take normal steps, like you're out for a stroll."

Out for a stroll. Right. More like out for an awkward and embarrassing stagger. Hadn't she snowshoed a few times with the Huards before they introduced her to downhill skiing and then snowboarding? In her memory, this seemed a lot easier.

"C'mon. You've got this."

His words of encouragement buoyed her. She moved her left leg a bit further from her right then stepped forward. A few more steps and the tension eased from her upper body. It wasn't anything like soaring down a mountainside, but the familiar ache of exertion in her leg muscles and the crisp fresh air renewed her enthusiasm. Before she knew it, they were past the trailhead and curving behind the Tully's house.

"See?" Jeremy smiled again. "It's not much different than walking, right?"

She banged the frames of her snowshoes together. *Shoot.* "Don't know about that." Eyes riveted on Angela's hot pink jacket in the distance, she concentrated on putting one snowshoe beside the other. But not too close. The threat of doing a face-plant loomed large.

Afternoon sunlight streamed through the barren tree branches, making the snow shine bright white. She squinted. Too bad she'd forgotten her goggles.

They trekked along in silence. When she felt certain the strange combination of wood, leather, and webbing would support her, she mustered her courage to give voice to the words she'd turned over and over in her mind. "Hey, listen. About—"

"—I'm so—"

Their words tumbled over one another. Alyssa stopped walking and waited, her breaths coming quickly.

"You first," Jeremy said, his expression guarded.

Great. She rushed the words before she lost her nerve. "I'm sorry I closed the door in your face. That was rude. You've been so kind and helpful since I got here and … I shouldn't have done that."

There. That wasn't so hard. No excuses, just a sincere apology.

"I'm sorry, too."

Wait. What? "Why?"

"You needed someone to listen, not offer unsolicited advice." He frowned. "I wanted to help and instead I sounded like I … didn't want you. That's not true. I do want you here."

She swallowed hard. Was he for real? It had been a long time—maybe never—since a guy apologized for his behavior with no strings attached.

Jeremy cleared his throat. "Say something. Please."

"I—I'm … I don't know what to say. It means a lot that you would apologize after the way I acted."

His features softened into a heart-stopping smile. "Alyssa. You deserve to be treated well."

The way that smile sent a shiver down her spine and the tenderness in his voice spurred her to action, and she moved away, killing the moment. "We should go. They keep stopping for us."

"Alyssa—"

Smashing down the snow, Alyssa willed her legs to move faster, determined to catch the rest of the group. They stood near a bend in the trail, a cluster of bright colors splashed on a winter-white background.

"Wait."

She looked back.

Jeremy came alongside her again. "I wanted to invite you to the Christmas Eve service tonight. Pretty sure I mentioned it before. Lots of singing and we'll finish by candlelight. It would be great if you could come."

"I'm not much of a church person anymore. My parents used to make me go all the time, but…" She trailed off and held both palms up, gesturing to their surroundings. "Being in nature like this is as spiritual as it gets for me. Don't you feel more peaceful, more centered, when you're outdoors?"

"It starts at seven."

She turned away without answering. His words pinged around in her mind, muddling her thoughts and triggering the urge to move. To run. Because old habits die hard, and as much as she wanted to believe that he wanted her, she couldn't risk being hurt again.

***

Jeremy sat in the back row of the church sanctuary, his jacket folded next to him, claiming the space on the aisle for Alyssa.

The ushers flanked the set of double doors nearby, encouraging people to find their seats. Up front, the pianist finished the prelude. Jeremy scanned the faces of the people hustling past. No Alyssa. What was she doing, anyway? Sitting in her room, watching classic movies on television? He should've just gone by the inn on his way to church and convinced her to come along.

Megan scooted closer, her shoulder bumping his as she made more room for people filling the last remaining seats beside her. She shot him a pointed look.

"I'm not giving up this seat. She still might show up."

Megan arched an eyebrow then flipped open the program.

The doors clicked shut, and Matt climbed the steps to the podium on stage. "Good evening, everyone. Merry Christmas."

"Merry Christmas," the crowd murmured.

"Please join me in prayer," he said.

Jeremy bowed his head but kept his eyes open. Just in case.

When the prayer was over, a family with three young children came forward and read a passage of scripture. Then they lit the candles in the Advent wreath.

The door opened behind him. He swiveled, his pulse accelerating.

Nope. Only Wyatt coming in late.

Wyatt's gaze flitted between Megan, the empty seat next to Jeremy, then back to Megan.

Jeremy glanced at her from the corner of his eye. She stiffened but stared straight ahead.

The worship leader invited them to stand. Wyatt moved on, crossing the sanctuary to the opposite side and taking a seat next to a cousin.

Jeremy nudged Megan with his elbow. "Wyatt's here."

"Shhh." She pretended to study the program, her mouth twitching.

So she did notice. He stifled a laugh. The familiar notes of "Go Tell It on the Mountain" filled the room, keeping him from asking any more questions. He glanced between her and Wyatt one more time. What was going on?

The next few songs were some of Jeremy's favorites, yet he barely mouthed the words as every movement in his peripheral vision caused him to stare at the doors again. By the time the pastor finished his brief message, Alyssa still hadn't made an appearance. An ache filled his gut. She'd said church wasn't her thing—that a spiritual experience for her meant being out in nature. How sad. While he observed the evidence of God's breathtaking creation every day in his own hometown, he struggled to convey how his relationship with the Lord was about more than a feeling. When he'd shared that he wanted her here—in Emerald Cove—and she'd visibly shut him down, he'd panicked and barely managed to invite her to tonight's service.

A woman sang a solo accompanied by a violin, and then the ushers came forward and passed around a basket full of small white candles inserted in the center of cardboard circles. When the basket reached them, he took one for himself and hesitated, then grabbed one for Alyssa, too. The lights dimmed and one by one, each person passed the flame to the next person, until the whole sanctuary glowed with the flickering of a couple hundred candle flames.

Jeremy felt the tension ease from his shoulders. No matter what else had happened, this single moment always realigned his focus on what he truly valued. Worship and celebration of the newborn King. Savior of the world.

Fabric rustled as someone slid into the seat next to him. A familiar citrusy scent wafted his way.

"Hey," Alyssa whispered in his ear. "I made it."

He felt a smile spread across his face. "Perfect timing." He touched the wick of her candle to the flame of his then passed it to her. She held the candle in her fingertips, her expression unreadable in the semidarkness.

His heart squeezed in his chest. There. He sensed it. Like the flickering flames cupped in their hands, he felt hope fighting for a cautious reentry. Hope that the hurts of the past would only be painful memories transformed into lessons learned. Hope that this beautiful woman beside him would know and understand her worth apart from all she'd achieved. He slipped his arm around her shoulders and pulled her close. While the audience around them sang "Silent Night," he pressed his lips to her ear and whispered, "I'm glad you're here."

She smiled up at him, eyes gleaming. In that moment, he recognized what he'd also secretly hoped since they'd collided on the mountain—that she'd want him in her life the way he wanted her.

13

"Mom, it's fine. I'm fine." Alyssa sat on the top step of the Tully's basement stairs, phone pressed to her ear.

"I just wish you weren't alone on Christmas."

The wistful tone in Mom's voice made Alyssa want to hang up. She'd managed to ignore the guilt for most of the day—until now. "I'm not alone."

A burst of laughter erupted in the background, mingling with Mom's response. Her brother-in-law was notorious for sticking hilarious gag gifts in people's stockings. She pictured them all sitting around, blowing air into whoopee cushions or posing for selfies with their new disguises. She gritted her teeth. So maybe there were one or two things she'd miss about not being at home today.

"I didn't hear what you said, Mom."

"I said, 'but you're not with family.'"

Alyssa gnawed on her thumbnail. "I'm with a nice family."

"How long will you stay?"

Jeremy's face flashed in her mind—lighting her candle last night in church, looking up at her yesterday while he helped with her snowshoes, and sitting beside her at dinner tonight. "I guess until it's time to move on." She lowered her voice. "I'll have to be in Aspen for the X-Games."

"That's almost a month from now."

"Don't worry. I'm fine." The more she said it, the sooner she might believe it.

"You're an adult, capable of making your own decisions. I just wish—"

"The powder here is epic. It's unreal. Like nothing I've ever experienced."

Mom laughed softly. "You were always one to follow great snow."

"You got it." Growing restless, Alyssa pushed to her feet.

159

"Do you want to talk to Dad or your sisters? They're finishing up dessert."

"No, I—I'd better get back. Wish them all a Merry Christmas."

"Are you sure? They'd love to chat."

"Merry Christmas, Mom."

"Merry Christmas, sweetie. I love you."

Alyssa ended the call. Whew. No mention of Nick and no questions about the pictures. She half expected one of her sisters to call back, though. They wouldn't be satisfied with a simple greeting sent via Mom. Setting the volume to silent, she pocketed the phone, then moved toward the gathering around the Tully's kitchen table.

"There you are." Jeremy met her in the archway between the kitchen and the hall. "Everything okay?"

"Yeah. Just wanted to call home before it got too late."

"I bet they were glad to hear from you."

"I guess." She lifted one shoulder and searched for someplace to stare besides his face. Or the pale blue sweater hugging his muscular biceps and emphasizing his broad shoulders.

"We've got a mean game of Pictionary going on in here. Want to jump in?"

"Um, I—"

"Look who's under the mistletoe!" Angela's voice carried above the others.

A chorus of "oooh's" followed by an adamant, "You have to kiss her" filled the air.

Alyssa's cheeks flushed as she glanced at the mistletoe dangling above their heads. How had she not noticed that until now?

Jeremy closed the distance between them, his deep blue eyes riveted on hers.

Her heart leaped into her throat. She should go. Make up an excuse and slip out of his reach. But she remained rooted in place, her feet somehow disobeying her brain's directive.

He leaned down, his head tilted.

She tipped her chin and closed her eyes.

He hooked a finger in one of her belt loops and gave a gentle tug, pulling her closer—a flirtatious move which took her by surprise and sent a tingling sensation zinging all the way to her toes. His lips brushed against hers. Soft. Cautious.

Their audience forgotten, she cupped her hands around his biceps, feeling the taut muscles under the wool material. Longing unfurled within her as he deepened the kiss. She responded, sliding her palms along his broad shoulders and then tunneling her fingers into the hair at the nape of his neck. At last she was in his arms, all her apprehension cast aside by his intoxicating touch.

An appreciative whistle interrupted them, and Jeremy pulled away much too soon.

Applause broke out. She kept her eyes closed, wanting very much to relive the moment and pull him in for another kiss.

"Merry Christmas," he whispered, his breath feathering her cheek.

She opened her eyes. His hands remained at her waist and those amazing lips of his curved into a sheepish grin. Her gaze lingered there. Pliant. Kissable. A hint of five o'clock shadow making her want to cup that jaw with her palm.

"Merry Christmas," she said after managing to find her voice.

He released his grasp, only to reach for her hand and lace his fingers through hers. "I'm not in the mood for Pictionary. You?"

She shook her head, thoughts muddled by his electrifying touch.

"Wow, that was some kiss," Angela teased.

She wasn't wrong. Alyssa dipped her head, letting her hair provide a shield from the curious stares.

"Ignore them," Jeremy said, his voice low. Husky. He didn't seem at all embarrassed to be kissing her like that in front of his family and friends. "How about a movie?"

She'd watch paint dry if it meant he kept holding her hand like that, the pad of his thumb caressing her skin. Following him into the family room, they stopped at the end of the sofa. *The Polar Express* played on the flat-screen television mounted on the far wall. Matt and Angela's kids were scattered across the carpet, wrapped in quilts or sitting on bean bags.

"Sorry." Jeremy squeezed her hand. "Not exactly a chick flick."

"It's okay. I love this one."

"Want to hang out here? These kids have to go home sometime. We'll call dibs on the next movie."

The next movie. That implied she'd be here a while. He didn't expect her to go back to the inn anytime soon. She felt welcome here. Like she belonged.

A yellow lab stood and stretched, tail wagging, then sidestepped a beanbag and trotted over to Jeremy, eyes riveted on his face.

He let go of Alyssa's hand. "Hazel, girl, what's going on?"

"Is that your dog?" Alyssa reached down and patted the soft fur on top of the dog's head, eager for a distraction after that very public display of affection. Hazel pressed her body against Alyssa's legs.

Jeremy chuckled as he gave the dog an affectionate pat. "Yep, this is Hazel. I'm feeling guilty for leaving her alone so much. She chewed up one of my shoes while we were snowshoeing yesterday." He gave the dog a playful nudge. "Point taken, Hazel. That's why your stocking is full of rawhides. Go lie down."

The dog whined and hung her head then flopped down beside the coffee table and heaved a sigh, head on her paws.

Jeremy crossed to the sofa opposite the Christmas tree, then sank into the corner, his arm resting on the back of the leather cushion.

Alyssa settled next to him, her leg against his, her lips still tingling from that incredible kiss. He slid his arm around her shoulders, giving her stomach yet another reason to turn cartwheels. She began to list them all. The delicious meal. Blake and Lauren sitting together, although fatigue etched both their faces. A tree swathed in twinkling lights and laughter around the table. Jeremy by her side. Their intimate moment under the mistletoe on instant replay in her mind. She snuggled into the crook of his arm and released a contented sigh. Could this day be any better?

***

The movie credits rolled on the television screen. Hazel's damp nose nudged Jeremy's hand. He chuckled softly. "Your timing couldn't be worse, Haze."

She whined and pranced around, her tail smacking the wooden coffee table littered with discarded wrapping paper, bows, and empty plates.

Alyssa stirred, her hair tickling his jaw.

He froze, hoping his voice hadn't disturbed her. He'd agreed to watch her favorite movie, *While You Were Sleeping*, but she'd fallen asleep even before the guy woke up from his coma. Mom, Wyatt, Megan, and Dad had traded Pictionary for a card game, and the murmur of their voices punctuated with occasional laughter drifted in from the kitchen. Before the movie had started, the rest of the Carters had gathered their exhausted children and said their goodbyes. Blake and Lauren had left, too. Still Alyssa slept, the two of them snuggled on one end of the sofa, her cheek pressed against his chest and her arm wrapped around his torso. The best Christmas gift ever.

Mom tiptoed in. "Want me to let Hazel out?"

"Please."

She clicked her tongue. "C'mon, Hazel. Let's go outside."

Hazel trotted toward the front door, her nails clicking on the hardwood in the entryway.

The Christmas tree's white lights bathed the room in a warm glow. Jeremy sank deeper into the couch and sighed. This was perfection. He threaded his hand through Alyssa's hair, letting his fingers trail through the silky strands. His pulse quickened at the memory of the kiss they'd shared underneath the mistletoe. It had taken every ounce of self-control he possessed to end it. If it weren't for a house full of people watching, especially the kids, he'd have kissed her again during the first half of the movie.

Oh, well. There was always tomorrow, right?

If she stays.

He dismissed the irritating thought as quickly as it came. Of course she'd stay. At least through the end of the month and the resort's grand reopening. Why wouldn't she? Sure, she couldn't stay forever. Snowboarding season kicked into high gear in the next few weeks. He wasn't naïve enough to think she'd blow off upcoming competitions for him. But he couldn't pretend his feelings for her hadn't grown stronger or that an amazing kiss hadn't just happened. More doubts pinged around in his mind, threatening to squelch his newfound happiness. They needed to talk—the pictures posted online, her apparent disinterest in anything faith-based, how she felt about a long-distance relationship. His heart fisted. What if she dodged any mention of grittier topics?

Between now and the grand opening, he'd have little free time. There was still so much to do. Chuck and Rachel had probably discovered more overlooked details while Jeremy had taken Christmas Eve and Christmas off. There was a lot riding on the resort's reopening, but he hated that Alyssa might feel she wasn't a priority in his life, too. Not to mention meaningful conversation would be tough if they hardly saw one another. Something told him if she didn't feel wanted, she'd find a reason to leave. And he didn't want to be that reason.

He drew a calming breath, wrestling with the anxiety creeping in. They'd survived an overnight in brutal winter conditions; surely a busy week wouldn't be their undoing. How hard could it be to carve out a few hours to spend together?

The front door opened and closed, and Hazel returned, snowflakes dotting her fur. She sniffed at his shirt sleeve then shimmied and shook with delight, the tags on her collar clinking together.

"Hazel. No." He held up his hand as a makeshift shield. Too late. Drops of moisture sprayed across his jeans.

Mom stifled a laugh. "Sorry. She came back in before I could grab a towel."

"Don't worry about it," Jeremy whispered. "It'll dry in a sec."

Obviously quite pleased with herself, Hazel sat down in the middle of the room, muzzle held high. He shook his head. She was something else.

Mom had a silver package tucked under her arm. "This was outside on the steps for Megan. Lucky girl. Looks like it came from a pretty fancy store."

"Huh. I wonder who that's from."

"Beats me. I'll let her know it's here."

"Wait." He motioned for her to come closer. "Let's wait until Wyatt goes home to give Megan the package."

Mom frowned. "Why?"

"Just—I think she'd rather not open it in front of … people." He stopped short of saying anything else. Megan was going to kill him for sharing that much, but if Wyatt had feelings for her, Jeremy didn't want him to have to watch her open a potentially extravagant gift from some other guy.

Mom hesitated, but she nodded then tucked the mysterious box under the tree.

Jeremy winked. "That's better."

"Whatever you say." She gathered up an abandoned cup and a few empty popcorn bowls left behind by Matt and Angela's kids. She paused on her way back to the kitchen, her gaze flitting from him to Alyssa. "Need anything?"

He couldn't stop the grin from spreading across his face. "Nope."

She tucked the cup under one arm then gave his shoulder a squeeze. "It's nice to see you so happy again, sweetie."

"Thanks."

Alone with Alyssa once more, he shifted slightly, then grabbed the remote and surfed to another channel, keeping the volume muted. He'd sit like this until morning if he could, holding Alyssa in his arms and pretending he didn't have a worry in the world.

He glanced briefly at his stocking hanging from the mantle, in its rightful place between Mom's and Megan's. This Christmas had felt unexpectedly festive. A few months ago—even a few weeks ago, really—he'd never have imagined feeling this content. As he gently rubbed his palm against Alyssa's upper arm, Mom's words stuck with him. She was right. For the first time in a long time he wasn't waiting for something. Or someone. Everything he needed was right here.

14

Near the bottom of the hill, Alyssa leaned back on her snowboard and skirted around a little girl learning to ski. The skis were linked at the tips by a twisty nylon cord, and the girl wobbled, arms outstretched for counterbalance. In her white and pink polka dot jacket and contrasting pink snow pants, the girl was about the cutest thing Alyssa had seen all day. Then again, she did have a thing for pink.

Easing to a stop, she rested her goggles on top of her hat and surveyed the mountainside. What little she could see of it, anyway. Thick fog shrouded the top of Miller's Ridge, while skiers and snowboarders dotted the lower runs. This place was packed.

Well played, Chuck.

His plan for an epic New Year's Eve grand opening had obviously worked. She glanced toward the shed, hoping to catch a glimpse of Jeremy. Too bad a busy day for the mountain meant seeing less of him.

A lot less of him. Since Christmas, she'd passed the time snowboarding, doing yoga, cross-training with snowshoes on the trails around town—anything she could think of to maintain her training regimen while Jeremy spent countless hours getting the resort ready for today.

She'd tried hard not to complain. After all, hadn't she dropped into his life unannounced? It wasn't like he could skip out on his commitments, especially this week. He'd made time for her, even in the middle of his chaotic schedule. Even though he was obviously exhausted, they'd spent every possible second together, ordering takeout from Randy's or The Fish House and eating at his place.

She'd stayed late every night, cocooned in his arms on the couch, with a movie playing in the background. The memory of his touch, igniting dangerous responses in her body, made her skin tingle just thinking about it. About him. His lips on hers, blazing a trail of kisses along her neck, and leaving her breathless—yet he'd managed to rein things in when they teetered on the edge of losing control. He never invited her into his bed. Never demanded more than she was willing to give.

It was close to one in the morning by the time he drove her back to the Carter's, and then he lingered on the porch for a long goodbye. Not once had she mentioned the social media posts. But he'd never asked, either. They were too happy together to bring it up now.

She sighed. Sooner or later, she'd have to talk to him about her commitments in January. Just the thought of buying her plane ticket back to Colorado planted an icy ball of dread in her stomach.

A snowboarder skidded to a stop beside her. "Alyssa?"

"Link?" She'd recognize those copper-colored dreadlocks anywhere. "What are you doing here?"

"Shredding this gnarly powder, girlie." He grinned and held out his gloved fist. "Sick three-sixty you pulled off back there, by the way."

"Thanks." She bumped his fist. "It's so foggy on top I didn't realize anybody was watching."

"You're hard to miss, stomping it like that. Is this where you've been hanging out?"

A harmless question, no doubt. She'd known Link since they both broke onto the scene eight years ago, and he pretty much only cared about one thing—snowboarding. Not gossip or other people's perceptions. Still, her old world colliding with the here-and-now set her on edge. She forced a smile. "Yeah. It's amazing, right?"

"True that." He shook his head. "We saw the pictures and video clips online, but it's even better in real life."

"Who are you here with?" Her throat tightened, and she scanned the snow nearby. Link and Nick weren't close friends. But they weren't enemies, either. The snowboarding community was pretty small. If word had spread about Emerald Cove, then…

"My usual posse. You've probably met them. We flew into Anchorage and rented a car."

Her mouth went dry. His usual posse. Who did that include? "Where are you staying?"

"At a hotel in town, the one on the corner by the pizza place. We couldn't get a room here—sold out."

"Are you going to be at the resort later? It's supposed to be rocking tonight."

"Absolutely." He grinned and readjusted his knit beanie. "Are you?"

"Alyssa?"

She turned toward the sound of Jeremy's voice, her pulse kicking up a notch as he walked up beside her then planted a kiss on her cheek.

Link would definitely have something to tell his friends now.

"Hey." She smiled up at him. "I was hoping you'd be finished soon."

"Me, too." He glanced at Link and gave him the standard guy greeting. Chin tip. Slight nod. "What's up?"

"Not much." Link slid his goggles back in place. "Y'all have fun tonight, all right?"

Jeremy watched him go. "Who's that?"

"Link. A snowboarder from the tour. He medaled in Sochi, too."

"Sweet." His gaze swung back to her, eyes twinkling. "I'm officially off-duty. At least until I have to meet the guys with the fireworks."

"Fireworks?"

"Yep. It wouldn't be New Year's Eve around here without fireworks. If the weather forecast is accurate, it's supposed to be a beautiful night."

"Can't wait." She tipped her head to one side, a smile playing at her lips. How awesome would it be to watch the fireworks from the resort's sprawling new patio, wrapped in his arms?

"Something on your mind?" Jeremy asked, arching one eyebrow.

"You. Me. Fireworks. A champagne toast."

His grin widened. "I like the way you think."

"Will it be dark soon?"

He chuckled. "Yes. But the show doesn't start until eleven-thirty."

"Dang it. That's like, ten hours from now. Do you have time to ski?"

"You'll be seen with a skier?" He arched an eyebrow. "I didn't think snowboarders hung out with the likes of us."

"For you, I'll make an exception."

"Be right back."

While he returned to the shed for his gear, Alyssa pulled an energy bar from her pocket and polished it off quickly. The dark chocolate and peanut butter concoction would have to do for now. Even if her stomach continued to growl, the opportunity for time with Jeremy was too perfect to miss.

Jeremy skied up beside her, goggles in place, a reddish tinge to his cheeks. His smile warmed her from the inside out. Every day spent in Emerald Cove birthed more daydreams about an ordinary, normal life spent with him. Yet today marked the end of the year. With the arrival of January, she'd be forced to confront her jam-packed schedule. Wasn't there a way she could have the best of both worlds? Didn't recording artists and actors juggle personal and professional roles? Filming on location balanced with real life in Montana or New Mexico or wherever they put down roots?

Roots. She shook her head. The notion had always seemed foreign, almost a threat to her freedom, until now.

"You okay?" Jeremy's arm brushed hers as they joined the end of the line waiting for the chairlift.

"Yeah." She bit her lip, catching another glimpse of Link's hair near the front of the line. He and two other guys took the next open chair. She scanned their jackets, hats, hair brushing their collars. Nothing looked familiar. Link would've told her if Nick was here, right? And would it matter if he was?

Jeremy nudged her. "You're quiet all of a sudden. Plotting your next run? Sorry, Chuck wouldn't let me build any rails or boxes in the middle of the mountain."

"No worries." She flashed a smile. If only her next ride was all she had on her mind.

***

Later that night, the tangy scent of appetizers wafted toward them as Jeremy weaved through the crowded lobby of the resort, Alyssa's fingers intertwined in his. Festive big band music played from the speakers, and guests mingled in small groups, drinks in hand. Waiters circulated with trays of sliders, stuffed mushrooms, and bacon-wrapped prosciutto, while a fire crackled in the fireplace. They worked their way to the front desk where Megan stood, wearing the resort's signature royal blue button-down shirt and black pants.

"Hey. I have something for you." Megan reached under the counter.

"You might need this. It's a balmy five degrees out there." She pushed a folded green-and-red plaid blanket toward them.

"Thanks." Jeremy released Alyssa's hand then tucked the blanket under his arm.

"How was your first week on the job?" Alyssa asked.

"Good." Megan shrugged. "I didn't really know what to expect, though."

"I can't believe Chuck put you at the front desk on New Year's Eve." Jeremy shook his head. "He's asking a lot."

Megan frowned. "Rachel's here if I have any problems. Chuck's probably still around, too."

"Probably." He didn't want her working at the resort at all, but she hadn't paid much attention to what he thought. Mom and Dad seemed thrilled to have her home and supported her willingness to find a job so quickly. Once this weekend was over, he'd sit down with her and get the full story about Seattle. Even if he had to pry it out of her.

"You're going to be fine," Alyssa said as raucous laughter broke out behind them. "See? People are here to have a good time. If they have a place to pass out later, you're all good."

Megan glanced at her computer. "We have two guests who still haven't checked in. Otherwise, we're sold out."

"Are you coming outside to watch the fireworks?" Alyssa glanced up at Jeremy and grinned. "I hear the view is amazing."

He let his gaze linger on hers, the air between them nearly crackling. "Yeah. Amazing." The fireworks were just an excuse to pull her close—a prelude to the kiss he planned to share with her in a few minutes when the clock struck twelve.

She nudged him with her elbow then looked away. Two splotches of color highlighted her cheekbones.

The phone at the desk rang, interrupting their moment. "You guys have fun," Megan said, then pressed the receiver to her ear. "Thank you for calling Emerald Cove Resort, this is Megan. How may I help you?"

Jeremy turned away from the counter, while Alyssa freed her hair from the confines of her new scarf. She looked fantastic in skinny jeans that hugged her curves in all the right places and a teal green sweater that made her eyes even more mesmerizing than usual.

"Nice scarf, by the way." Jeremy tugged on one end. The temptation to pull her even closer made his heart beat faster. Those fireworks couldn't happen soon enough.

"Thanks. Some guy gave it to me."

"Really? He has great taste."

She cocked her head to one side, fitting her gloves over her hands. "Does he?"

The gleam in her eyes and the attraction simmering between them sent warmth cascading through him. He returned her flirty smile with a wide grin. "True story."

"Thank you for thinking of me. You didn't have to get me anything."

"I know. But I couldn't resist. It reminded me so much of you." More truth. He'd rushed into the General Store on Christmas Eve, focused on finding last-minute gifts for Megan and his mom, when the scarf draped over a mannequin in the window stopped him in his tracks. He couldn't not buy it for Alyssa.

"C'mon. Let's go see these fireworks you've been bragging about."

Everyone else in the lobby obviously had the same idea. They fell in line behind the crowd flowing toward the front door.

"Did you want to grab some champagne for a toast?" Alyssa gestured to the bar nearby where a waitress circulated with a tray of glasses filled with the bubbling golden liquid.

Knowing Chuck, they were probably the plastic disposable kind. Still a popular notion, given the speed at which that tray was emptying. "Do you want to get it and I'll head on outside? If we want a spot by the heaters, we should hurry."

"I'll meet you out there." She squeezed his arm then turned and headed for the bar.

He watched her go, part of him wanting to call her back to his side. Champagne could wait. All he needed was her, nestled in the crook of his arm, the blanket draped across their shoulders. But if she wanted to toast the New Year, he wouldn't argue. Whatever her heart desired, he'd make it happen.

The automatic doors parted, and he followed the crowd outside. The frigid air swirled around him, and a taxi idling nearby snagged his attention. Huh. Interesting timing. Didn't Rachel say they were booked solid? A woman stepped out of the back seat, flipped her long platinum hair over her shoulder, then set a small suitcase down. His scalp prickled.

What in the world? He shook his head.

This wasn't an illusion. Celeste was there, moving toward him, like he'd envisioned so many times. Her knee-high boots, dark tights, and miniskirt emphasized legs that went for miles. The blanket slid from his grasp.

"Baby. You're here." She flung herself at him, staking her claim with arms looped around his neck. The floral scent of her perfume enveloped him as she pressed her body the length of his.

The last word darting through his mind before her mouth claimed his was *no.*

Murmurs rippled through the bystanders and a few applauded.

An icy chill raked Jeremy's spine. This wasn't right. He couldn't. She didn't. *Alyssa!* He broke contact.

"Mmm." Celeste scanned his face, her fingers toying with the hair at the nape of his neck, a dangerous smile on those ruby red lips. "It's been too long."

"Wh-what are you doing here?"

Her brow puckered. "I said I'd come. It just—"

"Jeremy?"

His stomach churned. *Please, no.* He turned slowly.

Alyssa stood behind him, holding two plastic glasses of champagne. Lower lip quivering, her eyes darted between him and Celeste.

"I—I can explain." He moved toward her, his heart in his throat.

"No explanation needed." She flung the glasses down and they shattered, splashing champagne on the snow-encrusted pavement.

Jeremy winced. This couldn't be happening. *Say something!* His mind raced, desperate to undo the damage.

Pain etched Alyssa's features as she jogged past him, sidestepping his outstretched hand. *No. No, no, no.*

"Jer, I didn't know…" Celeste stepped into his path, her mouth twisted in a pouty frown.

"Alyssa, wait." He ran after her, brushing off Celeste's attempt to intervene.

Alyssa climbed into the back of the same taxi that had delivered Celeste.

He lunged for the back door, but the driver accelerated, whisking her away. He jogged a few more steps into the parking lot, the pungent aroma of exhaust filling his nostrils. Fireworks exploded into the night sky, but he no longer cared. As the taxi turned onto the highway and its brake lights disappeared in the distance, a hollow ache filled his gut.

He had to go after her—convince her it wasn't what it looked like.

Another firework whistled into the sky with a pop and a crackle, its display drawing an enthusiastic response from the crowd gathered outside the resort. The purple and greenish afterglow illuminated the darkness, painting the snow in vibrant colors.

"Wasn't that Alyssa Huard?" Celeste hovered at his elbow.

Teeth clenched, he stared toward the highway. Words failed him. "Why?" He managed to choke it out.

"We had a deal, remember?" Her palm caressed his sleeve. "I'd meet you here as soon as my lease was up, and I could—"

"What lease? You told me you were crashing at your parents' place." Adrenaline coursed through him. He squared his shoulders, pinning her with an icy glare. He fought to keep his voice even. "I haven't heard from you in months."

"Things didn't go quite like I planned." Her gaze narrowed. "Looks like you found yourself a nice little distraction."

Spots peppered his vision. He wouldn't give her the satisfaction of losing his temper. "You shouldn't have come."

Her eyes widened.

Backing away from her persuasive touch, he turned and ran toward the parking lot, tugging his keys from his pocket. If he hurried, he could catch Alyssa before she barricaded herself in her bedroom. Or convinced someone to drive her to Colorado.

"I can make you forget her," Celeste called after him.

His chest tightened. He wasn't interested in forgetting Alyssa. How could he convince her that what she'd seen was nothing but lousy timing and a horrible misunderstanding?

***

Alyssa slammed her bedroom door, the sound echoing through the Carter's house.

Please, please, don't let them be here.

She'd caught a glimpse of Mrs. Carter earlier on the other side of the lobby at the resort. Hopefully they'd stayed to watch the fireworks. If she ran into them, they'd only ask questions she wasn't equipped to answer. Besides, they'd probably take Jeremy's side. Her stomach churned at the thought of anyone defending his behavior. Hot tears stung her eyes as she twisted the lock then jiggled the knob to confirm it was secure. Just in case. Other than the driver in the taxi still idling outside, there wasn't another soul she wanted to see right now.

Crossing to the dresser, she yanked open the drawer and grabbed a stack of clothes. Her phone vibrated in her pocket and she hesitated. Probably Jeremy, begging her to come back. She ignored the call and moved toward her suitcase lying on the floor in the corner. He could beg all he wanted. The image of that long-legged blonde wrapped around him was seared into her memory. There was nothing left to say.

She stacked the clothes in her suitcase then went back to the dresser for more. *Still so naïve, aren't you? How did you not see that coming?*

"I trusted him," she whispered, swiping at the moisture on her cheeks with the back of her hand. Was it wrong to believe there were still good guys in the world? He'd certainly fooled her. His empathetic gaze, concern for her safety, not to mention his gorgeous looks and electrifying touch. She'd clearly let her emotions cloud her judgement.

What else was new?

She grabbed her hoodie from the end of the bed, wadded it up, then flung it toward her suitcase. Stupid, stupid, stupid. Another sob broke loose, and she hurried into the bathroom and gathered her toiletries from the sink.

She heard the front door close, followed a moment later by footsteps in the hall. Shoot.

"Alyssa?" Jeremy's voice moved closer. "Are you in there?"

She froze. Heart pounding against her ribcage, she clutched her hairspray, moisturizer, and makeup remover tightly and glared at the door.

He knocked loudly. "Alyssa? Open up. Please. We need to talk."

Not a chance. She hooked her toe in the strap of her duffle bag and slid it closer, then crouched silently on the carpet and tucked the containers inside. She winced as the bottles clinked together.

The doorknob rattled. "Open the door."

"Go away," she called, anger boiling up like molten lava. What could he possibly say to soothe the sting of a betrayal like that?

"I'm not leaving until we talk."

She muttered an obscenity as she crammed the rest of her belongings into her bag then zipped it closed. Her snowboard sat out in the hall, less than a foot away from where Jeremy stood. She couldn't leave without her prized possession.

"That taxi's costing you a fortune. Why don't I tell him to go on—?"

"No!" Alyssa crossed the room, unlocked the door, and flung it open, adrenaline coursing through her veins. "Don't you dare."

Relief flooded Jeremy's face. "Thank God."

"Excuse me. I have to get my snowboard."

Hurt flashed in his eyes. "Please don't leave. We need to talk about this."

"No, we don't." She picked up her snowboard encased in its protective bag then hurried toward the front door.

"Wait. It wasn't what you think."

"Ha." She barked out a laugh. "Looked like a pretty meaningful kiss to me." Outside, the air chilled her flushed cheeks. Emotion clogged her throat as she hauled her board down the steps.

Jeremy jogged after her. "Why are you doing this? Why won't you listen to me?"

She gritted her teeth. "Go back to your girlfriend."

"She's *not* my girlfriend. We haven't talked in months. As far as I knew, we were over."

"Yeah? I don't think she got the memo," Alyssa yelled over her shoulder. Another wave of fresh tears stung her eyes as she propped her board on its end and reached for the back door of the taxi.

"Look, she kissed me. I didn't kiss her." He caught up and pressed his hand to her sleeve. "If you really believe that I'd cheat on someone, then you don't know me very well."

His words cut her to the quick. It was true. She didn't know him. Not like she thought she did. She tipped her chin up and glared at him. "You don't get it, do you? That kiss pretty much said it all. She obviously means something to you."

His eyes searched her face. "She did. Once. But not anymore."

"It might've been good to mention you still had a girlfriend."

A muscle in his jaw rippled. "I told you. She's not my girlfriend."

"And why would I believe anything you say now?" Alyssa opened the door and slid her board across the back seat. "I have to grab two more bags."

"Meter's running, sweetheart," the taxi driver said, his voice gravelly. "Take all the time you need."

She slammed the door then linked her arms across her chest. "I have to go."

"Alyssa, please. We're both upset. Don't leave—not like this."

Jeremy fisted his hands at his sides. The desperation in his voice and that pleading gaze almost convinced her. Almost.

"I trusted you—believed that you wanted me." Her voice broke and she huffed out a breath, her heart fisting. "I am the dumbest, most gullible girl on the planet."

"That's not true." Jeremy's voice was gruff. Strained. He moved closer, his hands outstretched. "I do want you, and I'm not giving up on us."

"There is no us." For the third time in less than an hour, she stepped around him and jogged back inside. More tears blurred her vision as she went to her room and collected her bags. Catching a glimpse of her reflection in the mirror, she scowled at the scarf Jeremy had given her, still looped around her neck. She quickly unwrapped it, balled it up, then tossed it in the bottom of the closet. The fewer souvenirs she carried, the better.

15

The deafening roar terrified him. Adrenaline pulsed through his veins, and he crawled toward the door, choking on the thick smoke, desperate to find a way out. Then the ceiling crashed in around him, while flames licked at the walls, snuffing out any hope of survival.

Where was Andrew?

His lungs screamed for oxygen, while panic squeezed his chest in a vise-like grip. The fire raged, consuming the walls and scorching his skin. Time was a precious commodity. He had to get out and find Andrew. He—

Gasping for air, Jeremy bolted up in bed. A cold sweat slicked his skin and dampened his T-shirt.

The nightmare was always the same—the fire blindsiding him and the sensation of suffocating. Complete helplessness. A desperation so palpable he could almost taste it.

A muted ring filled the silence. Eyes gritty, he shoved his hand under his flannel sheets, searching for his phone. Hazel pushed to her feet from her usual place at the end of the bed, the tags on her collar jangling as she shimmied and shook, ready to start her day.

"Go back to sleep, girl." His fingers located his cell phone and he retrieved it. Blake's number filled the screen. *Oh no. What happened?* His chest tightened as he accepted the call. "Hello?"

"Hey. Sorry to wake you. I know it's early," Blake said.

"What's up?" Jeremy propped on one elbow and glanced at the time on his alarm clock. Six-fifty.

"We're about ready to go. Wanted to make sure you were still able to take us to the airport."

Dang. Jeremy squeezed his eyes shut. He'd forgotten all about his promise to help. Blake had pulled him aside on Christmas and quietly shared his plan to whisk Lauren away to Cabo San Lucas on New Year's Day. As in today.

"Jeremy? You still there?"

"Yeah." Jeremy cleared his throat. "Yeah, I'm here. Sorry. What time do you leave?"

"Eight-thirty."

He'd better hustle. "I'll be there in a few minutes."

The events of the previous night came crashing back. Celeste. Fireworks. His heated argument with Alyssa before she took off in the taxi. He groaned inwardly.

"Wait." Blake's single plea made Jeremy's breath catch. *Please, please not another lecture or a list of a bazillion things that might go wrong while you're away.*

"I know you and I ... haven't gotten along lately. I—"

Jeremy stilled.

"We've—I've been so focused on myself that I've missed what's going on around me." Blake hesitated, then cleared his throat. "Meg told me what happened last night, and I—I know this is the worst time to talk, and you probably don't even want to talk about it, especially to me, but I just wanted you to know I'm sorry that happened."

Words failed him. Blake didn't dole out apologies or share sentimental thoughts casually. It took a lot for him to share what was on his heart. "Thanks." Jeremy choked out the word, battling back the wave of emotions cresting inside.

"See you in a few."

"Yep." Jeremy dropped the phone on the bed and scrubbed his hand across his face. Better to stop the conversation before they said anything to one another that might undo the fragile peace they'd just forged. Hazel's brown eyes toggled back and forth as she sank to her haunches with an impatient whimper.

"I know, I know. You're ready to get moving. Hold on, all right?" He needed a minute to savor an unexpected blessing in the midst of his heartache over Alyssa's departure.

Thank you, Lord.

Never did he think Blake would take the first step in addressing the brokenness in their relationship. It was hopefully the first of many tough discussions Jeremy would need to have with his brother if they had any hope of getting along like they once had.

Climbing out of bed, he grabbed a pair of jeans and a sweatshirt off the pile in the middle of the floor. His body ached from fatigue. Blake's words had bolstered his mood, but it was short-lived. Alyssa's absence left a deep, hollow ache inside. No matter how much his family loved and appreciated him, Jeremy couldn't forget all that he'd lost in just a few short minutes.

***

Alyssa jammed her sweatshirt between her head and the passenger window of Link's rental car. The hum of the tires plus the warm air blowing from the vents and the mesmerizing *whump whump* of the wipers on the windshield made her eyelids heavy. The sweet relief of sleep could be hers in a matter of minutes.

She'd spent the early morning hours slumped against her bags in the hallway outside Link's hotel room, mustering the courage to wake him up and beg him to drive her to the airport six hours away. Her eyes felt like sandpaper from crying. She longed to rest—anything to distract her from the pain. Maybe she should've just gone to the airport in Emerald Cove and waited for the next available seat on a flight out. But that meant sticking around and making it possible for Jeremy to find her, and that was the last thing she wanted.

"Hold on." Link tugged on her sleeve. "No sleeping if you're riding shotgun."

She lifted her head and studied him. "Seriously?"

"Seriously. Since you talked me into leaving a day early *and* driving to Anchorage, you have to keep me awake. Some of us didn't get much sleep last night, you know."

"I drove the first shift, remember? Why don't you let me sleep now and we'll trade again in a couple hours?"

"I'm not joking around, girlie. I think you'd better try and keep me awake if you want to make it to Anchorage in one piece."

"Fine. Whatever. I'll try to keep you awake. Why don't you finish your coffee?"

"I already did." Link adjusted a dial on the center console, and the hum of the defroster grew louder. "This is your idea so we're going to suffer in our sleep-deprived state together."

"You could've said no."

"Guess I'm a sucker for a girl in tears. Besides, you didn't seem like you'd take no for an answer."

He was right about that. The first flight this morning was booked, and she'd have to wait several hours once she got to Anchorage, too. But at least there, her chances of running into someone she knew were slim. She reached for one of the Styrofoam cups of coffee they'd bought at a dilapidated lodge a few miles back. The warm, sweet liquid coated her raw throat, but offered little relief. She'd cried until she didn't have anything left.

"What happened last night, anyway?"

She took another sip of her coffee and stared out the window. Snowbanks at least two stories high flanked both sides of the highway. Wet, dime-sized flakes fell with a vengeance and reflected in their headlights, creating a hypnotizing vortex of snow on the empty road in front of them. Link was right. The conditions had gone from bad to worse. They both needed to stay awake to navigate this storm.

"We don't have to talk about it if you don't want to," Link said.

"There's not much to say. I caught him kissing someone else."

"The guy with you on the hill yesterday?"

"That's the one."

Link shook his head, coppery dreadlocks brushing against his jacket. "Did he come looking for you? Maybe there's an explanation."

She released a humorless laugh. "I doubt it. Pretty hard to misinterpret what I saw." There was no way she'd give him a chance to deny his actions. He'd conveniently failed to mention the special someone in his life.

"Man, you've had a rough couple of months." Link shifted in his seat, hunching over the steering wheel as he strained to see out.

Her heart lurched. "So you know about the pictures?"

He nodded.

She drained the rest of her coffee even though her stomach threatened to revolt.

"I don't know about the guy at the resort kissing some other girl, but I do know this—you're much better off without Nick."

"Am I?" She twisted her empty cup in her hands.

"For sure."

"Why?"

Link shot her a look. "Do I really need to answer that?"

She stared out the window. "We had a good time together, Nick and me."

"Is that all you want from a relationship? A good time?"

"Sometimes." It sure beat the alternative—opening her heart only to have it handed back to her, worn and tattered. She'd careened recklessly down that path again and again. Stupid Jeremy had convinced her to go another round, too. Still, the results were the same.

"I'm all for living life with the throttle wide open, but once in a while you meet somebody who is worth the risk of slowing down. You get a glimpse of what it means to make a commitment, you know?"

She reached over and pressed her palm to his forehead. "Dude, I think you're feverish. I've never heard you utter the word 'commitment.'"

Link batted her hand away. "You can make jokes if you want, that's cool. I'm just saying you can do better than Nick. His only priority in life is keeping Nick happy, and I'd hate to see you get hurt again."

Too late. Alyssa swallowed hard against the emotions welling up. Jeremy's betrayal on the heels of Nick's thoughtless social media posts had reopened all the old wounds she'd worked so hard to mend. Even if there was a grain of truth in what Link said, she'd already made up her mind. Once they were back in Colorado, she'd throw herself into training for the X-Games. Nothing but first place in the competition would satisfy her. She'd show Nick, Jeremy, and the rest of the world she didn't need them.

***

Jeremy stared at the list of arrivals and departures posted in Emerald Cove's airport, noting the times and destinations of outbound flights. Was Alyssa here, waiting to board the eleven-fifteen for Anchorage? Or had she finagled a seat on the earlier flight with Blake and Lauren? Maybe she was hiding out, tucked in a corner, staring at her phone where no one would recognize her. His heart rate blipped at the thought, and he turned in a slow circle, surveying the small airport. What would it hurt to have a look around?

He quickly walked toward the opposite end of the building,

sidestepping the short line at the security checkpoint. He'd already said goodbye to Blake and Lauren, and they'd moved on to their gate.

Jeremy slowed in front of the mobile coffee cart and studied the waiting customers. The enticing aroma of freshly ground coffee beans wafted toward him, but he didn't have time to order anything. Almost twelve hours had dragged by since Alyssa had told him to get lost.

His gut clenched.

Despite the temptation to follow her taxi, he'd honored her request to leave and driven straight home. Still punching his pillow as the minutes and then hours ticked by, he'd second-guessed his decision again and again. What if he'd followed her? Tried—again—to convince her that she was the one he wanted? Loved?

The word made his pulse quicken. He did love her. Why didn't he tell her last night when he'd had the opportunity?

Their conversation had replayed in his mind as he stared into the darkness of his bedroom, Hazel snoring at his feet. He raked his hand through his hair, while the hurt and frustration churned him up like whitewater rapids on the river. She'd run. He'd unintentionally hurt her, and she'd left, because that's what she did when she was wounded. He scraped his palm across his face.

Leave it to Celeste to make an entrance at the worst possible moment.

He blew out a long breath as he reached the far side of the building. Families with teenagers and groups of people waited at the ticket counter, staring at their phones or drinking coffee. Luggage and ski equipment filled all the available space at their feet. A woman shifted a crying infant to her other shoulder and tried to comfort her while the man beside her wrestled with a stroller and car seat.

Jeremy slowed his steps, scanning faces. His gaze landed on a petite blonde with her back to him, slipping earbuds on. Her pink knit cap made his breath hitch. He skirted a group of snowboarders to get a closer look. She glanced up, her brown eyes widening when she caught him staring. Dang it. Jeremy looked away and altered his course, heading back toward the exit.

Near the automatic doors, he hesitated and turned in a slow circle one more time. What a stupid idea—scouting an airport for a woman who didn't want to be found. Maybe she'd rented a car or sweet-talked her way into somebody else's car—the chances of predicting what Alyssa might've done and then tracking her down grew slimmer with every passing minute.

He paused and stared out the wall of windows offering a view of the runway. A small jet taxied closer, its wing lights blinking orange in the falling snow. The intercom overhead announced an incoming flight as well as a gate change. The aroma of coffee tempted him again, so he joined the line at the cart to buy a cup. It might lessen the headache clamped around his brain.

While he waited to order, he surveyed the headlines on the newspapers and magazines filling the racks near the register. A cover photo of a breathtaking sunset over Cook Inlet near Anchorage caught his attention.

Jeremy read the bold letters silently, the image like a sucker punch to his gut. "Photo of the Year and other Grand Prize Winners Featured."

That could've been me. The ugly realization flashed through his mind, slamming into him like his own personal avalanche. Not that he craved the spotlight or needed to be the winner of a stupid magazine contest, but he had taken pictures that were equally as stunning. And they sat on a hard drive somewhere. Ignored. Unappreciated. Unseen.

A desire he thought Andrew's death had snuffed out sputtered to life, a subtle longing to get back out there. He missed the satisfying rush of capturing the moment and sharing it so others could appreciate it too. Most of all, he craved the adrenaline rush of chasing down that next beautiful image or experience and presenting it in a way no one else ever had.

There wasn't much in his life that sparked those feelings. Sure, he had his family. Work to do. Relatively good health. Slowly, he sensed his faith was back on track, maybe even growing. Baby steps for sure. But standing around, wishing for a girl who didn't want him, felt nothing like producing an award-winning photograph.

Maybe staying in Emerald Cove wasn't what he was supposed to be doing after all. Now that the resort was open, hadn't he done his penance? What if he stopped ignoring those calls and voice mail messages on his phone and pick up his camera again? He was done with the doubting and letting exciting opportunities pass him by. It was time to move on.

16

The next day, Alyssa huddled on one end of the chairlift as she rode to the top of the run with two other snowboarders, their incessant chatter driving her crazy. Too bad she'd forgotten her earbuds back at the condo. In three minutes, her seatmates had covered everything from their predictions for the X-Games, sick rails and boxes on the course below, and a freestyler's performance on the half-pipe trending on social media.

If only some of their enthusiasm would rub off on her. She drew a cleansing breath, trying to find her happy place. Maybe that was the problem. Despite being back in Colorado and on the mountain, training for the competition now only three weeks away, her happy place seemed ... elusive. Even the gray clouds hovering over Aspen matched her mood. Sullen. Ominous.

Was it the long trip from Alaska that zapped her energy? She'd flown all over the world and never felt this lousy.

Jeremy's pained expression as he stood in the Carter's driveway flashed through her mind.

Sheesh. Not again. She'd covered this already, hadn't she?

The lift deposited them at the top of the mountain, and she scooted off the edge of the bench, letting her board touch the packed snow first. She took her time, pushing with her free leg as she inched along, envisioning the first tricks she would put down. The other snowboarders cruised past her, still debating the pros and cons of the slopestyle course. She stopped and re-adjusted her goggles. Then her gloves. Tapped the top of her helmet twice like she always did. *Come on. Let's do this thing.*

Standing at the top of the run, she stared down the hill, scanning the boxes, rails, and jibs planted between her and the bottom of the course. Instead of mentally preparing for the ride, she heard the echo of Jeremy's laughter, saw that stupid dimple of his when he grinned ...

dang it. The woodsy scent of his cologne filtered through her memory, too.

"Enough," she whispered. Maybe she'd forgotten her earbuds and couldn't block out the images of what she'd left behind with heavy metal music, but she was a world-class athlete. Mental toughness came with the territory. She'd battled plenty of distractions before, right? This wasn't any different. From now on, it was just her and this mountain.

She leaned over and clipped her boot into the binding, then straightened and gave the run another look. Drawing a deep breath, she rolled her shoulders back, determined to find her happy place.

But nothing undid the listless feeling twisting through her insides. *Knock it off, Huard. Can't afford to fall apart now.* Before her negative thoughts completely sabotaged her run, she leaned forward and propelled her body down the slope.

Carving a long arc across the snow, with the icy wind stinging her cheeks, the tiniest hint of adrenaline pulsed through her extremities. But like an electrical current shorting out, she slid across the first box at a terrible angle and soared into the air, arms flailing. Her stomach lurched as she went airborne. At the last second, she recovered, and her board slapped against the snow. *Easy. Don't flip out. Find your groove.*

Her next two tricks felt smooth, almost effortless. The tension in her neck and shoulders loosened a fraction of an inch as she zoomed across the series of pipes jutting out of the snow. This was only a practice run, but she sensed plenty of people watching. Might as well show them her brief absence hadn't dampened her ability or her determination to perform at an elite level. The blue dye splashed in the snow mapped out a series of ramps coming up the middle of the slope. The perfect opportunity to nail that backflip she loved so much. Go big or go home, right?

She angled her snowboard toward the middle ramp. A niggle of doubt wormed its way into her gut, but as quickly as it came, she shoved the doubt aside. No time to alter her course now. Her pulse pounding, Alyssa bent her knees and got low, harnessing the energy she'd need to propel herself up the ramp, into the air, and nail the backflip. The bright blues, yellows, and reds of sponsors' logos and signs flew by in a blur as her board sailed up the steep grade. A surge of adrenaline burst within, sending her insides into that addicting freefall rush she craved.

Yes! The world spun by as her boots and board pointed toward the sky. Confidence soared. *You've got this.*

She'd celebrated too soon. Suddenly, she hurtled headfirst to the ground, and the bottom of her stomach dropped out. Desperate to correct before it was too late, she flailed through the air, then hit the snow hard, landing on her backside, sucking the wind right out of her. She tumbled downhill like a log until the edge of her board caught in the snow, yanking her boots out of their bindings.

When she finally came to a stop, her knees, shoulders, and backside protested. Cold snow stung her hands, and she squinted at the brightness. Somehow she'd lost her gloves and goggles.

The wolf whistle made her skin crawl. She stared up at the sky, her chest heaving as she fought to catch her breath. Snow crunched under somebody's boots as they jogged closer.

Coppery red dreadlocks, neon green goggles, and a mischievous grin filled her vision.

"Epic yard sale, girlie." Link leaned over her, hands on his knees. "Never seen ya go sideways quite like that before."

"Shut up."

"Yep, you're okay." He straightened. "Want some help?"

"Not from you."

He moved away for an instant then returned and held out her goggles and gloves. "You might need these later."

"Thanks." She pushed herself to a sitting position, gritting her teeth against the pain. She snatched her gear from Link. *Go away. Please.*

He offered a hand. "Take it slow."

She ignored him and turned away then forced herself to stand. Expecting the worst, she was pleasantly surprised when her legs cooperated and supported her weight.

"Are you sure you can walk?"

"I'm fine." She brushed past him and limped downhill to retrieve her snowboard.

"Alyssa…" Link's voice carried a hint of warning. She ignored him and grabbed her board.

Nick's familiar voice floated in the air.

Her heart sank. Of course he'd be here. But did he have to witness her humiliating spill?

Like a moth to a flame, she surveyed the crowd of people hanging out near the orange mesh barrier nearby. Nick stood close to a perky little snowboarder, giving one of her long blonde curls a flirtatious tug. She stared up at him, a giggle bubbling from her perfect mouth, then nudged him with her hip.

Alyssa narrowed her gaze. Hayley McFadden. How convenient.

She turned away, hot tears burning her eyelids as she limped off the course. *Do. Not. Cry.* They weren't worth it.

***

Jeremy stepped into Chuck's office and shut the door. His finger trembled as he pulled Chuck's camera from his backpack and then plugged it into the laptop on the desk. One picture. That's all. You can always delete it.

Heart kicking against his ribs, he quickly glanced at the schedule written on the whiteboard hanging on the wall. Chuck's messy scrawl confirmed he was out with clients on a full-day heli-skiing excursion. Good. If he was going to do this, he didn't need Chuck jawing at him about borrowing the camera—and the laptop—without permission.

The Northern Lights put on an epic performance over Emerald Cove last night. He'd been on his way home, crossing the parking lot from the resort to his truck, when he found a cluster of tourists huddled together, heads tipped back in awe. Instinct had taken over, and the familiar hum of adrenaline sent him hustling inside for the camera. He'd snapped more than a dozen pictures, determined to capture the brilliant greens and purples crackling across the inky black canvas of a January night sky.

Within minutes, he'd edited the best photo and uploaded it to his Facebook wall. His hand hovered over the keyboard as doubt pummeled him. It's not *that* great. Why are you even trying?

He scrolled up to delete the picture but stopped. It wasn't a perfect photo, but the fact that he'd managed to capture the Northern Lights at all was significant.

If he posted, it would be the first photo he'd shared in over a year. What if nobody noticed?

But if he didn't post, he'd never know what people thought of his work. And why did it even matter? Couldn't he just share a photo that he was proud of and get on with his life?

A knock at the door interrupted his second-guessing, and he quickly published the post.

"There you are." Megan paused in the doorway, arms linked across the front of her uniform. "Got a minute?"

Blood pounded in his ears as he stared at the computer screen. *Not really.* "What's up?"

"You have a guest asking for you."

Jeremy's gut clenched. Celeste. "Got it. Is she in the restaurant?"

"Lobby. Sitting by the fire."

"Thanks. I'll go talk to her." He pushed to his feet and crossed to the door.

Not three steps out of the office, a blonde in a low-cut sweater dress and knee-high leather boots collided with him.

"What are you doing here, Celeste?" He clasped her forearms with both hands to steady her, instantly regretting his decision. Warning bells sounded in his head.

"I've been looking all over for you." She smoothed her palms against his chest. "We haven't had a chance to talk yet."

"There's nothing to say. I already told you, you shouldn't have come."

"But you didn't mean it." She trapped her lip behind her teeth and let her hands slide north, a gesture that once upon a time would've made him putty in her hands.

"I meant every word." He stepped back, extracting himself from her clutches. "You and I were over a long time ago."

Her eyes flashed. "If this is about that Huard girl, you're wasting your time. She's just toying with you."

White hot anger boiled inside. He ground his molars, tempted to spar with her. *Don't.* He heeded the warning and brushed past her. "Have a safe trip home."

He strode through the lobby, blood pounding in his ears. What had he ever seen in her, anyway? Even if he didn't stand a chance with Alyssa, Celeste wasn't what he needed, either. He'd rather be single forever then drag his heart through that kind of dysfunction again.

Outside, Jeremy weaved through the skiers and snowboarders milling about, prepping for a day on the mountain. The storm had left more fresh powder than predicted, and, despite foggy conditions on top, people had flocked to the lifts. Chuck must be thrilled—all the late nights and the expensive rebuild were paying off. At least something was going right around here.

He made his way down to the shed, restless and craving a distraction.

The shed was empty, evidence Gunnar or one of the other employees had taken the snowcat out to maintain the hillside. Jeremy paced the small space like a caged animal. First, he stopped and reviewed the maintenance logs, then made sure they had plenty of oil on hand and checked to make sure the bag of vacuum splints was in its proper place on the shelf.

The sight of the red canvas bag sent memories tumbling through his mind—taking him back to that first night he'd met Alyssa. He braced his palm against the wall nearby and squeezed his eyes shut. Man, he missed her. That playful smile, the determined set of her mouth when she was convinced she was right, and even her citrusy shampoo when he'd curled around her in the sleeping bag, desperate to keep them both warm. His chest tightened. Sheesh, he couldn't go five minutes without thinking about her. How pathetic was that?

He straightened and moved toward the door. No sense wishing for what might have been. Alyssa's departure and total radio silence made her preferences clear. Pushing his thoughts of her aside, he scolded himself for getting distracted. He'd promised himself he'd stay focused, fight through the hurt and the guilt, and move on. Yet here he stood, hiding out in the shed, wallowing in self-pity.

No more.

A snowboarder carved a sweet line across the hillside, his confidence evident in his posture as he bent his knees then soared over a naturally made obstacle in the middle of the course. He kicked his feet up behind him for a quick board grab just before he returned to the snow and cruised downhill.

Alyssa's performance on the same mountain only days ago felt like a lifetime instead.

Good grief. Again with the pity party. *Dude, get a grip.*

His heart clenched. She might've left but she was still everywhere he turned.

It didn't matter, though. She wasn't coming back. And the sooner he accepted his new reality, the better.

17

Alyssa hobbled across the living room in her condominium, her phone and three ice packs in hand. The pain in her knee was a dull ache compared to the humiliation still gnawing at her, hours after that hideous spill on the mountain. Right in front of Nick and Hayley, of course. Her stomach knotted at the mental image of the two of them together.

"Oh, Nick, you're such a hottie." She mimicked Hayley's flirty singsong voice as she sank onto the leather couch. "Will you show me one of your epic moves?"

Alyssa made a gagging gesture then propped her foot on the coffee table. They were probably partying the night away at a club in Aspen right now. Or making out in a—

Whatever. They deserved each other. Wincing at the discomfort in her knee, she changed her mind and stretched out, extending both legs the length of the couch. Then she tugged on the cuff of her yoga pants, pulling it up slowly so she could assess the situation.

No swelling. A good sign. She poked at her knee cap gingerly. Maybe it had popped out of place for a second. Or the torque on her leg when she lost her board had caused a slight hyperextension. She'd still ice it, just in case. Despite her wounded pride, she'd have to get back on the mountain again tomorrow and give it another go.

Bracing herself for the stinging pain, she sandwiched the ice bags around her knee, sucking in a breath as they touched her bare skin. How could she fling herself off jumps, boxes, and rails but a few bags of ice turned her into a total wimp? She shivered against the cold then zipped up her microfleece jacket, grateful she'd thought to put that on over her T-shirt. With the timer on her phone set for twenty minutes, Alyssa tried to get comfortable, determined to ride out the initial pain until her skin went numb. Too bad there wasn't anything to numb the dark feelings blanketing her heart like a thick fog.

With only the hum of the refrigerator in the kitchen to keep her company, she quickly grew restless. Tempted to scroll through her social media accounts, her finger hovered over one of the apps on her phone. The wounds were still too tender, though. She couldn't risk seeing something that might send her into a total meltdown. Besides, she might stumble upon a reminder of Jeremy or Emerald Cove. Her chest tightened. Nope. Definitely not going there.

She traded her phone for the remote control, aimed it at the television, then surfed through the channels. Nothing seemed appealing until she landed on a major network's coverage of the national figure skating championships. Shoot. *Dani.* Palming her forehead, she moaned out loud. How could she forget Dani was competing this week?

She glanced at the TV again. Wait. This was the pairs competition. Maybe that meant the women hadn't skated yet. She reached for her phone and mentally calculated the time difference between Colorado and Boston. Probably not a good idea to call. It was almost ten p.m. there. Dani was an early-to-bed kind of girl, especially during competitions. She'd send a text message instead. It was the least she could do.

Hey, just wanted to wish you good luck this week. I hope you kick some serious butt. Skate your way to the top of the podium, k?

Alyssa pressed 'send' then nested her phone against her chest. It chimed less than a minute later.

How's Alaska?

Alyssa hesitated. She didn't want to talk about it.

I left yesterday. Back in Aspen training for the X-Games.

She sent the message then stared at the TV. A new couple glided across the ice, performing a series of elaborate twists that culminated with the lady soaring in her partner's arms, stretched overhead.

Her phone rang in her hand. She checked the screen. Dani. Alyssa answered the call. "Hey."

"So you left already? What's up with that?" Dani said, her voice hushed.

"Why are you being so quiet?"

"Because I'm supposed to be sleeping."

"You didn't have to call me." Alyssa snagged another pillow and wedged it behind her head. "We can catch up later."

"Nice try. I thought you'd met somebody up there. Did he come to Colorado with you?"

"No."

"So…"

"It didn't work out."

"You're joking. What happened?"

Her throat constricted. "He rang in the new year lip-locked with some other chick."

Dani gasped. "Oh, Alyssa. I'm so sorry. How—I mean—did you catch them kissing?"

"Yep. I went to get champagne for the toast. We were supposed to go outside and watch the fireworks together. Then I turned around and she was all over him."

"How do you know it wasn't an accident? Sometimes people are all jacked up on New Year's Eve. They get caught up in the moment and just grab whoever's closest and plant one on 'em."

"I wish that were true."

"How do you know it isn't?"

"Because he told me. She's his ex-girlfriend."

"What? Where did she come from?"

"Who knows. Who cares. It doesn't even matter. He was obviously happy to see her." Jealousy knifed at her insides as she replayed Jeremy and what's-her-name's intimate embrace. Again.

"Did he tell you he was happy to see her?"

"No. Not exactly."

"So you asked him and he said—"

"Geez, what's up with the twenty questions? Whose side are you on, anyway?" She squeezed her eyes shut. Her words were way harsh.

Dani's silence was measured. "There isn't a side. I'm just trying to understand what happened. Because you and I, we're friends. This is what we do for each other … listen and try to figure things out. Together."

Alyssa blew out a breath. "I know. I—I'm sorry. I didn't mean to bite your head off."

"It's okay. I forgive you."

Forgiveness. How did Dani toss that word around so easily? And she meant it, too. Stuff seemed to float right off of her, as if it never even happened. Meanwhile, Alyssa held on to her junk for ages, dragging it around like deadweight.

"Alyssa? Are you still there?"

"Yeah." She stared at the ceiling, her insides twisted in knots. "I'm here."

"Listen, I know you hate it when I preach at you, so I won't. I'll try to speak 'snowboarder' for a minute, okay?"

Alyssa smiled. "Can't wait."

"Be quiet for a sec. You need to hear this."

Her smile faded. Everything in her wanted to drop the phone and cover her ears, blocking out the world just as she'd done so many times as a child. But Dani was different. She had no reason to care about a wild-child snowboarder, yet she did. Alyssa gritted her teeth. Fine. She'd listen. Really listen.

"When you stand at the top of the run, you can't see the bottom, right? Sure, there are signs with sponsors' names and that weird blue dye marking the slides, maybe some rods sticking out of the snowbank, but still a ton of unknowns."

"What does this have to do with Jeremy kissing his ex-girlfriend?"

"Shhh. I'm not finished."

Alyssa clamped her mouth shut.

"You always make your next trick a little bigger than the last one, right? If it's a midair board grab the first time, maybe you'll lay down a sick five-forty on the next run…"

Alyssa bit her lip to keep from laughing. Dani was trying so hard to make it sound legit.

"Relationships aren't much different than snowboarding. You have to go big. Put yourself out there. I know you've been hurt, and I don't blame you for giving up. But Jeremy sounded like a really nice guy, and I'd hate for you to wreck a good thing just because you're scared."

Alyssa picked at a loose thread on the hem of her T-shirt, weighing Dani's advice. "It's just not that easy."

"But it's so worth it, sweetie."

Dani's claim pricked the dark emotions waging within. Was it worth it? Could she risk her heart yet again? Alyssa pulled the phone away and glanced at the time. "It's getting late there. I'd better let you go."

"Please promise me you'll think about what I said."

I can't promise anything. "Thanks for calling me. Good luck this week."

"Love ya, Alyssa. I'll be praying for you."

A lump formed in her throat. "'Bye."

She ended the call and tossed her phone aside. Resting her forearm across her eyes, she tried to staunch the tears that threatened to fall.

Even if Dani was right, there wasn't anything Alyssa could do about it. She'd ruined her chances with Jeremy. If it wasn't her lack of honesty that ran him off, leaving in a taxi when he'd asked her to stay definitely sealed her fate. As much as she missed him, she couldn't stand the thought of getting hurt again.

Face it. You aren't relationship material.

***

Jeremy crumpled his napkin and launched it toward the trash can in the corner of Chuck's office. It fell short, landing on the carpet. He sighed and pushed back his chair. Matt and Angela Carter's oldest, Josh, sat on the other side of the desk, his order of chicken fingers and french fries quickly disappearing from his plate while he stared at his iPad, engrossed in a basketball game. Jeremy had run into the Carters outside the resort and spent most of the afternoon skiing with them. Matt and Angela had eventually taken their other kids home, and Jeremy promised to drop Josh off later.

Jeremy retrieved the napkin and tossed it in the can. "You about ready to go?"

"Now?"

"Pretty soon. I've got to let Hazel out before she does some serious damage to my place."

"I'm not finished."

"You can finish your dinner. Then we need to leave."

"But there's still twelve minutes left in the game."

Jeremy gritted his teeth. "I'll get you home in time to watch the end. You'll only miss a couple of minutes."

"Aw, man." Josh shook his head and dragged another fry through a puddle of ketchup. "It's tied at thirty-eight. What if they score while we're in the car and I miss it?"

"Then you can catch the replay. Maybe your mom will let you turn the TV on as soon as you walk in the door." Jeremy fought to remain calm. Patient. Unaffected by Josh's attitude. They'd had a good time. He didn't mind hanging out with Blake and Lauren's nephew—it had kept his mind off Alyssa's absence—but he was exhausted and ready to call it a night.

Before Josh fired off another objection, Jeremy's phone rang. He pulled it from his back pocket and answered the call. "Hello?"

"Hey, it's me." Megan's tone was hushed. "I'm at the front desk. You have a visitor."

Not again. His gut clenched. "Celeste's still here?"

"No, she checked out a couple of hours ago. This is a gentleman from Seattle. Says he's with a magazine and you're expecting him?"

"I thought that was tomorrow." Jeremy's heart rate accelerated as he rounded the desk and dug through his backpack for the reminder he'd scrawled on the back of an envelope.

"Shall I ask him to wait in the bar?"

"Um ... hang on a sec." Jeremy located the paper under a bottle of water and tugged it free. *Wednesday. 7PM.* The black ink on white paper was a stark notice.

Shoot. That was five minutes from now. He dropped the envelope back into his bag and hurried to the door.

Josh's eyes tracked his every move, and Jeremy stopped mid-stride. What was he supposed to do now? Couldn't drag Josh to a job interview—an interview he'd intentionally not mentioned to anyone. He cleared his throat. "Yeah, that sounds good. I'll be right there."

"My shift is just about over. Want me to take Josh home too?"

Jeremy blew out a breath. "Please. That would be awesome."

He hung up then glanced down at his navy-blue sweater and dark-washed jeans. Not a suit and tie but at least it was presentable.

Josh's brow furrowed. "Who was that?"

"Megan. Change of plans. She'll take you home. I have a meeting I forgot about."

"Sweet." Josh's expression brightened. "She'll let me watch the end of the game."

Jeremy raked his fingers through his hair. "Probably. You'll have to work all that out with her."

"She'll totally say yes." Josh jumped to his feet. "Can we go now?"

Jeremy chuckled. "Grab your stuff. I'll walk you out to the front desk."

"Yes!" Josh pumped his fist in the air, tucked the iPad under his arm, then trotted out of the office.

Jeremy stared after him. "Thanks for skiing with me," he called to Josh's retreating backside.

Out at the front desk, Megan pinned him with her inquisitive stare. "Good luck."

His mouth felt dry as sandpaper. She'd pepper him with twenty questions later. He cleared his throat. "Thanks."

Josh's instant replay of the basketball game's first half filled the air as Jeremy walked into the restaurant. The hostess at the podium offered a friendly smile. "Hey, Jeremy. What's up?"

Jeremy scanned the dimly lit room until he found a man wearing a suit coat seated at a table near the windows. "I'm meeting a friend. Thanks." He moved past, hoping Megan hadn't shared the guest's identity with anyone at the resort. He wasn't interested in supplying the local rumor mill with any more fodder.

The man stood as Jeremy approached the table. "Hi, Jeremy. Doug Kelton, editor of *Explore* magazine."

Jeremy shook his outstretched hand. "Nice to meet you, sir. I'm sorry to keep you waiting."

"Not a problem." Doug sat back down. "I'm sure this is a busy time."

"I appreciate you coming all this way to meet with me. Seattle isn't exactly close."

"I'm meeting family here tomorrow. We wanted to check out the resort and do some skiing."

They paused their conversation while the server took their order for drinks and an appetizer. When she moved on, Doug leaned forward, his piercing gray eyes locked on Jeremy's. "Let's cut to the chase. Your photos are incredible. That shot you posted on Facebook of the

Northern Lights is stunning. The hits on your blog were impressive, and your social media following was phenomenal before you shut it all down. If you're ready, I'd like to talk with you about an assignment in California. Big Sur."

Jeremy swallowed hard. Not far from Andrew's hometown. "With all due respect, sir, why me?"

"Like I said, given your impressive portfolio, my team and I feel you have the artistic ability and creative experience to give our readers the photojournalism they're expecting. You're extremely talented—brimming with raw potential. But I understand you've stepped away from social media for a season and empathize with your need to fully recover from any personal setbacks."

For a season. He looked away. It was much longer than that. He'd had plenty of space and time. What if he didn't ever fully recover? Maybe this was as good as he'd ever get. "What's the expectation in terms of timing? Is this a one-time assignment, or are there ongoing opportunities?"

"We're open to discussing additional opportunities if this goes well and you find you're interested in regular assignments."

Jeremy shifted. He'd be able to come back to Emerald Cove and see his family. At least every other month or so. "Full benefits?"

"We are looking for a full-time photojournalist, yes. I think you'll find our benefits and compensation very attractive. And if your social media platform continues to grow like we expect, there might be additional bonuses based on advertiser's investments. We recognize this is an unorthodox job description that, as you've learned firsthand, carries some inherent risks. We also believe our offer is on par, if not better, than anything a similar publication might offer."

Assuming they were offering. Jeremy fiddled with the napkin-wrapped silverware on the table. Doug didn't have to know there wasn't anyone else pursuing him.

"If you accept our offer, we hope it is the beginning of a long and productive relationship."

Jeremy's chest tightened. Traveling and experiencing the world from behind the lens of his camera? That certainly sounded tempting. Maybe his dreams of returning to the life he'd once loved didn't have to be ignored. This wasn't quite how he envisioned it happening, but that wasn't a reason to reject the magazine's offer. "How long do I have to decide?"

"Six days. We'd like to have you in California late next week."

His Northern Lights photo had received hundreds of likes and dozens of shares. Hadn't he decided he needed to move on, to take control of life instead of sitting back and waiting for something good to happen? Maybe this opportunity was his sign—confirmation that it was time to step into a new year with a renewed focus.

Jeremy nodded. "Thank you for the offer. I'm honored. You'll have an answer soon."

18

Alyssa rolled up her yoga mat then reached for her water bottle. The other participants in the hot yoga class huddled in clusters, talking quietly. She crossed the room to her knapsack on the floor and dug around inside until she found a towel. The pain in her knee had almost disappeared. Thank goodness. Yesterday's wipeout was a close call. She blotted at the sweat on her forehead and the back of her neck, then dropped the towel back inside her bag.

Hopefully, Lance wouldn't mind if she arrived a little sweaty to their ten o'clock meeting. There certainly wasn't time to shower. She'd cut it close, taking a hot yoga class right before she planned to meet him. But the hotel coffee shop was two floors below. And she'd needed the structure of a class to re-center her focus this morning. Between fitful sleep filled with dreams of Jeremy and Dani's advice spinning through her mind, her thoughts were all over the place. Not at all ideal for training for a competition. Or forgetting a certain Alaskan heartbreaker.

She sighed as she left the workout area then made her way down the corridor. Aspen's most popular hotel hummed with activity. Alyssa joined several couples and a family with young children waiting for the elevator. Two young blonde girls dressed in matching dresses and leggings clung to their parents' hands. They looked so much like Mrs. Carter's granddaughters, Emmy and Ava. Alyssa's heart ached.

The bell chimed, and the doors parted. They all filed in, their incessant questions and almost palpable energy filling the air.

Alyssa bit her lip. So far, her efforts to leave Emerald Cove in her wake and not look back had been a colossal failure. Maybe in time, it would get easier. She'd focus on her career, winning a medal at the X-Games, expanding her sportswear product line, and eventually there wouldn't be space in her head for those painful memories.

The elevator stopped on her floor and the doors parted. "Excuse me, please." She squeezed by the adorable family, exhaling with relief once she'd escaped that cuteness overload. Inside the crowded coffee shop, she found Lance at a table for two near the back, nursing a Venti-size paper cup and staring at his iPad.

"Hey." She dropped her yoga mat and knapsack to the floor then slid into the chair opposite his. "Happy New Year."

"Same to you." Lance flashed a sheepish grin. "I wasn't sure if you'd show up or not."

She frowned. "I probably deserve that."

"Everything okay?"

"Yep. Let's get to work." She leaned closer and examined the calendar on his screen. "What's on your agenda?"

"Do you want to order coffee or anything first?" He angled his head toward the counter. "They make killer mochas."

"No thanks. I've got my water." She retrieved her bottle. "I'll make a smoothie when I get back to my place."

Lance arched an eyebrow. "Who are you? What have you done with the real Alyssa?"

"Ha-ha." She shot him a pointed look. "You wanted me to focus. So here I am. The re-focused, not-distracted-by-a-boy Alyssa. Let's do this thing."

"Hallelujah."

She ignored his smart remark. "What did you want to talk about first?"

"Before I forget, here are your tickets to the benefit." He pulled an envelope from his pocket and pushed it across the table. "My wife and I have a conflict, so we won't be able to go, but I'm sure you'll find a plus one."

"The kickoff to the X-Games?" She stared at the envelope, her stomach tightening. All of her old crowd would be there for sure. "I was planning on skipping this year."

He slid the tickets closer. "Take them anyway, in case you change your mind. It's a good time. Great food, too. The proceeds from the silent auction benefit pediatric cancer."

Perfect. Nothing like a little guilt to motivate her. "I'll think about it." She tucked the envelope inside her knapsack. "What else?"

"This just in. The Grammy people called. They'd like you to make an appearance during the awards show next month."

Her breath hitched. "You're kidding."

"For real." He scanned the screen. "February sixteenth in LA."

"Wait." Alyssa set down her water and reached for her phone. "It doesn't conflict with any competition dates, right?"

Lance hesitated. "I didn't check yet. The awards are on a Sunday night, so unless you're traveling, you should be set."

She opened the calendar app on her phone and scrolled to the middle of February. "I'm supposed to be in San Diego on Tuesday the eighteenth for a shoot."

He frowned over the rim of his coffee cup. "Is this for Verge, too?"

"No. The new line for Pioneer Outfitters."

"Perfect. Then you'll need to be in Vail at the end of the month for Verge's US competition. Does that leave enough time to practice?"

"I'll make it work."

"That's what I like to hear." He drummed his fingers on the table, quickly scanning the screen. "Let's talk about international competitions. Are you stoked for the World Championships? That's the week after Vail. My assistant is supposed to book your flights this week."

"Austria, right?" Her pulse accelerated at the mention of her favorite competition. "If I medal at the X-Games, then win the US Open, Worlds should be a cake walk."

Something flickered in Lance's eyes. "Absolutely." He reached for his coffee again.

She narrowed her gaze. "What was that?"

"Nothing. I agreed with you. I bet you'll stomp all over the competition."

"You had a funny look on your face. What aren't you telling me?"

He took a long sip. She fisted her hands in her lap, willing him to say whatever was on his mind. She could handle it.

"This is an intense three months we've outlined here. Are you sure you're prepared, mentally and physically?"

"You said to come back ready to hit it hard. This is me. Hitting it hard."

"I admire your drive." He measured his words, gray eyes scanning her face. "Is Alaska a thing of the past?"

Bingo. The key detail he'd been fishing for all along. She tipped her chin up. "You don't need to worry. There's nothing for me in Emerald Cove anymore."

Lance nodded. "Good." He made a fist and held it out. "Proud of you, girl."

She bumped his fist and gave him a weak smile. "Thanks."

If only it were true. Emerald Cove—and Jeremy—were never far from her thoughts. Maybe if she kept saying the words, "There's nothing for me in Emerald Cove, there's nothing for me in Emerald Cove," out loud, her heart would finally believe it.

***

Jeremy stood at his kitchen sink, wrinkling his nose at the congealed food clinging to the plates and bowls stacked on the counter and wishing Megan hadn't dropped by uninvited. Good grief. He should've cleaned this up a long time ago. Fruit Loops? How long had those been sitting there? He scraped them into the garbage disposal. Gross. Once the dishes were done, he'd start packing his suitcases for California.

"You've got to go see her." Megan leaned against the counter beside him. "What do you have to lose?"

Everything. He turned the hot water on. "I already told you, I have to pack. Then I'm leaving for San Francisco to be there in time to catch a ride down to Carmel. If I want this job, I have to prove myself by showing up at the first shoot, ready to go. There's no way I can make it to Aspen right now."

"Since when do you want to take pictures for a magazine? Why not open your own gallery here?"

He scrubbed harder at the bowl in his hands. "Knock it off, Megan. I don't need your approval."

Her stony silence confirmed he'd hurt her. "That's true. You don't. I'd just hate to see you screw up a good thing."

Hazel flopped at his feet with a dramatic whine. He gave her an empathetic glance as she draped one paw across her snout. *I feel ya, girl.* He didn't want to deal with this, either. The last few days since the interview and his decision to take the job left him spent. He didn't have the energy to argue with Megan. "I can see you've put a lot of thought into my personal life." He turned off the water and set the bowl in the drying rack. "What's up with that?"

"You're moping around when there's an easy solution."

He snorted. "Yeah? What's that?"

"Get on a plane to Colorado, doofus." She nudged his shoulder with her hand. "It's so simple."

"I beg to differ, little sis. Alyssa left, remember? In case you didn't get the memo, she's never looked back, either."

"Women want to be pursued."

He ground his teeth and scrubbed at a foreign substance stuck to a dinner plate. "Not that woman. She'd rather run the other direction."

"She's probably scared. Maybe something happened in a past relationship that freaked her out."

He couldn't argue with that. The brief snippets of her childhood she'd shared made his heart ache. Not to mention the pictures. No wonder she wrestled with building healthy relationships.

"You don't think she'd love it if you showed up at the X-Games and cheered her on?"

"I'm gonna stop trying to figure out what she'd love. It's my New Year's resolution."

"Ha. Since when do you make resolutions?"

He shot a pointed glance her way. "You know, for a girl who seems to be in pretty deep, you're sure handing out a lot of relationship advice."

Her face paled. "What are you talking about?"

"Flowers you threw away, a Christmas gift from Nordstrom you didn't open … I'm sure if I checked your phone there'd be texts and voice mails from the mystery man, and don't even get me started on the way Wyatt looks at you." Jeremy turned the water back on and rinsed off the dish before placing it in the drying rack.

"How did you know about the present from Nordstrom?"

"Mom put it under the tree on Christmas. What was in it?"

"I'm not telling you." She examined her fingernails. "There's nothing going on between me and Wyatt, either."

"I bet there could be, if you'd stop giving him the cold shoulder." Jeremy studied her. "He's a good guy, Megan."

She sighed and shoved her hands inside her coat pockets. "I'm not here to talk about Wyatt, or any other guy besides you. Would you *please* just listen to me?"

"All right, I'm listening." He shut off the water then dried his hands on what was possibly the only clean dish towel in the whole place. "What's your plan to resurrect my love life?"

"I already checked the flights and the X-Games schedule online. If you leave tomorrow, you could be there in time to watch the finals. Which Alyssa qualified for, by the way."

"You're kidding, right?"

She arched one eyebrow. "About which part? The flights or her qualifying?"

He clenched the towel in his fist. "Both."

Megan sucked in a breath. "You'll go?"

Packing, resigning from his job at the resort, asking Doug for a few extra days to consider the offer, finding someone to stay with Hazel … the details flew at him rapid-fire. He tipped his head back and stared at the ceiling. "No. Maybe. I don't know."

"That's almost a yes." She whipped out her phone. "I knew I'd convince you."

Wait. What was he thinking? This was a terrible idea. "Not so fast, quick-draw." He reached over and pressed his palm over the screen. She'd book his flight if he wasn't careful. "What if I get all the way down there and she won't give me the time of day? Then I'm stuck in Aspen, after I just asked my future boss for special treatment, and I've wasted a bunch of time and money."

"Better than standing here wishing things were different."

Oh. She had a point. He'd wasted far too much time wishing his circumstances would change. Nursing his wounds. Playing the blame game. Was this a long shot at a second chance? Or another foolish decision that would only lead to more heartache?

"You know what? Forget it. I'm not going to Colorado or anywhere else to track Alyssa down. It's over."

There. He'd made another decision. Stood his ground—no waffling to please somebody else.

He turned away, his sister's disappointed expression needling him. If this was the right thing to do, why couldn't he shake the hollowness inside?

19

Alyssa tugged the zipper closed on her little black dress then stepped back and examined her reflection in the full-length mirror. A French twist and chandelier earrings completed the look. Too bad nothing could ease the hurt rooted deep inside. Apparently, there weren't any cosmetics on the market to patch a broken heart. She sighed and turned away. Good thing this benefit was for a good cause. Otherwise she'd be on the couch in her sweats, binge-watching *Fixer Upper*.

Her doorbell chimed, and she hesitated. Who could that be? The condos all around her were rented. Maybe a neighbor needed to borrow an egg or a cup of sugar. They'd knocked on the wrong door, given the status of her empty pantry.

She walked down the hallway to the front door and glanced through the peephole.

Dani stood on the other side, making a silly face.

Alyssa squealed, turned the deadbolt, and flung open the door. "What are you doing here?"

Dani crossed the threshold and threw her arms around Alyssa. "I'm your plus one."

"No way." Alyssa stepped back and admired Dani's flawless, intricate updo and rich red lipstick—an exact match for the stylish dress peeking beneath her wool coat. "What about your next competition?"

"Even figure skaters need a day off now and then. Besides, my parents promised my brother they'd help him move this week, so I tagged along." Dani glanced around Alyssa's condo, her smile fading. "Wow, I love what you've done with the place?"

Alyssa scanned the barren walls—empty except for the one snowboarding poster she'd tacked over the couch. A couple of magazines and half-finished gourmet popcorn bags were all that adorned her glass coffee table.

"What do you have against picture frames? Or candles?"

"Stop." Alyssa turned away, cringing. "I haven't had time to get settled."

"Uh-huh." Dani trailed after her. "A card table? Really?"

Alyssa stopped next to the rickety table and metal folding chair she'd pushed against the wall in the breakfast nook. "Who needs a kitchen table? That's what the couch is for."

Dani groaned. "Oh, my word."

Alyssa headed back to the bedroom and the dreaded high heels she'd bought to match her dress. "It's not like I'm having anybody over," she murmured, fishing the velvety sling backs from their box on her closet floor.

When she returned to the living room, she held up the shoes like a peace offering. "Do you approve?"

Dani's brown eyes widened. "Those are stunning." She inched closer, her fingers caressing the tiny bow affixed to the toe. "I'm in love."

Alyssa chuckled. "How are we even friends?"

Dani faked a pout. "I'm good for you and you know it. Put those on and let's go. I've got a car waiting."

"What? Why? The benefit's only a couple of blocks from here."

Dani's gaze flitted to Alyssa's shoes. "Sweetie, those aren't meant for snow. C'mon. The benefit starts in fifteen minutes."

Alyssa teetered after her, second-guessing her decision to wear those shoes all the way to the car idling beside the curb.

In the back of the sedan, Dani buckled her seat belt then gave Alyssa's hand a quick pat. "Relax. It'll be fun."

"Hope so." Alyssa buckled her own belt and gave her condo a longing glance. Why had she accepted the tickets from Lance, anyway? So what if the money raised tonight funded more research for pediatric cancer? Couldn't she make a donation instead and skip all the hoopla?

"You're trying to figure out how to get out of this, aren't you?"

Alyssa clasped and unclasped the sequined clutch in her lap as the Uber driver eased away from the curb. "I'd rather be snowboarding."

"Of course you would."

A few minutes later, they slowed to a stop in the circular driveway, and Alyssa stared out the window at the well-dressed crowd flowing into the convention center.

"C'mon." Dani nudged her shoulder. "You can do this."

"All right, all right." Alyssa pushed open the door then stepped out onto the sidewalk, shivering as the cold air swirled around her bare legs.

Dani slammed the door, linked her elbow through Alyssa's, and tugged her toward the imposing glass-and-steel structure.

"Chin up, girlfriend. A little swagger wouldn't hurt, either." Dani kept her voice low. "Remember, you're a world-class athlete and you belong here."

"What are—"

Nick filled her peripheral vision. Hayley clung to his arm, a gold-sequined miniskirt revealing shapely, spray-tanned legs.

Alyssa's steps faltered.

"Nope." Dani jerked her forward. "Don't go there."

Alyssa clamped her mouth closed and followed Dani inside. Plush carpeting, modern art adorning the walls, and an ice sculpture of two swans in the center of the buffet table took her breath away.

"Let's keep moving." Dani steered her deeper into the crowd.

"Where are we going?"

"As far away from those two as we can get."

"Why don't we just go home?" Alyssa stumbled after her. "I really don't want to be here."

Dani didn't stop walking until they arrived at coat check. She shrugged out of her jacket then passed it to the attendant. "We aren't leaving. That would be cowardly. Never let 'em see you sweat, remember?"

"Too late." Alyssa wiped her clammy palms on her jacket before Dani reached for it.

"Let's grab a drink and check out the silent auction items."

Goosebumps pebbled Alyssa's arms, and she hugged her tiny purse to her chest. "I don't think I can handle a public confrontation tonight."

"Don't worry. There won't be one. That's why I'm here."

They worked their way back to the bar, and Dani ordered a diet soda and water with lemon. While they waited, Alyssa shot a nervous glance around the spacious ballroom. Any glimpse of a gold skirt sent her pulse sky-rocketing. Thankfully, the benefit summoned a huge turnout. While she recognized several skiers, snowboarders, and celebrities, the two she desperately hoped to avoid seemed to be keeping their distance.

"Here." Dani pressed a glass into Alyssa's hand and angled her head toward the far wall. "Let's grab that table for two instead."

No argument there. Alyssa eased through the crowd, protecting her drink as she zeroed in on the empty, tall table tucked away from the action like an oasis in the desert.

She clambered onto the stool and sat down, her feet already thanking her for the sweet relief. Lifting her drink to her lips, she took a long sip, letting the soda coat her parched throat.

Dani slid effortlessly onto the stool opposite Alyssa. "Let's talk about what's really bothering you."

Alyssa narrowed her gaze. Meaningful conversation and plumbing the depths of her tangled emotions weren't really on her agenda. She slid halfway off the stool again. "On second thought, I'm dying to bid on an all-inclusive package in Cabo, aren't you?"

"Not so fast." Dani grasped her arm. "We haven't had a chance to catch up since you left Alaska. What's the latest?"

"Nothing." Alyssa lifted one shoulder, pretending not to care.

"Why don't you text him?" Dani took a sip of her fruit-infused water.

"And say what? 'No worries about kissing somebody else. Wanna follow me around the world and carry my snowboard?'"

Dani rolled her eyes. "I'm sure that would totally win him over."

"There's nothing left to say. I told him exactly what I thought of him kissing someone else. If he wants to apologize—"

"Did you give him a chance?"

Alyssa bit her lip. "Not exactly."

"So you left that night and told him…"

"That there wasn't an 'us'." Alyssa cringed. "Probably not helpful, right?"

Dani's red lips formed an O.

Alyssa stared into her cup, jiggling the ice. "It doesn't matter. He won't come after me. Why would he?"

Empathy filled Dani's eyes. "Because you're worth it, that's why."

"Stop."

"It's true. You're smart, funny, an incredible athlete... He probably fell madly in love the first second he saw you."

"Doubt it. I was pretty rude."

"Stop negating everything I say. Believe you have value. I know you've had a hard time. But you've been redeemed from the mess. This might be a wonderful relationship if you'd quit sabotaging it."

"I didn't sabotage it."

Dani arched an eyebrow.

"Okay, maybe a little."

"Then do something. Make amends. Call him up."

Alyssa puffed her cheeks and blew out a long breath. "I have to win the X-Games first. I promised Lance I'd stay focused."

***

Jeremy grabbed Hazel's dog food from his truck then slammed the door. A bitter wind sliced through the air, and he shivered as he shouldered the kibble and hustled back toward the house. He hated leaving Hazel behind, but she couldn't tag along on his trip to California. Thankfully, Megan had agreed to watch her.

He nudged open the door, hurried inside, then lowered the bag to the floor with a grunt. Hazel trotted over, tail wagging.

"There you go, girl. I know Megan's gonna—"

Heated voices erupted from the kitchen. Jeremy paused, his fingers buried in Hazel's slick fur.

"Mom, I know. Okay?" Megan's voice raised an octave. "Spare me the lecture because I promise you I've—"

"We're not here to lecture you, honey. This comes as a huge shock to us." Dad sounded like he was barely holding it together.

Jeremy gave Hazel another pat then glanced around. Should he leave? That conversation—whatever it was about—sounded intense. But leaving for ten days without saying goodbye to his parents and Megan was rude. He made his way quietly into the kitchen.

"Hey, sweetie." Mom swiped at the tears on her cheeks.

"Dad." Jeremy glanced from Dad to Megan, sitting at the table, eyes red-rimmed. "What's going on?"

"Megan was just sharing some big news with us." Dad's jaw tightened, and he stared at the floor.

Jeremy's gut clenched.

"I'm pregnant." Megan sniffed. "That's the big news."

Holy moly. His mind raced. The flowers, the gifts, her unexpected decision to not go back to Seattle after the holidays. Never suspected *that* was the reason. "I—uh—I…"

He licked his lips, struggling to come up with some sort of encouraging word.

"Don't bother trying to say something positive. It only gets worse." Megan huffed out a breath and dabbed at her eyes with a crumpled tissue. "I had an affair. With the assistant volleyball coach."

"Oh, Megan." Mom's fingers fluttered as she clapped her hand over her mouth.

"Isn't he married?" Dad growled, his face reddening.

"That's why it's called an affair, Dad." Megan stood. "I don't want to talk about this anymore." She turned and rushed upstairs.

Silence filled the kitchen. Jeremy scrubbed his palm across his face. Her *coach?* What kind of a guy took advantage of one of his athletes like that?

Mom sighed and mopped at her tears again. "We don't expect you to miss your trip because of this."

"I know. I'll go in a few minutes."

Dad cleared his throat. "I can drive you to the airport. Let me grab my wallet." He stood and left the room.

Mom watched him go, her brow furrowed, then shifted her attention back to Jeremy. "It's a shame you'll miss Blake and Lauren coming home tomorrow. Have you told them about your new job?"

Jeremy's chest tightened. "Not yet."

"We all have a lot on our minds." Mom frowned. "Blake is not going to be happy when he finds out Megan is pregnant."

"I'm sorry I couldn't stick around to help out more." Another reason why leaving now wasn't the best decision.

Mom studied him. "No one expected you to. You know that, right?"

"I honestly don't know what people expect anymore." Jeremy glanced at the floor again, scuffing his boot against the beige tile. So much for just coming inside to say goodbye.

"What do you mean?" Dad asked, shrugging into his winter jacket.

"People seem to have a hard time letting stuff go. They still blame me for burning down the lodge. Blake thinks I'll never get my act together. I screwed up and ruined things with Alyssa. I feel like I let a lot of people down—got caught up in my own stuff. *Again.*"

"Sweetheart." Mom pressed her hand against his sleeve. "The people who caused the lodge to burn down are adults. They make their own choices. No one blames you. Besides, the grand opening was spectacular. You aren't responsible for your brother's challenges, or Megan's or anyone else's. Is this guilt the reason you've stayed around Emerald Cove?"

Jeremy nodded. "Part of the reason."

"We're not trying to get rid of you or anything," Dad said. "But what else is keeping you around?"

Jeremy blew out a long breath. This wasn't the time or the place, but words came anyway. "I thought about leaving. A few times. Something always held me back. Fear, mostly. My anxiety about another awful accident happening. Besides, it's comfortable there. I have my role and I play it well—Blake's slightly irresponsible younger brother, outdoorsy dude, and has-been reality TV star. This time I wanted to prove to all of you, and myself, that I could do something right. Working at the resort, looking out for people I care about was a way—both were easy ways to help my family and make my community love me again."

"At little cost to you."

Dad's comment pricked at Jeremy's conscience. He challenged Dad's inquisitive gaze with his own. "What do you mean?"

"There's nothing wrong with living in Emerald Cove and making family a priority. Except when it's an excuse to hide from the world and ignore your God-given gifts."

"I'm not—"

Dad held up his hand to silence Jeremy. "Let me finish. You're a talented photographer. An incredible whitewater guide and an expert kayaker. Even though you took a hiatus, and the TV show ended, you still have so much to offer. Don't let your doubts and fears keep you from exploring and doing what you love. The only person who cares if your life mirrors Blake's is you."

Oh-kay. Jeremy gritted his teeth and looked away. *Don't hold back, Dad.*

"I think what your father and I are trying to say is that we're proud of you," Mom said. "We want you to be happy. More importantly, we want you to use the gifts God gave you. We're concerned that hanging around here is keeping you from both."

Jeremy stared at the TV in the family room, where scenes from the X-Games splashed across the giant flat screen. A snowboarder shot down the hillside and launched off a box, catapulting into the air.

Alyssa.

She was what made him happy. Loving her was truly what gave him a purpose. He stood and planted a kiss on Mom's cheek. "Take good care of Megan. I'll call you when I land in California."

She pulled him into a quick hug. "Have a good time, sweetie."

"Thanks." He followed Dad toward the door, stopping to give Hazel a last-minute ear scratch.

She licked his hand, her eyes uncertain. Add 'leaving the best dog in the world' to his list of drawbacks about saying yes to this job. Yet he knew without a doubt this was a trip he had to take. More than completing a photojournalism assignment, he had to pursue closure. Visiting Andrew's family was the first step in that process.

20

"I can't finish this."

Alyssa pushed aside her plate, leaving the remnants of her ham and cheese omelet. Her knee bounced incessantly under the table, mimicking the way her stomach felt. With only a few hours before her last round of competition, she needed to find a way to manage her emotions and focus on her goal of winning.

Mom and Dad sat across from her in their hotel suite, where they'd invited Alyssa to have breakfast before the X-Game finals. Dad put down the newspaper, his eyes filled with concern. "Everything okay?"

"Too anxious to eat." She stood and paced from the table to the sliding glass door and back again, jamming her hands in the pockets of her hoodie. This wasn't like her—battling nerves and self-doubt when she was at the top of the leaderboard heading into the last day of competition. But Dani's words at the benefit had stayed with her, burrowing deep into her mind. Refusing to let her forget Jeremy or the possibility of a relationship with him.

She sighed and flopped back into her chair at the table.

Mom rose from the table and went to the refrigerator. "How about some yogurt and granola?"

"Sure. Whatever."

Dad folded the sports section and set it aside. "Does this have anything to do with that young man you met in Alaska?"

"No. Yes. I don't know." She groaned and tipped her head back, staring at the ceiling. Why now? Why couldn't she put all these convoluted feelings aside and deal with them later?

"Is he here?" Dad asked.

"Probably not." Alyssa straightened and met her Dad's gaze. "I told him I didn't want to see him again."

"I'm guessing that isn't exactly what you meant to say."

She bit her lip then shook her head.

Mom returned with a container of yogurt, a carton of blueberries, and some granola. "Here. I'll get you a spoon."

Alyssa pulled the foil lid from the carton and added a few blueberries then stirred in some granola. Dad waited patiently for her to elaborate. She frowned. How to put what happened with Jeremy into words?

"So when did things fall apart? You sounded ... content to be there at Christmas." Mom passed her the spoon and frowned. "It's about the pictures, isn't it?"

The spoon slipped from Alyssa's fingers and clattered to the table. Her breath caught. She forced herself to look at her parents. "You saw the pictures?"

Mom reached for Dad's hand, then she nodded slowly, a sheen of moisture coating her eyes.

"Sweetie, we're here to help." Dad smiled tenderly. "We only want what's best for you. It makes us sad when you don't share what's going on in your life—the good and the bad. So tell us what happened. From the beginning."

Alyssa swallowed hard. "I didn't want to tell you because I knew what you'd say," she whispered.

"What did you think we would say?" The hurt was evident in Mom's voice, making Alyssa regret her decision to avoid her parents even more.

"The same thing you've told me whenever I've made a questionable choice—that I shouldn't have gotten involved with Nick. He was trouble. Only cared about himself."

"Were your perceptions accurate?" Dad asked. "Is he what you thought he'd be?"

Alyssa nodded and dipped her spoon in her yogurt. She still couldn't bring herself to eat.

"Nick's the one responsible for the pictures?" Mom asked. "Did he take them or just post them?"

"Both. He took me to a party, gave me something to drink, then followed me to the hot tub—the rest is a little fuzzy, but I know I wasn't the only girl who—took off my top." She ducked her chin. As if that justified her behavior. Hadn't she led the group to jump in? "The next day we were competing at Copper Mountain, and I caught him showing his friends something on his phone—"

Her voice broke, reliving the humiliation all over again. Why had she let Nick persuade her to go to that party? Accepted another drink even when she'd known she'd had too much already?

"That's why you left unexpectedly." Dad finished the story.

"I'm sorry if I upset you. Leaving felt like the only option. I couldn't deal with the embarrassment, not in front of all my friends. Lance. You guys. The media. I already had to be in Alaska to film a commercial, so I went early. Then I met Jeremy, and everything I was struggling with here vanished. At least for a little while." Her heart cartwheeled at the memory of finding solace with Jeremy—protecting her from hypothermia on the mountain, inviting her to spend the holidays with his family, sharing tender kisses. "Too bad I found a way to mess it all up."

"Oh, honey." Mom reached across the table and placed her hand over Alyssa's. "What happened?"

"I stayed in Emerald Cove to spend more time with Jeremy and get to know his family. But I couldn't shake this feeling that something wasn't quite right. Then I figured I was just worried about how to balance a career and a relationship—haven't exactly done a stellar job of that in the past."

"Did he know about the pictures online?"

Alyssa winced at Dad's question. She stared at the table then lifted one shoulder. "I—I don't know. We never talked about it."

"So that's not the reason the relationship didn't work?" Mom gave her Alyssa's hand a gentle squeeze. "Talk to us. Please. We want to help."

Alyssa drew a wobbly breath. "Jeremy and I made plans to watch the fireworks on New Year's Eve. They'd reopened this renovated resort, and it was a big night. Then this gorgeous girl showed up and threw herself into his arms. I—I lost my mind. All I could think about was how stupid I'd been to trust him." Hot tears stung her eyes and she gritted her teeth. "I mean, really. How many times do I have to be betrayed before I finally get a clue?"

Mom pushed back her chair, skirted the table, knelt at Alyssa's side, and slid her arms around her. "I'm so sorry. We had no idea."

Alyssa pressed her temple against Mom's as a dam burst inside. The tears flowed. Finally. A safe place to fall.

"Is there any chance at all that perhaps you misunderstood?" Mom stroked Alyssa's hair. "Maybe this Jeremy is a good guy and the mystery woman's kiss wasn't what it looked like?"

"Here's the thing. He tried to stop me from leaving, told me it wasn't what it looked like. But I didn't believe him, and then I did what I do best—I left at the first sign of conflict." She swiped at the tears on her cheeks. "Why do I always run from my problems?"

"Because it's easy," Mom whispered, her eyes glistening with fresh tears.

"Have you considered maybe you need to recalculate which way you run?"

Dad's question confused her. "What?"

"Your mom and I have never pushed you to embrace a God you didn't believe in. Sometimes I wonder if your success on a snowboard only perpetuated your belief that you didn't need anyone."

She nodded. "Probably."

"Don't misunderstand." Dad's kind eyes crinkled at the corners as he offered a gentle smile. "We're super proud of you. If your career still needs to be your main focus, then I think that's wonderful. But don't let it be your only focus."

She hung her head. It was easier to let snowboarding be the only thing that mattered. Then the rest of life didn't hurt so much.

"We've tried our best to live out our relationship as a positive example and steer you away from people we thought might be harmful. But you're an adult now and responsible for your own choices. If that means a serious relationship with Jeremy, or somebody else down the road, we really hope someday you'll find the courage to let that kind of love into your life."

Alyssa met his gaze, too defeated to shun his wisdom like she had countless times before.

"People will often disappoint you, sweetheart. Brokenness and conflict are a part of being human." Mom slid her arm around Alyssa's shoulders, her expression full of tenderness. "I know you're probably tired of your lame parents spouting the same thing again and again, but the truth never changes. Genuine love doesn't run at the first sign of trouble."

"I have trust issues." Alyssa's mouth formed a weak smile. "Shocking, I know."

Mom chuckled softly. "We all do. It's hard to let go of our own agendas and believe someone else might have our best interests in mind."

"Loving someone is a daily decision," Dad said. "You have to choose to trust. It isn't easy. And living a life of faith doesn't earn much credibility in the world these days. But if you're willing, I think you might find giving your heart away is more rewarding than trying to keep someone out. You don't have to carry such heavy loads all by yourself."

A sweet relief rushed in. She didn't roll her eyes at Dad's insights, as she often had in the past. The hurt and bitterness wouldn't magically evaporate, but this time she was willing to admit that she couldn't keep binding her wounds alone.

***

Jeremy eased his rental car to the curb in front of a modest Spanish-style one-level on a quiet street in Carmel-by-the-Sea. Andrew's childhood home was just as he'd described it. The mature trees stood like centurions on either side of the wide front windows, and the lush green lawn appeared freshly mowed.

His mouth dry as sandpaper, Jeremy turned off the ignition then climbed out of the compact vehicle. Even though he'd called Andrew's wife, Misti, and asked permission to stop by, dread still coiled his insides in knots.

The California sunshine warmed his face, and he hesitated, whispering a prayer for strength and courage. He hadn't seen Misti or her daughter since Andrew's funeral, a fact he wasn't particularly proud of. Imprisoned by his own issues, struggling to overcome the guilt and regret, he'd felt ill-equipped to reach out. It was easier to just not call or text.

He drew a cleansing breath and walked up the driveway. This

conversation was a long-time coming. Before he reached the front door, it flew open, and a little girl with Andrew's eyes and Misti's smile stared up at him.

"What'cha doin'?" she asked, her brow puckered.

A smile tugged at his lips. "I've come to see you."

She quirked her lips to one side. "Oh. Lemme get my mom."

Jeremy waited patiently, admiring the containers of succulents and vibrant flowers decorating the modest porch. Only in California could he find beautiful things blooming in the middle of winter.

"Hi, Jeremy." Misti appeared in the hallway, with the little girl trailing behind her. "Please come in."

"Hi, Misti." He stepped inside. "It's great to see you."

"I see you've met Mackenzie." She pulled him into a quick hug. "It's good to see you, too. Thanks for stopping by."

He tensed in her welcoming embrace, a lump forming in his throat. He wanted to tell her that Mackenzie was beautiful, and Andrew would be so proud, but words failed him. He managed to pat Misti's shoulder awkwardly then stepped aside while she closed the door behind him.

Looking fit and healthy in a long white shirt and red leggings, Misti wore her dark hair pulled back in a simple ponytail. "Follow me. We were just having a tea party in the family room."

Jeremy smiled as the little girl alternated between hopping on one leg and skipping along the hallway, occasionally peeking over her shoulder at him.

"Mackenzie, can you offer Mr. Jeremy a cup of tea, please?" Misti cleared a blanket and a stuffed lamb off the brown leather sofa. "Have a seat."

He cleared his throat and sat on one end. "Thank you."

"Cweam and shuga?" Mackenzie asked, kneeling on the floor at his feet, an impressive array of plastic cups and saucers scattered across the carpet.

"Both, please."

"All right." Mackenzie poured imaginary liquid from a pink-and-white teapot, her tongue lodged in the corner of her lips.

Jeremy swallowed hard. Her mannerisms, creativity, and almost everything about her reminded him so much of her dad. He chanced a look at Misti, sitting across from him on the loveseat, her bare feet tucked under her.

"Pretty amazing, huh?" she asked, one brow arched.

"She's almost a carbon copy," he whispered.

Misti's smile illuminated her face. "I know it. Such a blessing, having a little bit of him walking around in the world with me."

"Misti, I—"

"Jeremy, wait. If you're here to apologize, you don't need to." Misti's expression grew serious. "Andrew knew what he was doing. His job was risky. Filming a TV show in Alaska was risky. Every time he left on a trip, we both knew he might not make it home."

"But he told me he needed to get home. To you. That you were expecting. I persuaded him to stay." Jeremy fisted his hands in his lap. "If I'd listened to him, things might've turned out differently."

"Maybe. Maybe not. We'll never know for sure." She leaned forward and squeezed his arm with her hand. "Please stop carrying this guilt around. It's too heavy."

Mackenzie brought him a tiny saucer and a cup. "Dis one's yours. Dwink up."

Jeremy grinned and accepted her offering. "Thank you."

Her gaze stayed riveted on him, no doubt waiting for him to sample the tea. He tipped the dainty cup to his lips and slurped loudly. "Mmmm, delicious."

Mackenzie's innocent giggle bubbled from her lips, and Jeremy felt an invisible weight lift.

Misti's eyes met his over the rim of her own tea cup. "See?"

He nodded, acknowledging that she was right. "Thank you for being so gracious."

"Life is way too short to hang onto things we have no business clinging to." Her smile wobbled for an instant, then she drew a deep breath. "Andrew would want us to move on. To live out our callings. He'd be disappointed if we were just sitting around, too sad or angry to do anything productive."

They spent a few minutes reminiscing about their favorite moments with Andrew, enjoying more imaginary tea and scones created by

Mackenzie, before saying their goodbyes. Jeremy promised to keep in touch, and thanked Misti again for extending grace and forgiveness. He drove away, grateful that he'd made the effort to reach out, despite the fear and anxiety that had almost convinced him to not even try.

Late that afternoon, he impatiently waited his turn to get off the crowded airplane and then made his way into the Denver airport. If he hurried, he could rent a car and be in Aspen by midnight. His phone chimed, and he paused to fish it from his pocket. Doug's name and number filled the screen.

"Hello?"

"Hi, Jeremy. It's Doug."

"Hey." He stepped out of the way of the passengers streaming into the terminal. "What's up?"

"I'm looking at your photos from Big Sur right now. These are fantastic."

"Thank you."

"How did it feel, taking pictures again?"

"Good. Really good." He glanced around, looking for a quick option for dinner. The smell of cheeseburgers and fries from a nearby pub wafted toward him, and his stomach growled. He hadn't eaten much on the flight from San Francisco, and he hated to lose precious minutes at a restaurant, but he couldn't drive to Aspen without food.

"We'd like to offer you another assignment. This one's in Austin, Texas." Doug's voice pulled him back to the conversation.

"Here's the thing." Jeremy measured his words carefully. "I've given this a lot of thought, and I'm grateful for the opportunity to get back to work, but I'm afraid I can't commit to traveling to Austin. Or anywhere else right now."

Silence filled the line. "I'm sorry to hear that. Is there anything I could offer to sweeten the deal? We could have you in and out of Austin by the end of next week."

"Next week will be too late." He didn't have any idea where Alyssa's schedule would take her next, but based on what he'd gleaned from online, Austria and the World Championships were likely on her itinerary. Once she left the country, it would be weeks or possibly even months before he could see her. Tell her how he felt. Try and convince her one more time that they still had a chance.

"All right then. You do what you've got to do, I guess," Doug said. "Good luck, Jeremy."

"Thank you."

Jeremy ended the call, pocketed his phone, then grabbed his wheeled suitcase and towed it behind him through the airport. Ever since he'd spoken with Misti, he'd felt about a thousand times lighter. No longer burdened with guilt and regret, he felt free to pursue what he really wanted. While Doug's offer had given him a quick ego boost, the thought of losing Alyssa forever snuffed out any enthusiasm he had for taking on another new assignment.

But what if she didn't want anything to do with him?

Shoving those worries aside, he moved quickly through the crowded terminal to the closest rental car counter.

The line snaked across the linoleum floor, impatient travelers jockeying for position at the first company's desk. Luggage carts overflowed with skis, snowboards, and suitcases while the hum of conversation and phones chiming punctuated the air.

"This storm's going to be a doozy. They're saying twenty-four to thirty-six inches, whiteout conditions in the next couple of hours." The woman waiting behind him relayed the weather forecast to her companion.

Dread pitted his stomach. He should've known trying to rent a car during peak ski season was a ridiculous idea. Even if he secured a car, driving through a blizzard wasn't smart. Jeremy surveyed the crowded terminal, then moved to the next line, which wasn't much shorter. While he waited, he used an app on his phone to try and locate a company with cars available. Nothing came up.

He raked a hand through his hair and turned in a slow circle. The lines had grown longer, and disgruntled customers pressed in, news of the impending storm amping up their anxiety. There had to be a way to get to Aspen tonight. He scrolled to another app, holding his breath that there was at least one adventurous ride-sharing opportunity left.

A few minutes later, he grabbed his suitcase, stepped out of line at the rental car company, and hurried to the automatic doors leading outside.

The cold air nipped at his cheeks as he waited for his Uber to arrive. *Hold on, Alyssa. I'm coming.*

***

Alyssa strapped in then swiveled on her board, making sure her boots were tight and locked in place. Hip-hop music blasted from the speakers behind the starting gate, and she bobbed her head along to the contagious beat. It wasn't her jam but that didn't matter. She'd lay down sick tricks anyway. The X-Games were all about making a statement, and she'd come here to prove that no matter what life threw at her, she'd still dominate.

Adrenaline pulsed through her veins as she straightened to her full height then tapped her helmet twice with her right glove. One last tug on her goggles and she was set.

"Find your center," she whispered, visualizing her first trick off the rail. The jumps were intense this week—more than one snowboarder had bit it hard coming off that first rail. She wouldn't be adding to the body count. Hayley had made a statement with a gnarly trick on her final run and chopped away at Alyssa's comfortable lead. Only five points ahead now, she'd have to stomp it if she was still going to win gold today.

Dad's cowbell rang out in the distance, and she bit back a smile as she scanned the empty run, envisioning her family filling the top row of the crowded bleachers at the bottom of the hill. Despite the pressure of close competition, the crystal clear blue sky and golden sunlight inspired her. A television camera zoomed in on her as the announcer called her name over the loudspeaker, launching a thousand butterflies in her abdomen. Not now. No way. She didn't have time for nerves.

Hadn't she practiced until her legs were like Jell-O? All that extra time on the trampolines, the stretching, the yoga classes—it all came down to this. Loose. Confident. Calm. She owned this run.

Gritting her teeth, she dropped into her run and found her groove right away. A rail loomed large and she angled the nose of her board toward it, picking up speed. She hit it just right, the familiar *swoosh* of her board gliding across the obstacle giving her that familiar rush. With the wind in her face, she sailed off the end of the jib, grabbed the back of her board near her heel, rotated in two full circles, and landed on the snow in the sweet spot. She rode away, the familiar wave of satisfaction washing over her. This was perfect.

The front 1080 mute is yours. Own it. Alyssa winced at the deviant thought pinging around in her head. Sure, she'd tried three revolutions on a trampoline, and even with a harness, but never in a competition and definitely not at the X-Games. A failed trick here would be devastating.

What have you got to lose?

Everything.

She rode toward the next jump, her pulse pounding. Still undecided, she went with an easier trick, hoping to impress the judges with a little flair yet playing it safe while the internal debate still warred within. Stomp a complex trick like the 1080 for the first time and she'd claim a space in the record books. Undoubtedly the gold medal, too. Fall on her face, lose to Hayley, and never live it down.

She carved a line across the snow, her heart in her throat as her board ate up the distance to the ramp. It was now or never. Alyssa shot up the curve then went airborne, the world flashing by in a blur as she propelled her body through three complete revolutions, left hand clutching the center of the board between her toes.

"Oh my—"

The words died on her tongue as she let go of the board and thrust her arms out to the sides, fighting for balance as her snowboard hit the snow hard. The impact traveled from her heels up to her spine and she grunted. That was going to hurt later. But the roar of approval from the crowd on the other side of the barrier quickly overpowered any thoughts of future aches and pains.

She skidded to a stop in front of the raucous crowd, a spray of snow shooting into the air from underneath her board. A television camera was in her face, and her breaths came quickly, releasing little puffs of white vapor as she scanned the spectators. Dad's cowbell clanged like crazy, fans whipped pink rowdy rags, and two tweener girls waved a giant banner with "Huard's Hooligans" spelled in block letters.

"Way to go, Alyssa!"

She offered a grin and a thumbs up in the general direction of the cheer then leaned down and loosened her bindings. When she straightened, she stole a quick glance at the scoreboard. The judges hadn't posted anything yet, but she couldn't not check. A replay of her performance on the JumboTron captured her attention instead. Applause rippled across the crowd when she stomped the 1080 at the end.

"Check it out," someone shouted behind her. "Scores are up."

She pivoted and swallowed hard as the numbers registered in her head. She blinked then looked again. First place. By a mere six points.

"Yes!" She thrust both arms in the air, a wide grin spreading across her face. Finally. All of her hard work had paid off.

"Congratulations!" Her fans pressed against the barrier at the end of the course, their cheers and applause sending an exhilarating rush through her whole body.

"We love you!"

"Will you sign this, please?" The child's request was too precious to ignore.

"Of course." Alyssa took the permanent marker and scrawled her name across the photo the little girl offered.

The next several minutes flew by as she worked the crowd and autographed everything from hats to bare skin.

"Last one." Lance had found his way to her and wedged himself between Alyssa and the barrier. "She's got to get to the podium for the awards ceremony."

Relieved, Alyssa reached around Lance and handed the hat and marker back to the enthusiastic fan. "Thanks," she murmured to Lance then turned away to grab her board.

"How about one more? Please? I've come a long way."

The familiar voice paralyzed her. Heart pounding, she turned, her eyes traveling from his winter boots and dark-washed jeans to the pink T-shirt under his parka and the temporary 'H' tattooed on his cheek. Lance, the curious onlookers, her family—all of it melted into the background.

"Jeremy?"

His mouth curved up in a tentative smile. "You stomped it out there. Nicely done."

"Thanks." She licked her dry lips, words failing her as she stared into his deep blue eyes.

"May I talk to you? It won't take long. Promise."

"Alyssa—" Lance grasped her sleeve.

As if he could stop her. Nothing would keep her from this moment. She loved Jeremy.

The realization sent her heart into a swan dive, breaking free from the doubt and uncertainty that had held her prisoner for far too long.

"Here." She pressed her snowboard to Lance's chest. "Hold this for a sec."

She bridged the gap separating her from Jeremy, propelled by the intensity of his gaze, pulling her to him. Dozens of fans pressed in, snapping pictures with their phones. She was beyond caring.

"You came," she said, her voice breathy. So many things she wanted to say. Needed to say. "I have to—"

His lips found hers, tender yet reassuring.

He wanted her. She yielded to his kiss, leaning into his embrace as his arms tightened around her. The kiss deepened, and she slid her fingers into his hair, losing herself in the moment.

A whoop of delight went up from the onlookers, reminding her they weren't alone.

They came up for air, and his eyes opened, lips still lingering close to hers.

"I love you," she said, desperate to share her feelings.

His eyes darkened, pulling her further into their depths. "I love you, too."

His mouth claimed hers once more, and she savored the kiss. Her pulse raced, and warmth spread all the way to her toes. This was better than any award, endorsement, stomped trick, or record-setting performance. He hadn't given up on her, even when she deserved to be forgotten.

Lance cleared his throat. "I hate to interrupt, but you've got a medal to claim."

Jeremy pulled away, resting his forehead against hers. "Hold that thought."

"They can't start without me." She linked her fingers at the nape of his neck, her confidence buoyed by the tenderness in his gaze. "There's something I have to tell you. I've … done a lot of things I'm not proud of, things I thought wouldn't matter because I was having fun and life was all about the good times." She frowned. "I've realized there are consequences for my actions. When I hurt people I love…" Her voice broke.

"If this is about an ex-boyfriend or those pictures, none of it matters to me."

Her breath caught in her chest. "How did you—when did—"

"I saw them online, right after you came to Emerald Cove." He cupped her cheek with his hand and brushed another gentle kiss to her lips. "It's in the past. Where it belongs."

She blinked back the tears. "I'm sorry for the way I treated you and those hurtful things I said to you that night … and accused you of—"

"Shhh." His eyes pierced hers. "All is forgiven." He pulled a familiar scarf from inside his jacket. "Wait. Before you go, I have something for you. I think you forgot this when you left."

She grinned as he draped it around her neck. "Thank you for not giving up on us."

Warmth filled his eyes. "Never. Go enjoy your moment on the podium."

Her fingers skimmed the sleeves of his jacket then trailed across his palms. Now that he'd held her close again, she hated to let him out of her sight. "Say you won't go."

He grabbed her hand and pressed a quick kiss to her palm. "I'll always wait for you, Alyssa."

Epilogue

Hurry up, hurry up, hurry up. Jeremy stood inside the new gallery he'd opened in downtown Emerald Cove, willing his guests to make a decision or find their way toward the door. He pretended to straighten one of his framed prints, a stunning image of Denali he'd taken earlier this spring then proudly displayed on the brick wall nearby.

"Want me to stay and lock up?" Megan asked.

Jeremy glanced at her, leaning against the counter nearby, fanning her face with one of Blake and Lauren's whitewater rafting and kayaking brochures. Poor thing. She tugged at her black cotton dress stretched taut over her very pregnant stomach. "No way." He shook his head. "I can't do that to you. Why don't you go on home?"

"No arguments from me." She sighed and reached for her purse from under the register. "Thank you."

"Not a problem." He checked the time again. The gallery was supposed to close five minutes ago. Still the customers lingered, admiring a stunning black-and-white of Horsetail Falls one of his friends had taken, while discussing the pros and cons of displaying the picture in their home.

Jeremy groaned silently. His gallery had received an enthusiastic welcome from the community, and since the summer tourists started trickling in to town over the last few weeks, he'd sold quite a few pictures. Normally he was thrilled when people hung around. But not tonight. Couldn't they wander toward the waterfront and enjoy the live entertainment or something? As soon as they walked out the door, he'd slam that deadbolt, flip the sign in the window to closed, and sprint to his truck. Forty-five minutes tops and he'd be at the airport, a one-man welcoming committee for Alyssa's arrival.

And what a welcome it would be.

Five months had passed since he'd stood on that hillside in Aspen, held Alyssa in his arms again, and promised to wait for her. It felt like he'd lived a whole lifetime since then, finding his new normal as a photographer and gallery owner while still missing her so much it hurt.

The wait was almost over, though. If he could ever get these people to move on.

"Nice to meet you, Jeremy." The party of four waved goodbye and headed toward the door. "You have a lovely gallery."

"Thanks for coming by." Jeremy offered a polite smile. Would it be obnoxious to walk them out? He trailed them, stopping to wipe non-existent dust off the edge of a frame, until they stepped outside. The bell on the door jingled, and then they were gone.

"Sweet. Thank you, Lord." He crossed the gallery in long strides, his boots clicking against the hardwood floors. He was desperate to get out of there before another interruption delayed him. But he wasn't quite fast enough. The door pushed open and a vision in a royal blue sleeveless dress filled the doorway, the late afternoon sun glowing like a halo behind her.

"Oh my."

Alyssa grinned. "Do you know where a girl could sign up for a decent photography class around here?"

He feigned irritation. "Sorry, we're closed. I have to get to the airport."

Her smile faded. "Bummer. Guess I'll come back tomorrow."

"Not on your life." His legs ate up the distance between them while his heart pounded in his chest.

She stepped inside, the bells jingling against the handle as the door swung closed.

He reached around and twisted the deadbolt, then kept his hand planted firmly beside her on the door. Honey-brown waves cascaded across her slender shoulders, and he boldly tunneled his fingers through the silky strands until he gently cupped her head in his palm.

Alyssa arched an eyebrow. "Is this how you welcome all potential customers?"

"Only the most beautiful ones." He leaned closer, his mouth only inches from hers.

"I see." Her gaze slid to his lips.

He tilted his head and claimed her mouth with his, softly at first, struggling to exercise restraint. Her familiar citrusy scent enveloped him as he slipped his hand around her waist and pulled her closer, letting her know how much he'd missed her. Skype, FaceTime, dozens of text messages—watching her snowboard live on television—none of it compared to holding her close again, savoring the warmth of her touch.

Pulling back, he caressed her bare arms with his fingertips.

"Well, hello." Her full lips formed a teasing smile. "I missed you, too."

"You're killing me, woman." He searched her face. "What are you doing here? I thought I was supposed to pick you up."

"I couldn't stand to wait a second longer, so I jumped on an earlier flight." She pressed her palm to his cheek and kissed him slowly, stealing all rational thought. His arms encircled her waist again and he lifted her off her feet, losing himself in the heady buzz of her embrace.

It was all he could do to break contact and rein in his dangerous thoughts.

She released a contented sigh. "I suppose we'll have plenty of time to get reacquainted."

"Absolutely. I'm not letting you leave this zip code for a very long time."

"Good to know. I'm officially unemployed, by the way." She twined her fingers through his. "Do you think Emerald Cove is the place to open an outdoor apparel store?"

He lifted her hand to his lips and kissed her knuckles, the words slowly registering. "What did you say?"

"I've given a lot of thought to what it means to be in a healthy, committed relationship." Her face grew serious. "My parents and my sisters are married, but I haven't had much experience myself. If anything, I'm a great example of what not to do."

Jeremy's heart squeezed in his chest as she looked away for an instant, a hint of regret surfacing in her expression. "That's all in the past, remember?"

"Let me finish. Please." She tipped her chin up, a warmth and a lightness he hadn't seen before filling her eyes. It swept him up and sent his heart careening into overdrive. "For a long time, I didn't think I deserved to be loved like that. And then there was you—looking out for me, protecting me, putting up with my sassiness…"

He grinned. "I love your sassiness. It's one of my favorite things about you."

Pink tinged her cheeks. "Be serious. Or else I'll never get to say what I had planned."

He cleared his throat. "Sorry."

"I thought I could be content with my snowboarding. Seeing the world from the tallest mountains made me feel invincible. But since I've met you I've realized there's more to life than laying down cool tricks. My parents have reminded me that faith in myself is not what's most important, and I don't want to keep running from you or from a relationship with the God I've tried to pretend didn't exist."

Jeremy's heart cartwheeled. He kept quiet and waited for her to finish.

"Since you and I have been apart, I've also realized that I—I'm not the same without you. I need you, Jeremy Tully. So if you're willing to let me into your world, I want to see what it's like to live in the same town. It doesn't matter where, as long as we're together. And I want to hang out with your family and go to church with you ... maybe see what being an Alaska girl is all about."

He released his grasp on her hands just long enough to splay his hands across the small of her back and stare deep into her fathomless eyes. "I need you, too," he said, his voice thick with emotion. "I've imagined you coming here and telling me you wanted to be a part of my life so many times. You have no idea how much it means to hear those words. Thank you."

Her gaze roamed his face. "I love you."

"I love you, too." He sealed the declaration with another kiss.

THE END

Connect with the Author

Thank you for taking the time to read *Say You Won't Go*. For those of you who have been with me from the beginning, thank you for your patience. I know the release of this novel took much longer than any of us anticipated. From the moment Jeremy swaggered onto the page in my first novel, *Unraveled*, I knew he'd eventually demand his own story. Instead, my real life took center stage as my family faced a series of plot twists that took us through a three-year season of tremendous difficulty. While I tried to keep writing, it was very challenging to be creative when circumstances were not at all what we'd anticipated. Looking back, I can say with absolute certainty that God is good and He is faithful, and we leaned into His promises. By His grace, we emerged on the other side of our storms deeply anchored in our faith. Whatever you're going through right now, I hope my novels serve as a source of inspiration, a pleasant yet temporary escape from your current reality, and remind you of the hope that is found in walking with a God who loves you unconditionally.

I'd love to connect with you, so please visit HeidiMcCahan.com where you'll find a box on the right sidebar inviting you to subscribe to my author e-newsletter. My goal is to provide exclusive content for all subscribers, so you'll receive a free novella once your subscription is confirmed, as well as sneak peeks of future cover designs, breaking news about upcoming titles and giveaways, and occasionally an opportunity to join my street team and help spread the word about my books.

I'm a huge fan of social media and you can find me on Facebook and Twitter as @heidimccahan or @heidimccahan.author on Instagram.

One last shameless plug for authors everywhere: the best way you can help an author create and publish more books is tell your friends how much you love the books you've read. If you'd take a few minutes to leave an honest review of *Say You Won't Go* on Goodreads and Amazon, it would mean so much.

Thank you!

Sincerely,
Heidi

Acknowledgements

I'm so grateful for the many people in my life who make this writing journey sweeter. While the creative part of the process happens day after day, one word at a time, the production of a book requires a team effort. This novel would not be possible without the following:

First, to my husband Steve, I couldn't write a single word without your unconditional love and support. You graciously "share" me with a lot of fictional friends and never complain. You've tolerated more than your fair share of mediocre meals, handled the chores I've neglected with patience and grace, and cheered me on when I was certain I couldn't keep going. Thank you from the bottom of my heart. I am blessed to call you mine.

To our three boys, thank you for the laughter, the hugs, and most of all, your love. I hope watching your mom chase her big dreams inspires you to chase yours, too.

To my parents, Dave and Nancy, I'm certain you're my biggest fans. Thank you for always being in my corner, helping me find new readers and praying without ceasing. Your faith journey and commitment to one another is better than any love story I could ever craft. Thank you for teaching me what it means to walk closely with the Lord.

To my sister Heather and her family, thank you for your encouraging words and for telling your friends about my books.

Thank you to my awesome extended family for supporting my dream, encouraging me to keep writing, and celebrating my successes. No matter where I go, I know I will find a member of the Rea family, who will offer a warm smile and share a great story.

Jessie Kirkland, you are a gift. Thank you for your tireless efforts, encouraging words and abundant grace. Your professionalism and fearlessness are unmatched, and I'm proud to be a part of Kirkland Media Management.

Sally Bradley, Lesley Ann McDaniel, Leslie L. McKee, and Jessica Dunning, your remarkable editing skills and keen insights helped this story become all that it could be. It needed some tough love and I'm glad you all delivered. Thank you very much!

Lynnette Bonner, the first glimpse of this cover took my breath away. I love it so much! Thank you for helping make this book beautiful.

To Anna and Megan, my dear friends and first readers, I'm grateful for you. Thank you again for listening, reading those early drafts, and most of all thank you for the gift of your friendship.

To my team at Story Matters, you rock! I couldn't launch these books without you. Your boundless enthusiasm, generosity and kind words have blessed me so. Thank you.

To my writing friends flung far and wide across the world, thank you for being kindred spirits. My people. You get me and I am fortunate to be on this wild ride with each of you.

Finally, thank you to God, who crafts the best stories. Your plot twists and cliffhangers ultimately point us all to your reckless and extravagant love. Great is your faithfulness. Thank you for planting this story in my heart and giving me the opportunity to share it with others.

About the Author

HEIDI MCCAHAN is a Pacific Northwest girl at heart, but currently resides in North Carolina with her husband and three boys. When she isn't writing inspirational romance, Heidi can usually be found reading a book, enjoying a cup of coffee and avoiding the laundry pile. She's also a huge fan of dark chocolate and her adorable goldendoodle, Finn.

Made in the USA
Columbia, SC
04 November 2018